Genetic Memory

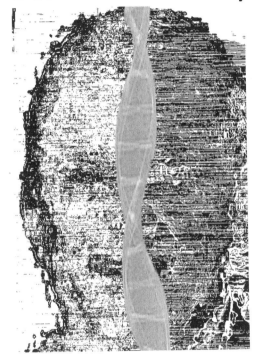

By Tim Dunn

This is a work of fiction. All incidents and dialogue and all characters, with the exception of well-known ancient historical figures, are products of the author's imagination and are not to be construed as real. Where real life historical figures appear, the situations, incidents and dialogues concerning those persons are entirely fictional and are not intended to depict actual events or to change the fictional nature of the work. Some ancient historical events and quotations are represented as real, and in these cases readers are encouraged to verify sources and come to their own conclusions regarding the veracity of such passages. In all other respects, any resemblance to actual events, locales, or persons, living or dead, is entirely coincidental.

DEDICATION

This work is dedicated to the people we love that lost their capacity to remember.

ACKNOWLEDGMENTS

When you have a full time day job, you only have a certain amount of free time available. Each moment I am locked away in a room writing a story is another moment away from my personal life. Thanks to my wife for her support of my every endeavor. She realizes that my ultimate goal is to expose people to the saving grace of the gospel of Jesus Christ and an eternal relationship with God.

Much appreciation to my son for his creative contributions and the ideas he provides me when I hit a block. Once again he has contributed, with permission, a few lines of text and code to help round out the story.

To those folks who enthusiastically supported, read and enjoyed the fictional Autobiography of Tom Dory, 'Monomania'... you know who you are, thank you! And thanks for your patience.

Thank you to my Lord and Savior, Jesus Christ

INTRODUCTION

I've been told the style of my writing tends to be subtle, abstract and thought provoking at times, but I also try to keep it as simple as the sunrise and sunset that we sometimes take for granted. My first book, Monomania, was a blend of ideas that were conceived before I was a believer, and the spiritual beliefs that I hold dear to my heart today. Inspired by the wonderful story of 'Lazarus and the Rich Man' in Luke 16:19 - 31, I wrote about the fictional character's faith journey and the result of choices during the relentless struggle between flesh and spirit. If you have not yet read 'Monomania', no worries. Each piece should be able to stand on its own, however if did you read the first book then 'Genetic Memory' should help clear some things up for you. And if it has been a while since you read 'Monomania', don't worry about it, just enjoy the moment.

This story, Genetic Memory, is part two of that fictional voyage and takes readers on an historic journey using modern fictional characters while expanding on the concepts found in the first book; Dreams and the images they produce are real and exist in the life and mind of the person that imagined them. Memories are always there and available for us to tap into. And when we live within them it sometimes seems like our brain files them away and they end up in a different file cabinet. We think that if we could organize them in a consistent, repeatable fashion that it would help ensure our recollections and they would be exactly as the events originally occurred.

The notions offered in this book invite us to suppose that our memory is a collection of memories and that there is a compilation process that occurs across our brain. That there is a complex construction built by the cells and systems, assembled and reassembled into the final product - our memory. Then from there, layer in the memories passed on through our genetic code and suddenly the possibilities of what we know and remember become limitless.

This is a work of fiction. It was written purely as an adventure for your entertainment. It is in no way intended to re-interpret, add to or take away from the true word of God. If you have never read God's word or if you have not read it for a while, my hope is that you will read the bible, discover God's truth, embrace it and apply it to your life as you build a personal relationship with Him.

If you enjoy my stories please write a review and let others know.

Most importantly, if you already have a personal relationship with God, let others know about that and what it means to you.

TIM DUNN

"Infinity is made up of inner space and outer space. Mankind sits at the midpoint. Infinity is physical, but eternity is spiritual,"

Quote from Tom Dory's journal

CHAPTER 1

"Cheri, the official documents arrived. No more Skip Chalmers. From now on I will always be known and remembered as Adam Dory!"

"That's um, really great Skip, I mean Adam. I guess I didn't know you were changing your name," Cheri responded hesitantly. Cheri and Skip had been dating and spending a lot of time together for the past three months and the news of his name change was somewhat of a surprise. She thought she knew him, but was learning just how much she didn't know.

Cheri thought, *'He is now Adam Dory. Still the same six foot tall, two hundred ten pound, muscular, brown hair, green eyed handsome young man, just a new name. So I guess that's not so bad.'* She had to know why he did it. She decided to let him go on with his story and simply by listening he would tell her everything. At least she hoped so.

Skip had just turned eighteen years old and was no longer a ward of the court. He explained how his name was given to him when he was in an orphanage as a baby, which was also news to her. He grew up in many different homes over the years and the parents Cheri had met were the last in a long line of foster parents. No one ever adopted Skip.

He decided a long time ago that on his eighteenth birthday he would submit all the paperwork and officially and forever change his name to Adam Dory. After explaining what he did, he paused and went silent and Cheri was on the edge of her seat waiting to hear why he did it. Adam simply hung his head and rested it in his hands and sighed deep and long, "Don't you want to know why, Cheri?"

"Yes, Adam, yes, I do."

Adam lifted his head and smiled. His whole life he wanted someone to share his story with and Cheri was his best friend and girlfriend. He trusted her. Even though they recently started dating, they had known each other for almost two years. He paused and looked deep into her bright blues eyes.

Cheri slid her fingers along her long blonde hair to move it behind her ear as she sat forward in her chair. When she leaned forward Adam could smell her perfume and his eyes shifted to her slender figure then back to her eyes again and he proceeded to tell his story. From the beginning. As he remembered it.

Many of the details were fuzzy but he remembered his first foster family. He was four or five years old and a young couple with two other children were his parents. It was like he just appeared into life, into their home, into reality, for the very first time.

Adam remembered the other two children, a boy and a girl were a little older than he was. The girl was closer to his age and very nice to him. The boy picked on him when no one was watching. Nothing bad, just little kid stuff, annoying for the most part.

The parents were very kind and took him to church and Sunday school and made sure he was always clean and well fed. He had his own bedroom and had his own toys. He remembered a lady would always come by and check up on him. He didn't know it then but he now knows it was the social worker.

One day the lady came and took him away. He doesn't know why, he just remembers showing up at a new home one day. Adam thought there was somewhere he went in between homes but cannot really recall. Maybe it was a big brick building with other kids. Maybe?

At any rate, in the new home there was only a man and woman that took care of him. They had no other kids. Adam was pretty much spoiled with material things and attention. The people seemed real sincere about their affection towards him. They took him to the carnival and the theme park and bought him souvenirs. They also took him to church every week. Adam remembered the bible stories and the nice people at the church.

Adam couldn't recall the names of the man and woman but he explained to Cheri that they expressed interest in adopting him. Cheri listened intently as Adam shared how the young couple took him to family events and he was beginning to feel like he had a real home, a place he would stay for the rest of his life.

Cheri thought about her home. The loving care and trust that comes with a stable family. Her mother and father were never divorced, both were her biological parents. They lived in the same house in the same neighborhood her whole life. Not boring, just predictable, secure.

He went on to explain that family lasted about two years, then one day the man never came home. The wife was distraught. She wasn't going to be able to take care of him by herself. She was 'sorry Skip'. So he had to go to another home. She wasn't going to let him go until the social worker found a new home for him. She was very sorrowful. She cried a lot. Then he never saw her again.

Adam welled up in tears as he thought about her. As he recalled another loss. His hope of a real family ripped away again. He wondered, *'Why did that man leave? Was it my sleep walking?'* The knot in his gut tightened.

"Adam, that is so sad," Cheri held back her own tears as she felt the anguish of Adam's childhood, "Please tell me everything you can remember. Let it out."

The next home Adam went to was small and dirty. The transfer between homes happened at the same time the State switched social workers. The people were mean and uncaring.

He was about eight years old at the time and had no friends. He was very sad in that home.

One night he locked himself in his bedroom and the man stood outside knocking the whole evening. The man was cussing and yelling and saying, "You are going to pay when I get my hands on you Skip." That was the last thing he remembered about that home.

There was a gap in Adam's memory from the time he was eight until he was ten years old. He thinks he just blocked it out of his mind. It must have been pretty bad. "I don't know, it's like part of my life disappeared," Adam sighed.

From the time he was ten until he was fourteen he stayed with the same family. He had made some friends and was feeling like maybe life would all work out for him. There were two girls that his foster parents called his step-sisters. He was told that he was their older brother and should always set a good example and protect them.

Then one day, he was sent away. The foster parents thought he was a danger to the girls. They were really scared. They didn't understand, even after Adam had tried to explain, it only made things worse. They didn't understand the sleep walking. They couldn't comprehend the dreams he was having. They gave up on him.

"What was so scary about sleepwalking and your dreams that they sent you away?" Cheri was perplexed that anyone would be afraid of a sleepwalker that easily, "Did you hurt the girls?"

"No, never. I could never, I really loved them like sisters. I don't understand why they never believed me. I am not crazy. I just have very lively dreams. They are real, and sometimes I walk around as if I am actually there."

"Where Adam?"

"Wherever my mind takes me."

Cheri asked, "What happened after they sent you away?"

"I was put into a state institution and poked and prodded for about a year and then ended up here."

"What do you mean, poked and prodded?"

"Never mind, forget I said that."

"No, Adam, that's serious. What do you mean and does anyone else know about it? Your parents?" Cheri pressed him.

"No one else knows, except the people who did it. It wasn't so bad, no big deal."

"If it's no big deal then tell me about it."

"They would strap me to a chair and hold my eyes open and make me take tests and there were wires connected to my head and they watched me on camera all day, every day for a whole year. Then they let me go." Adam was shaking and sweating as he rapidly concluded.

"Who? Who are they?"

"I don't know. They looked like scientists, acted like psychiatrists and talked like doctors. It was weird. I'd like to forget about it."

"Adam, we should tell the police about this. People can't do those things, and..."

Adam interrupted, "Stop! Cheri, no. I let them. I agreed. I wanted to know why I am the way I am. Why I sleepwalk and why it always feels so real. Why it *is* so real."

Cheri was looking up at the ceiling, shaking her head. It was becoming too much for her to understand and comprehend all at once and so fast and..."Cheri! " Adam hollered and snapped her out of it.

"Adam, I don't..."

"Please," he stopped her again in mid-sentence, "Hang in there with me on this. I've shared it all. You said you were ready and wanted to know. You must think I am some kind of freak, but I'm not. The scientists found nothing. They told me I would grow out of it and it was just an active imagination. It seems like..."

Cheri interrupted this time, "Adam. Do you still have the dreams and the sleepwalking?" She thought it best to put herself aside and let this be about Adam. She cared deeply about him and nothing should get between them. He was bearing his soul and she wanted to see it all.

Adam hung his head and after a long pause he raised his eyes until they locked on Cheri's, "More than ever." He was scared.

He imagined Cheri running for the door and never coming back. Suddenly a peace came over him. He believed it was because for the first time in his life he actually let it out. It was freeing.

Adam continued talking about his most recent dreams for a few more minutes. He described adventures that would carry on for years and he would awaken only to realize he was dreaming for a few hours. Instead of outgrowing it he was growing into it. More strength and control.

Cheri continued listening intently the whole time, never taking her eyes off him. Adam finished telling his history, he shrugged and said, "That's it for now. If I remember anything else I'll let you know."

"Adam. You are soooo sweet. Thank you so much for sharing that. It means so much to me. I feel much closer to you now," Cheri kissed him on the forehead and said, "Just so you know, when I turn eighteen next month, I won't be changing my name. You can still call me Cheri Thompson. And if you play your cards right, maybe even Cheri Dory someday."

Adam smiled and said, "Cheri. There is one more thing."

Her eyes lit up in anticipation, "What is it Adam?"

He lifted his shirt and revealed a scar on his left side that ran from his ribcage to his hip.

"You've shown me that scar before. You had your appendix removed, right?" Cheri's questioning look poked at Adam's heart for letting her believe that. Although he never said it was his appendix, Cheri always assumed it, he just never corrected her before, until now.

"Cheri, my appendix is on my right side."

"Oh, Adam, what happened to you? Who did that to you?"

"Are you sure you want to know everything about me Cheri?"

"Of course."

"Do you promise not to freak out, or judge me, and no matter what you see and hear next, you won't leave me?"

Cheri had goose bumps and a cool sweat developing under her armpits as she stuttered, "Adam, you are starting to scare me."

"If you are scared, then you are not ready and I'll wait for another time," Adam sighed, "I would never hurt you."

His whole demeanor shifted from confidence to defeat, but Cheri sensed it, so she responded quickly, "Adam, I promise I will stay with you. You are very brave for sharing all of this with me and I trust you. Just tell me, is this the last thing you have to share?"

"Follow me."

Adam led her to his bedroom. Adam still lived with his foster parents and they were not home from work yet. Adam and Cheri always hung out at Adam's since high school was over and they both had graduated. The first few weeks of summer was a time of freedom for them to get to know each other. Quality time that eluded them during the school year.

Cheri stopped abruptly outside his bedroom.

"Cheri, its ok, I want to show you something, it's in my closet."

"Keep the bedroom door open Adam. I don't want your parents getting the wrong idea if they come home."

"They won't be here for another hour, but I'll keep it open, come on inside."

Adam opened his closet door and waved Cheri in. She hesitantly approached, looking past Adam to see what was in there besides his clothes and shoes. Adam pulled a string that was attached to a light bulb in the ceiling. There was a click, a hum and a purple glow from the bulb. It was a black light.

Adam said, "Are you ready?"

"Okay."

Adam pulled up his shirt to reveal the scar. It was about an inch wide and several inches long. Under the black light it looked very different. Cheri could see inside Adam's body. There was no skin. The muscle was separated exposing his intestines. They were slimy and moving as he breathed and looked very real. Like a movie she saw about surgeries.

Cheri reached forward to touch it and her finger went into his side. She screamed.

7

CHAPTER 2

"Calm down, Cheri, please," Adam pleaded as he wrapped his arms around her. Cheri was trembling and Adam was beginning to regret how far he took things today. He second guessed whether he could trust her and thoughts were racing through his mind , *'What if she calls the police, or tells my foster parents, or her parents, or if anyone finds out, what will I do now!'*

"Skip! I mean Adam! What the heck is going on!" Cheri was screaming and trying to shake free of Adam's hold on her. Adam was gentle but firm in his grip, only to keep her contained until she got ahold of herself. As soon as Adam released her she ran out the front door and down the street. He decided to let her go and not to pursue.

Adam slowly and methodically walked outside, perused the area, and moved cautiously down the street toward a girl lying on the neighbor's lawn, curled up in a ball and sobbing.

"It'll be alright Cheri," Adam placed his hand gently on her shoulder. She uncurled, sat up and looked into his eyes. Tears were streaming down her cheeks as she whimpered.

"Adam, I need to get going. We'll talk again in two weeks."

"Two Weeks! What?"

"Did you forget?" Cheri asked.

"Wait, what? Oh yeah. Bible camp. You leave already tonight?"

"Yes, and I'll come see you as soon as I return. I promise," Cheri said as she turned and walked away.

'Let her go. It'll be fine. Relax. She needs time to reflect on all of this. You'll see her in two weeks.' Adam's thoughts raced as he shivered and trembled. Adam turned away, walked back to the house, into his bedroom, sat down on his bed and wept himself into exhaustion.

Going against everything he always implored himself to shed any memories of the past, or connections to his biological parents, other than his name, Adam sits in front of his computer and types 'Tom Dory' into the blank field of the internet search engine. He pauses, closes his eyes and reflects on his crappy childhood and ponders what this new information will bring. Will he travel deeper into a dark hole where rats and skeletons share stories of his family traits and treasons? Or will it unlock colorful mysteries and provide answers to unasked questions in a flurry of time gone by, dropping the shackles of fear and anger allowing freedom to move forward? Will he embrace and offer forgiveness either way?

'Click', Adam taps the enter key. When he opens his eyes the screen indicates there are eleven thousand two hundred fifty three matches. *'What the heck did I just do?'* He takes a deep breath and clicks on the first match. It leads him to a social networking site of a twelve year old boy in West Virginia named Tom Dory.

'Back Button.'

'Tap on second match.'

Again, irrelevant.

'Advanced search.' The thought of this search begins giving Adam serious anxiety. He only suspected a connection, but feared the truth. *Tom Dory Mentally Insane*

'Click', three matches.

First Match, 'click', PAGE ERROR.

Second match, 'click'. Adware Site.
Third Match, *'Walk away now Adam.'*
'Press the button you chicken shit.'
'Don't go there.'
'Grow a pair. Man up. Who cares?'
'Forget it.'
'Do it!'

A knock at the door sends Adam's heart into temporary arrhythmia and he spins around in his chair to the sound of creaking hinges.

"Hello Adam," an elderly woman with white hair, severely wrinkled skin and yellowing teeth stands in the doorway. There is a dim blue glow of light behind her. Adam does not recognize her. Confusion sets in.

'Who is she and how does she know my name?'

The woman moves methodically to Adam's side, reaches over his shoulder and presses the enter key on the computer's keyboard, 'click'.

Music began playing in the middle of a song. Adam bolted upright in his bed, shook his head, looked around his room, reached across his bed and turned off the alarm on his clock radio.

'Who was that woman in my dream?'

Buzzzz, buzzzz. Adam's cell phone starting vibrating on his nightstand. He picked it up and the caller ID displayed 'CHERI'.

"Sup??" he answered it.

"A few of us rode into town and I am outside the store near camp and thought I'd call and see how you were doing," Cheri's voice was soft, reassuring and sweetness in Adam's ear.

"Good. I am good... I am sorry for..."

"Skip, everything is fine between us," she wanted to stop him from revisiting what happened last week. Everything wasn't totally fine with Cheri, but she knew she needed the time away to process it all and wanted to keep the relationship intact just in case she did come to a place of peace with him and his freaky mind.

'Do I really think he is a freak,' Cheri wondered. Maybe she shouldn't have called him yet. Maybe she should cut the conversation short and...

"Cheri? Are you still there?" Adam's breathing sounded heavy.

"Yes, I need to go, I see everyone getting on the bus..."

"OK, thanks for the call, I guess. Can you remember to call me Adam from now on?"

"Bye Adam," Cheri wished she hadn't even called and expressed it out loud as she was hanging up, "Crap!"

"I heard that," Adam said to no one on the other end of the line. He began wondering what she meant by that. If it was meant for him or maybe she saw the bus pulling away without her. Yes. The latter sounded good.

Cheri was raised in a Christian home and was attending bible camp for the seventh time. She had a lot of great memories and her faith had grown very strong in the past year. She was truly understanding what it meant to have a relationship with God.

Cheri never drank alcohol, never did drugs, never had sex and she was very happy inside. She was confident and at peace. She avoided television and movies that had adult ratings and chose family oriented themes. Life was good to her and she had joy. She smiled at the bus driver and sat next to her friends, ready for a fun filled day.

Adam jumped in the shower to get ready for his day. It was Saturday so he could do everything or nothing. He chose to do something. He chose to follow his dream and find out the secrets of his lineage and who his parents were and why they left him behind.

Adam, showered and dressed, sitting at the desk in front of his computer screen, opened an internet web browser and typed into the blank field of the search engine, 'Tom Dory Mentally Insane".

'Click'. Three matches. Adam immediately chose the third match and hit enter.

MILTON MEDICAL INSTITUTE website started to paint across the screen. The link had led him directly to an article posted on the site a few weeks ago. *'When does reality become odder than fiction?'* He mused.

A picture of young Tom Dory was posted in the article. It looked strikingly similar to Adam. He knew it was his father. The article was more of an obituary that anything else. Privacy laws didn't really allow for much information to be shared.

The story mentioned that seventeen years earlier Tom Dory had been prepared for release but died in his sleep the evening before he would have been sent out into the world again. Tom was the first 'student' in a program utilizing a new technique that has since graduated twenty five others from the Milton Medical Institute.

Adam closed the browser. The county offices were only open until noon so he had to leave now if he wanted to take advantage of the next two hours searching their archives for information on his parents.

"Skip would you like some breakfast?" his foster mom poked her head into his bedroom. She was so kind. Her brown hair was graying around the temples and wrinkles appeared next to the corner of her eyes as she smiled.

"No thanks, I am heading out, I'll be back after lunch, so I'll join you for dinner. And remember, I changed my name to Adam."

She held her smile until he was out of her sight, walked into the living room and said to Adam's foster father, "What are we going to do about him? He can't stay here forever. He's an adult now. He even changed his name. He's probably having sex with that little girly friend of his the whole time we are at work, he..."

"Let it go," the foster father said in a cold stoic tone, "He'll be fine. He just needs a little more time, Doris."

"He needs a job, Chuck! That's what he needs," she stomped out of the living room and into the kitchen to prepare breakfast.

Chuck was getting close to retirement and had worked a long hard life of physical labor. His heart and mind were as calloused as his hands. He didn't want to care about the simple things anymore. His muscular frame was sagging from gravity as was his enthusiasm for Doris' constant nagging and senseless inter-relational skills. The office job he recently landed was his way to coast the rest of the way.

Chuck continued reading the morning paper. He never noticed the article on page three. Never noticed the photograph. He had no reason to. Sondra Farber should mean nothing to him. He should have never heard of her so his eyes, almost deliberately, skimmed right past it and onto page four, a story of a local gang that was disbanded by years of relentless police work. The officer was given an award for merit.

In the meantime, back at camp, Cheri couldn't stop thinking about the scar. She wanted answers. A voice inside her kept saying, *'Call him back'*. She began dialing Adam's number. Her fingers were trembling with each movement across the touch screen. *'Maybe I should text him?'* *'Call Him.'* She called.

Buzzzz, buzzzz. Adam's cell phone starting vibrating. He had left it on the kitchen counter. Doris, his foster mom heard it, picked it up and the caller ID displayed 'CHERI'. Doris' has a reputation as the town crier. 'A real gossip', many women in the neighborhood had called her behind her back. She has to know everything.

She did not hesitate to answer. She was crafty and deliberately allowed the person on the other end to speak first before she revealed herself. It was a way for her to possibly get some information. Her memory was rock solid for her age and her body fit like an athlete. First glance you would not know she recently turned sixty. She liked to maintain control and was still good at it.

The voice on the other end of the line was shaky, "Tell me about the scar Adam. Why did it do that, that, I don't know what to call it...how was I able to see inside it with the black light on?"

Doris waited silently to see if Cheri would expose more.

Cheri felt a chill and continued, "Adam, please talk to me. Adam?"

"Oh, hello Cheri," Doris disclosed herself, "Adam's not here right now. He left his phone..."

A dull hum echoed into Cheri's head. She knew of Doris' reputation and her skin began tingling as she sunk to the ground in a subconscious stupor of the realization of what she had just done. She hung up the phone and whispered, "Oh Adam, I am so sorry."

One of the camp counselors walked past and noticed Cheri was distraught, "Are you ok Cheri?"

Cheri looked her in the eyes and asked, "What if good is really evil and evil is good?"

"It is. In the eyes of evil," the counselor turned and walked away as she said it. Her point was made and Cheri understood it.

CHAPTER 3

Adam was excited to learn more about his family's background. He had a burst of energy and a tingly rush of anticipation of what he would find out today. He didn't have many friends; in fact, Cheri was really his only real friend. As he thought about calling her to tell her about his adventure, his hand instinctively reached for his phone, but it wasn't on his hip.

He remembered setting the phone down on the counter. He realized she wasn't ready to talk to him anyway. *'I hope Doris doesn't snoop around in my phone,'* he thought because he never deletes his text messages. He didn't have a clue that Doris had fresh information on him that he would need to explain away later.

As he neared his destination his thoughts flashed back to a memory of the previous night's dreams. His mind was telling him there was significance to what happened in the dream and his research today would open up more answers.

In the dream he was standing upon a rocky ledge overlooking a field. It had some vegetation but was covered mostly in dirt, sand and stone. An older man, dressed like an Arab, wearing a long gown and head coverings approached him. The man's face was weathered and tough like a wrinkled football. His eyes were milky and his breath like stale yogurt was warm as he spoke, "חקל דמא",the man said it in a growling whisper as he pointed out over the field.

Adam did not understand the language but he repeated it back to the man how he heard it, "Akeldama?"

The man nodded his head up and down in affirmation.

When Adam woke up the next morning he had written the word on a piece of paper that was now tucked away safely in his front left shirt pocket. He was going to look up the meaning of the word before he had left for the county offices but in his excitement to get going he had forgotten. Arriving at the public building, he decided he would use the county's computer to find its meaning.

The brakes of the bus screeched as it rolled to a stop in front of the county offices. Adam stood up and walked past the row of passengers to the front doors as the hydraulics pressed them open and fresh air rolled past the sweaty, overweight driver.

Adam had a bounce in his step as he hopped onto the pavement and accelerated his pace toward the building. A brisk wind hit his face causing his eyes to slightly water reminding him that winter was not too far off.

He entered the building and perused the building directory to confirm which office number the public records would be in. C411. Of course, same place where he was when he did his name change paperwork. Adam turned to his left and walked over to the elevator and pressed the up arrow.

Ding. The doors opened and a tall, elegant woman was standing inside. She was wearing a white, blue and beige skirt that revealed the smoothest, most perfect thighs attached to the rest of her hourglass figure with stunning natural blonde hair and impeccable blue eyes. Adam thought her smile could have been on every toothpaste ad in the world. A dentist's worst client, a doctor's worst patient, she was flawless and needed no one or nothing to make her better.

She brushed Adam's shoulder as she exited and he stepped inside. He pressed the number four but it didn't light up so he pressed it again as the doors closed. It still did not light up and the elevator began ascending. Adam pressed the number five and as the button lit the elevator stopped and the doors opened.

The number 4 was posted on each side of the wall where the doors opened. The light must have been burnt out. Adam exited the elevator and followed the signs to office C411. He passed a few hallway benches and some restrooms, turned the corner and walked into the offices of county records.

A cardboard sign that read '*be back in ten minutes*' rested on the counter. Adam looked around and there were empty desks and active computer screens lit up with icons and documents, but no people. He figured he would just wait it out when he was startled by a tap on his right shoulder. Adam twitched and turned to look and all he saw was a hand.

"I'm down here," a white haired woman that stood several inches under five feet tall giggled and smiled as Adam looked down at her.

"Can I help you young man?" She asked.

"Um, yes. I wanted to look up some public records. I am looking for information on my biological parents, Tom and, and...," Adam could not remember the name of his birth mother so he finished his answer with, "Thomas Dory."

His mother's name was not on his birth certificate and he was drawing a blank. Adam was getting agitated with himself and shifted his stance when an elderly man with graying dark hair and a hunch in his gait approached him and the old woman.

"I remember you from the other day. The boy who wanted his name changed," the old man said as he pointed at Adam.

"Yes. I am here to find information on my birth parents."

"Oh, so now you want to know. Changed yer mind, eh?" the old man's eyes pressed together in suspicion, "Why the change of heart?"

Adam wanted to tell him it was none of his business, but instead said, "I am ready for what I might find. I was unsure if I wanted to know. But I really do."

"Follow me," the man grunted as he turned and walked toward another room inside the C411 offices. He pulled out a ring full of keys and fumbled with them for several minutes until he found one that opened the door.

The door creaked loudly on its hinges as it swung inward. The room let out a musty odor and dust was visibly floating in the ray of light that shone through a crack in the window blind. Five foot tall metal file cabinets lined the walls and shelves full of cardboard boxes filled the center of the room.

Adam noticed a file cabinet with a label A -D on the top drawer, "That one," he said and pointed.

"Nope," the old man replied and pointed to a cardboard box on the second shelf, "The one labeled DI - DY. We'll probably find their file in the middle of that one."

Adam went right at it, pulled the box off the shelf, set it on a table and started rummaging thru the files when a hand grabbed his left shoulder, "Hold on young fella," the old man pulled Adam back from the contents of the box, "Those are public records, yes, but we have a process of retrieval. I will find the file and then you can review the contents. Did the gal up front get a copy of your identification?"

"Yes, of course," Adam lied, because he didn't want to waste any more time.

"What was the name you are looking for?" asked the clerk.

"Tom Dory," Adam let out an exasperated sigh.

"Ah, here it is. It looks like..." before he finished Adam grabbed the folder from his hand, "... like there isn't much in there. Knock yourself out kid," the old man grunted as he stepped back away from Adam.

There were three pieces of paper in the folder. A birth certificate, a release form from Milton Medical Institute, and a copy of Tom's death certificate. Adam reached into the box and flipped through the folders to see if there was another. *There must be more.'* The clerk let him have at it as he chuckled cynically under his breath at Adam's disappointment.

"Can I get copies of these, please?" Adam politely requested.

"Twenty-five cents each and a three dollar processing fee."

Adam rolled his eyes and replied, "Whatever."

"You can wait up front in the lobby."

After about fifteen minutes the clerk came back with the copies and handed them to Adam. He reeked of cigarettes.

"Thanks for waiting. Your request for copies crossed into my break time."

"How do I get a job like this?" Adam asked with a smirk on his face.

"Excuse me?" the old man responded with belligerence.

"Thanks for your help today, and have a great afternoon," Adam smiled and walked out of the county offices.

As he was walking to the bus stop he quickly scanned the four pages in the folder. Adam whispered to himself as he turned to look back toward the building, "I swear there were only three pages in the file." He looked up and noticed the clerk moving away from the window on the fourth floor.

The fourth piece of paper was from Milton. It was an internal letter from Sondra Farber to Dr. Benjamin Skinner. She was requesting the elimination of the trial vitamin from Tom Dory's daily supplement regiment. Her reason **was** *'increased despondency from the patient. Withdrawal and periodic catatonic states.'*

After making a few calls into the county offices, Chuck had fallen into a peaceful sleep on his recliner when Doris abruptly woke him by asking, "Did you know about his scar?"

Chuck grunted and cleared his throat, "Huh? Scar? Who has a scar?"

"Adam's scar. Did you know about it?"

"Doris. I was resting nicely. What are you talking about?"

She began rambling, "He left his phone and it rang and when I answered I didn't say anything and then Cheri thought it was Adam and she said something about a scar and then I told her Adam wasn't here and then ..."

Chuck hollered, "Stop!" He paused, took a deep breath and said, "I hate when you do that. You make no sense when you carry on at a hundred miles an hour and mash all your thoughts together. It's so damn annoying. Just shut the hell up and leave me alone."

Adam's foster parents stared into each other's eyes waiting for the other person to flinch, both holding their ground and finally Doris broke and stormed out of the room stomping her feet.

Adam stepped onto the bus to head back to his house. He knew he would have to keep the file a secret from his parents, especially Doris. *'Doris, that's right. My phone. God only knows what she's been doing with it for the past couple hours.'* He stared out the window and thought about Sondra Farber. He needed to find her, and talk to her. She would know more about his father.

"Excuse me sir, you dropped this," a young boy handed Adam one of the pages from the file.

"Thanks," Adam said as he looked down at the paper. It was the release form. It said 'the specimen had been successfully extracted from the patient'.

'What specimen? I need to find Sondra.' Adam dozed off. The bus drove mightily off to complete its route.

Adam is standing at the base of a hill looking up. Dust is blowing sand in a warm breeze. There is a stench in the air. There are three trees on the hill. They are in the shape of a cross and there is a man hanging from each one of them. *'I have been here before.'*

The ground shakes and there is a flash of light. Calm and tranquility embrace him. Adam feels nothing. A figure of a being is hovering over him. Anxiety nudges him. Adam hears thoughts in his mind, *'I will take you to see God. Then you will know what he knows.'* He thinks it is an angel.

Adam looks down at his own chest and he can see through his own skin past the ribcage into his heart. His heart is black. As the angel turns and moves away, its light dims and the figure fades.

The bus lurches to a halt thrusting Adam's face into the back of the seat in front of him wakening him abruptly. Adam noticed he was the only one left on the bus and he missed his stop a mile back. He rushed to the front of the bus and hopped off. The hydraulics released, *psssst*, and the bus started to roll away when Adam realized he forgot the file.

"Wait!" Adam yelled as he jumped up and down waving his arms.

The bus driver stopped the vehicle and opened the door. Adam ran to his seat, grabbed the file, said "Thanks," hopped off the bus and headed down the street toward home. He whispered to no one in particular, "I have an appointment with God."

As he walked toward his house from the bus stop he looked at the paper in the file. It had the number of Milton Medical Clinic listed on the back. Adam decided he would call there first, but he needed to sneak back home and retrieve his phone.

Adam set out to find Sondra Farber. Something told him she would still be in the clinic. Something also told him he would be meeting her soon.

CHAPTER 4

Doris never got the chance to confront Adam about the scar. He snuck in the house, took his phone and disappeared for the rest of the evening. No note, no communication, he just left. Doris was concerned about him. He was only coming home during the day, leaving evidence he was alive by polishing off food.

Yes, she was frustrated with him, but that was common with teenage boys and their mother. Even though she was his foster mother she had raised him for the past several years. She actually loved the boy.

Chuck was a different story. Chuck was indifferent to the boy, to the whole situation for that matter. They interacted like a father and son at times, they would play ball, or laugh at stupid guy things, go to a football game now and then, but it seemed superficial to Doris.

"Chuck, I am worried about Adam. He didn't sleep here again last night," Doris had a quiver in her voice.

"He'll be fine. He's eating just fine. Probably found him a little..."

"Don't go there Chuck. Is that all you ever think about. Is that all you ever talk about?" Doris was raising her voice.

"I can call the cops and say we have a missing person."

"Maybe we should Chuck."

"Perfect. So officer, he is missing at night and then my food is missing when I come home from work, so we know he's alive, he just doesn't sleep here. Do you realize how stupid this sounds, Doris?" Chuck had enough, "Besides, let's not draw attention to him if we don't need to, okay."

Doris whimpered for a few seconds and left the room. Chuck sat back in his recliner and read the newspaper. He knew Adam would be just fine. He was a young man and could take care of himself. The women always worried.

Adam's arms and legs are bound by thick ropes tightly pressed against his skin digging into and burning his flesh. He is covered only by a small cotton cloth that covers his waist to his thighs. Slivers of wood are burrowing into Adam's back and he feels his ligaments being stretched with each clicking sound. Stabbing pain.

The world looks upside down. Suddenly he is flipped upwards and around until the rack stops on a forty-five degree angle. Adam chokes up some fluid that burns his throat and he begins gagging and coughing. There is a burning sensation in his throat and Adam awakens. He bolts upright in his bed and spits some bile from his mouth into a cup next to his bed.

He reaches over and turns on the light next to his bed. He shakes off the apostasy in his head and ponders what occurred. The people were speaking Spanish and he was being tortured for some reason. He had an acid reflux episode which woke him from the dream. *'Did the acid reflux cause the dream or did the dream cause the acid reflux?'*

Adam turns on the television to shake the graven images from his mind and get grounded in reality. There is a toll free number on the screen and a woman is talking about a new sleep vitamin. An infomercial boasting, "Free trial. Not released to the public. Earn money while you sleep. Call now."

The woman in the commercial is Sondra Farber. He recognizes her. He has seen her before. This is the first time he has seen this commercial. He had seen her before he came to this place. She was the woman in his dreams. The one in the coffee shop? Adam's mind is racing to piece it together.

A soft voice whispers into his ear and he feels a light touch on his right shoulder, "Adam, wake up."

Adam opened his eyes and questioned, "How long have I been here?"

He was in a room painted all white. Very sterile environment. He was on a bed staring up at her. She was dressed like a clinician. She was the woman in the commercial. It was coming back to him. He called her a few days ago. He found her.

"You came in a couple nights ago, remember? You only sleep here. It was the agreement we made."

In a demanding voice Adam said, "How do you know my Father?"

Sondra did not respond. She turned away and simply said, "Good morning to you too Adam."

"How did you know my father?" a bit of anger was entering Adam's tone.

Sondra knew she couldn't and shouldn't push it. She knew this day would come. It was time. Time to tell Adam all he needed to know and only what he needed to know. She turned toward Adam and said, "He was in a clinical trial for my employer, Dr. Benjamin Skinner. You can ask me anything you would like," her motives were selfish but she wanted him to believe otherwise.

"Tell me about Skinner."

"Eccentric, rich, brilliant. Made a fortune in real estate and other investments. Tall, handsome for his age. Married, one child, one granddaughter. Loving, but distant," Sondra repeated the last word while staring at the ceiling, "Distant."

Despite her odious memories of Ben, Sondra was ecstatic that Adam showed up after all these years. Now that he was an adult, there were no State agencies that could keep him from volunteering for the study. No oversight or roadblocks that would keep her from Adam. His identity was hidden.

"When did you first meet him? Tom Dory that is," Adam pressed on realizing she held the answers he longed for.

Sondra hesitated and Adam picked up on it. She had to be open and honest or he would not trust her enough for her to get what *she* wanted. Sondra wanted to know if the experiment on Tom and now Adam actually worked so she told the truth, "We met in high school. We were very good friends. Your dad asked me out on a date once, but I was dating someone else at the time so it never happened, but we were always close friends."

Adam pressed for more, "How did he, or why did he get involved with Ben Skinner?"

"Me. He did it for me. I asked him to do it as a favor for me, to join the trial for the revolutionary new 'Sleep Vitamin'. At the time we couldn't afford to pay people to join the trial so we had no committed test subjects. People weren't even willing to try it for free because even though it was a vitamin, the government labeled it a drug due to one of the ingredients."

"What ingredient?" he asked.

Sondra disregarded his question and continued her monologue, "People were very suspect of the whole project. Ben, uh Doctor Skinner, had a sketchy reputation in the industry and the press made sure to publish it, so Tom signed up at my request."

He wondered why she referred to the Doctor as Ben. She must have known him well.

"Was he married to or with my mother at the time?" Adam wanted the whole story and it seemed like Sondra was willing to share it.

"Yes. She was with him and they were married."

"Did she know about it?"

"Yes," Sondra was not going to elaborate any more unless Adam asked open questions.

"How did she react?" Adam realized he needed to get Sondra to open up again.

"Your mother signed up for the trials with him."

Adam's head dropped and he sighed, "Do I share both their memories?"

Sondra reached over and touched Adam's shoulder, "It's not very likely, your mother dropped out of the program after one session, just like all the other candidates…except Tom."

"Why did she drop out?"

"Bad side effects."

"Like what?" Adam had to keep asking to get deeper understanding.

"I cannot disclose that."

"Why not?"

"Patient confidentiality," she was stretching the truth because nothing up to this point was treated as confidential.

"Bullshit!" Adam was quickly getting agitated.

"You are a sagacious young man! Okay fine, you want it, you got it," Sondra gave him a stare down and continued, "She hallucinated for sixteen hours from the minimum dose administered. We were all freaked out wondering if she would ever come out of it. The images she described were terrifying, to all of us. Your dad even dropped out of the program for a few months."

"Why did he come back? I am assuming he came back."

"The dreams. And the memories. For Tom, it was more about the dreams."

"What?" Adam started thinking about his dreams. As long as he could remember, his dreams were surreal yet as real as the scar on his side. He began to wonder if he was insane. If anything was real. He thought, *'Am I sitting in a wheelchair in an institution somewhere imagining all this right now?'*

"He came back because of the dreams," Sondra confirmed.

"What about the dreams?"

"He couldn't get enough. He believed he could move between realities and conquer both. He experimented with ideas beyond all our imaginations."

Adam's mind was wandering and he disregarded Sondra's last statement as he said, "I see John and Billy. I don't like them but I don't know why."

Sondra was taken aback but excited at the same time. There was a slight tremble in her voice that went undetected, "They were your father's friends. I do mean, were. John dated your mother when he and Tom, um, your father, were best friends. She broke it off with John and then a couple years later hooked up with your dad. John was never okay with that. It never bothered your dad that much since it was in the past."

Sondra drew in a deep breath and continued, "Until one night when they were all together, Johnny, Johnny's girlfriend, your mom and dad, Billy and Billy's girlfriend. Johnny got drunk and got in Tom's face about how much fun he had being intimate with your mom. Your dad got really upset and started beating the crap out of Johnny."

She paused for effect, "Billy pulled your dad off of John and the two of them, Billy and John, beat your dad silly. That was the end of those friendships. Everyone was drinking that night and it got out of hand."

Adam had a puzzled look on his face, "How do you know all of this?"

"I was at the party. I didn't see Johnny and Billy again until they showed up one day for the clinical trials. I believed the only reason they did it was because they found out your father was in the program and they just wanted to taunt him again. They were immature jerks."

Adam was taking it all in. He was wondering why Sondra was so open with information, yet she kept sharing, "I didn't want Skinner to let them in the program but he felt it would stimulate some possibilities with your father's trial. You see, Tom Dory was his prize subject."

"What was the ingredient?" Adam asked.

"Ingredient?"

"Yes, earlier you mentioned the government was regulating the trial because of one of the ingredients. What was it?" he asked.

"It was a derivative of mescaline. Lophophora williamsii is a small, spineless cactus with psychoactive alkaloids, particularly mescaline. Peyote," she explained.

"Peyote?" Adam heard of it but didn't understand.

Sondra responded, "My definition is that it's a poison, that doesn't kill. It takes a human's physical and mental state and alters it so dramatically that the person gets extremely ill and near death, then they think they see God."

"Did they all go insane?" Adam asked.

"Who?"

"My father, Billy and Johnny. Did, they, all, go, insane?"

"Yes."

Adam jumped topic to his next question, "Who is the old lady I frequently see?"

Sondra paused, shifted her stance and said, "I am not sure."

Adam scratched the back of his head inquisitively and said, "Please, do tell."

"Possibly Tom's grandmother," Sondra said. She knew it was her but didn't want Adam to go too far down that path of questioning. It was a complex web that could entrap and entangle a young mind. She didn't think that telling Adam that Ben Skinner was Tom Dory's father-in-law would do anything more than confuse him. She would save that for a later day.

"Sondra?"

"Yes, Adam?"

"The visions and memories are so real that most of the time they feel like my memories."

"Tell me more Adam." It's what she wanted. The deepest secrets of his mind.

Adam's stomach gurgled and he let loose a little gas caused by the anxiety of his thoughts, but he could not hold back any longer so he blurted it out really fast, "Am I Tom Dory?"

Sondra was taken aback and her shoulders drew her back into her chair.

Adam slowed his breathing and the delivery of his words, "Am, I, Tom, Dory?"

CHAPTER 5

"How far back do your memories go?" Sondra's words trembled with excitement.

"They have always been in my mind. I can even recall opening my eyes as an infant."

Sondra felt a tingling sensation in her spine, like she was about to win the jackpot on a slot machine and all the coins were going to start clinging in the bottom of the collection tray so she went in for the winning pull, "What do you remember before you opened your eyes, Adam?"

Adam felt sleep deprived and it challenged him to go back in time. The farther back he traveled in his mind, the more nauseated he would get. His ears would pierce with pain accompanied by sirens of tinnitus and his head felt like it wanted to explode from the pressure buildup in his forehead.

He closed his eyes very tight and held them closed the whole time he spoke, "I could hear the voice of a young woman, saying *'Good morning, Tom.'* I tried to respond. The words were coming out but there was no sound. I tried harder and harder to make the words come out audibly but there was no noise," he paused.

"And?" Sondra prodded.

"My body ached everywhere as if someone or something was beating me with a club. I felt an urge to urinate. There was an intermittent ringing in my ears that faded in and out and drowned out the external sounds."

"The woman speaking mentioned the name Amy then it sounded like a doctor summoned her. I felt something wet and warm brushing against my face and I heard a clip clop, clip clop, clip clop. The woman said something about my friends, Billy and John and I could feel something hard and cold on the back of my head. "

"Then I could hear an old man's voice talking about a group session and some old men dying. Then the man referenced a guy named Jerry crossing over from the other side. Then I remember the old man saying that 'Tom's case is unique'."

"I remember seeing a blue pickup truck and then I was in long narrow hallway with thousands of open doors. Blurriness and nausea started consuming me. Tunnel vision rushed through my eyes and mind. Blurred concentric circles merged into one and assortments of doors began appearing before me. The doors were lined up uniformly on each side and there was light shining through them. Then doors began to close, one at a time, and I could see a faint blue light in the distance."

"There was a mirror up ahead on my right. As I approached it, the reflection of a man, my father I believe, wavered in the glass. In the distance I could hear weeping. It grew louder as each door closed. Then suddenly it became very cold and very bright and I could not breath for a few seconds," Adam paused as he tried to recollect if there was anything else, "And that's all I remember."

Sondra had to summon her body to breathe. She was blown away by the detail of the memories Adam had just shared so she asked, "How do you know you were an infant? What I mean to ask is what makes you think that you can actually remember those things since the day you were born?"

Adam smiled and replied, "Because that's all I remember before I felt a slap on my butt and I gasped for air and screamed in agony from the whole experience."

Sondra's mouth was hanging open and she let out a gasp, "Oh my goodness. Adam, do you realize those were your memories as you were being born?" She got more than she ever imagined out of him. If it was truly his earliest memory, what if she could take him further back with the experiment? Sondra's mind was racing with excitement. She could dig deep into Adam's Genetic Memory!

"Sondra? Sondra! Hello, are you there?" Adam had been responding to her question and she was so deep in thought she didn't hear a word he said.

"Sorry Adam. What did you say?"

"I said yes. It was horrifying. It was warm and dark one moment and then crushing pain throughout my body, for what felt like forever, then freezing cold and bright and something slapping my bare ass. Unbelievable! I shiver every time I relive it in my mind," Adam was visibly shaking as the words trembled off his tongue, "And I can't help but think that I am Tom Dory."

"Adam, it was a collision of memories from your father's life that flashed in your mind while you were in the womb at the very moment you were being born into this world. That's what makes it so confusing," Sondra was referring to what Adam dreamed as he was being born, "All of your father's memories collided and created a story, a lifetime that your mind reassembled and displayed from the time you exited the birth canal to when you finally woke up in the incubator."

"Finally woke up? You say it like I was in some kind of catatonic state."

"You were."

"So are you telling me my mind was inactive until birth?"

"No, what I am saying is that for the time being that is as far back as you can remember for some reason," Sondra sighed and continued, "While in the womb and as a newborn in the lab we were monitoring your brainwaves. Your EEG readings were the most active of any recorded human and right after you were born we thought we lost you. Everything went blank, you paled and froze. Everyone thought the overwhelming brain activity put you into shock. When you came back, Doctor Skinner was convinced you would recall everything in your father's memory as you were being born."

"Not anymore. Or at least now that I know what is happening," Adam was pale and sweat beaded on his upper lip as he opened up Pandora's Box to Sondra.

"Sondra?"

"Yes."

"What time did Skinner die?" Adam inquired.

"Why?"

"What time was I born?"

"Why do you ask Adam?"

"Things I remember force the questions," Adam looked away, dropped his head and closed his eyes. It was like he was sleeping or dreaming while engaging in dialog.

"What are the deeper questions?" Sondra had her suspicions but wanted Adam to open up.

"When you stop answering my questions with a question, maybe I'll let you know," Adam expressed his frustration.

"Approximately the same time. You were born about the same time as Skinner was pronounced dead. Same time as your father passed away," Sondra whispered and sighed, "But it doesn't mean anything, really."

Adam jumped to another random question, "How long ago did I start the trial? How long have you been experimenting with me?"

"You know the answer to that. We started a week ago when you called the toll free number and inquired about the trial. Remember?" Sondra answered nervously.

Adam sensed she was hiding something but didn't want her to think he was paranoid or that he was experiencing side effects. She told him from the beginning that at the first sign of any adverse reactions she would stop the trial immediately. He had to make sure he was always calm and steady in his demeanor.

"Sondra, were there any experiments done on me before last week?" He wished he could take the question back but the words already became sound.

"Seriously Tom?" Sondra acted flabbergasted.

"Did you just call me Tom?" Adam leaned over; dry heaved and began to cough.

Sondra jumped up from her seat and grabbed the Styrofoam cup next to Adam's bed, "Here, drink some water."

Adam took a sip and choked out, "Thanks."

"Damn it Adam. We are stopping the trial effective immediately," Sondra said it with conviction, but didn't really mean it. She wanted Adam to think she would stop it so that he would push on. Reverse Psychology. He took the bait.

"I am fine. I must have eaten too much pizza."

"Adam, I am referring to your paranoid comments about previous experiments and hearing things that were not spoken," Sondra was staring directly into his eyes when she spoke, but Adam was convinced her mouth never moved.

Then Sondra's mouth did move and the words audibly filled the air, "Ok, take it easy on the pizza."

Adam just smiled and nodded even though he was scared on the inside.

Sondra pressed him for more information, "Tell me what you meant before when you said that now you know what is happening."

"The last thing I remember before I woke up was that I was being tortured."

"*What?*"

"It was as if I were a prisoner on some sort of torture device. It was a historical moment in time. Like it was really happening. It seemed primitive by today's standards."

"*What?*"

"Sondra, stop saying what!"

"Adam, it's working. Your memories are going back in time."

"No duh," Adam shook his head in disbelief that she finally caught up to the concept. She was supposed to be the clinician. He was simply the test case. Little did she know he had his secrets also. He knew she slipped up and called him Tom. He knew he had to be prepared for her on-going head games.

"You know we're in this together, Adam?"

"Yeah, I know. I take the vitamins, I get the side effects and you get the research paper."

Her eyebrows tilted together and Sondra looked confused when she replied, "You came to me, remember? You are free to leave anytime. We can stop the payments immediately if you'd like. Just say the word."

"Seriously?" Adam raised his voice, "Twenty-five dollars covers bus fair and a crappy dinner."

"You originally said you didn't care about the money. You told me you wanted to uncover your past," Sondra pushed back.

Cheri was back from camp and wanted to see Adam. He wasn't answering his phone and Doris claimed she hadn't seen him for a long time. She told Cheri he wasn't sleeping there, only eating during the day, leaving a mess and disappearing again.

Adam had left the clinic and was on the bus back to the house to grab some breakfast. He always got off one stop past the house so he could stake out the place to make sure no one was around before he went in.

No cars were around and the house looked closed up. He peeked over the fence and there were no signs of his parents. He opened the gate and walked past the old maple tree toward the back door of the house.

"Hello Adam," a female voice echoed in his ears and he jumped and his body shook.

"Cheri?" Adam gulped, "What are you doing here? You scared the crap out of me."

"Nice to see you too Adam," she sarcastically replied.

"Oh, no, I didn't mean anything, I mean, it's good to see you, and I just thought you were maybe done with me."

Cheri stood and stared into Adam's eyes with a perplexed look on her face. She knew this would be a bad idea. Maybe he was just some weirdo and she should get as far away from him as possible, but something in her heart desired to be around him, to care for him.

"I'll just go," Cheri turned away.

"Adam gently grabbed her arm, "No, please stay."

"Where have you been?"

"It's a long story. Come on in, I'll make you some breakfast. But we gotta make it quick in case Doris comes home."

"Adam, Doris is worried sick about you. And she knows about the scar."

Adam's head snapped around and his eyes widened with fright, "What makes you say that?"

"I told her."

"You what? Why?"

"It was an accident," Cheri stepped back as she said it because Adam's face was reddening.

"How much does she know?" Adam had a slight growl in his tone.

"Nothing really. She answered your phone and didn't say anything and I spoke first and I said tell me about the scar and then she reveled herself. That's all."

Adam sighed, "No biggie. I'll tell her it was appendix surgery when I was little."

"But your appendix is on the other side."

"I know, but most people don't really know, and they accept that answer. Just like you never knew the difference. Peanut butter and jelly sound good?" Adam smiled.

"Sounds good," Cheri smiled back, but was nervous about how things could have gone if Adam wasn't satisfied with the conversation. She had never seen him lose it, but he seemed edgy. More volatile than usual.

"Let's talk," Adam said.

He told Cheri all about the documents in the file and how he found Sondra Farber and that he was doing the vitamin trial so he could figure out his past. He told her about the angel in his dream and that he wanted to learn about good and evil and see God.

"Adam, can I say something?" She interrupted him.

"Sure."

She took hold of his hands, "Look into my eyes when I tell you this."

"Ok, what's up?"

Cheri said, "When I was at camp, I had a long talk with one of the counselors. We talked about good and evil, angels and demons."

"Cool," Adam replied and leaned in to hear more.

"The lady told me that it's possible that angels and demons all look the same because they all were angels when they were created. It may not be the beauty versus beast like we're used to seeing them portrayed in books and movies. She told me the head demon, named Satan, appears as an angel of light," Cheri looked away for a moment.

"And?" Adam wanted her to finish.

Cheri looked deep into Adam's eyes and said, "What if the angel you saw was really a demon?"

"How can you tell the difference?" Adam asked.

Cheri tilted her head and replied slow and methodically, "Light and hope as opposed to darkness and despair."

He thought to himself and recalled the vision, *There was light but what kind of light? Did I feel hope of what I was told about seeing God or was it a desire placed at the inception by the angel speaking to me?* He struggled to discern. As he placed himself in the moment of the dream his heart was feeling the despair but his mind, filled with excitement, insisted he press on.

CHAPTER 6

"Are you recording this?" Sondra excitedly asked the young lady monitoring all the equipment, vital signs, monitors and sound capture devices. Adam was speaking in his sleep. It was a foreign language.

"Yes," she replied with a lisp from the silver stud embedded in her tongue. The young aide had an attitude toward Sondra, to authority for that matter, and she displayed it with her piercings, rebel tattoos and short colored hair. A work of abstract art on the outside, a brilliant young and developing medical mind on the inside.

"Of course Amy," Sondra responded with a smile and a wink. Sondra knew the young lady would grow out of it someday and learn to appreciate and respect how the world operates. 'The girl has unlimited potential' she would explain to the administrators every time they wanted to send her packing for her demonstrable issues towards leaders and business owners.

Amy was a genius and Sondra knew it. The girl skipped a grade and went into the University a year sooner than her peers. The girl tested out of intro classes with her ACT scores and could probably pass her MCAT's if she took them today as a freshman.

"It's Aramaic," the young aide blurted out her random thought.

"Say what?" Sondra wasn't sure she heard it correctly.

"Aramaic. Ancient dialect. Adam is speaking Aramaic. Only four words.   Like he's repeating what he's hearing," she explained.

Sondra asked, "Are you certain?"

"Yes. I am studying religions and the languages along with ancient manuscripts. Electives," she smiled and winked back at Sondra. Always wanting to 'one-up' her superior to intimidate and never show weakness. Something her grandfather taught her when she was a little girl.

"What did he say? *In Aramaic*," Sondra emphasized the last two words.

"Off with his head!" the girl growled out the words to reflect the way she heard Adam speak them.

Sondra gasped, "We should wake him…"

"He's fine Sondra."

"Amy, you know I trust your judgment but…"

"If you trust my judgment Sondra, there are no buts."

"Keep recording. I want to review it with him as soon as he wakes up. I am going to get some coffee. Want anything?" Sondra asked as she approached the door.

"Low fat Latte', extra hot, double shot."

"The usual then," Sondra smiled and walked out. The clinic only offered regular coffee with powdered cream and sweetener.

Adam's EEG reading was off the charts, in a good way. Amy rubbed the pearl piercing in her nose, sat back in her chair and thought, '*I wonder where he is right now*'.

Amy recalled her last debrief with Adam. He was soaked in sweat, shivering, yet calm and confident. In that session Adam told her, "Sometimes, when your psyche travels, you watch your dreams and other times you live your dreams." Staring at the EEG readings it dawned on her, Adam does both.

Adam is in peak R.E.M. sleep. He is standing in an ancient structure made of stone. Although his mind knows it is ancient it appears to have been built recently. People are moving around him as if he doesn't exist, yet he can see and hear every detail clearly as if it is real and he is standing among them.

The people are wearing robes, or togas, tied at the waist by rope. Some are adorned with gold and jewels, others are plain. The servants are the plain ones. The servants are also barefoot and the elite, the adorned, wear sandals. *'A king's palace?'*

A servant carrying a platter of fresh fruits and nuts approaches him and offers it to him. Adam reaches forward and helps himself to some of the food. He can taste the freshness of the juices as they coat his throat with sweetness. Adam smiles but the female servant merely stares back at him with a stoic expression.

Adam looks at where he is sitting. He is on a large chair that rests above everyone else. It is made of gold and silver with beautiful artwork etched into the arms and legs. The backing is padded and covered with a silky material. *'Am I the King?'*

His question is answered as a deep resounding voice comes from next to him and shouts, "رأسه مع قبالة". Adam is sitting next to the King. Adam realizes he is merely the prince.

Several large men are dragging another scrawny, boney, naked, dirty, unshaven and beaten man toward him and the King. Another man steps forward, unsheathes a sword and with a single stroke decapitates the man as the others are holding him with his arms back.

Adam will remember those words forever. The image burns in his mind as the man's cranium hits the floor and rolls toward him, eyes wide open staring directly into Adam's eyes. Rich burgundy blood pooling on the palace floor under the head. The King had commanded the beheading.

Adam drops his own head to his chest, closes his eyes and wonders, *'What kind of world do we live in?'* He lifts his head and reopens his eyes, hoping he is no longer dreaming. A voice inside him whispers, *'There is a greater King than he'*.

Everything he sees is blurry. It looks like the outline of a face. He hears sound, like a muffled grumbling voice, "Hell am you k. Ad r o."

"Hello Adam, are you ok?" Amy whispered the words into his ear for the third time.

"Your eyes are open, you must be awake now."

"Can I have some water?" Adam asked. His voice was dry and cracked.

Amy smiled and handed him a cup of ice water. Adam's hand trembled and twitched as he took the cup and placed the straw into his mouth.

"Ahhh. So good," Adam said as he sat up in the bed.

"Where were you Adam?" Amy asked.

The door to the room flung open and cool air rushed in giving Adam a chill.

"Here's your Latte', I see our patient is awake," Sondra handed a steaming cup of black coffee to Amy.

"Patient?" Adam frowned the question.

"That's what we have to call anyone in the trial. It sounds better than 'test subject', doesn't it?" Sondra rolled her eyes and said, "Are you always this grumpy when you first wake up?"

"I was just asking him where he was this time," Amy said with a smile and a wink at Sondra, hoping that Sondra would step back and let her work with Adam this time.

"Of course, please continue," Sondra replied.

Adam looked up at the clock and realized he was supposed to meet Cheri for breakfast in forty minutes. If he left right away he would make the next bus and be on time for once.

"I gotta go. Let's talk about it tonight," Adam said.

Amy wasn't going to give up that easy so she quickly asked, "Was that Hebrew you were speaking?"

Adam was half way out of the bed with one foot on the floor when he froze and stared directly at Amy. Neither of them moved. It was a stand-off. A few more seconds of silence passed when Adam jumped off the bed and headed for the door.

"I'll see you tonight," Adam said as he closed the door behind him, leaving Amy and Sondra alone and frustrated.

Cheri was smiling and glowing with excitement when Adam stepped off the bus. He was actually a few minutes early. She ran to greet him. She was concerned about his apparent obsession with the clinical trial because his sleep patterns were getting more and more random and he looked like he was wearing down physically. Today he looked pretty good and she was happy to see him.

"Hi Cheri," Adam said as he gave her a big hug.

Cheri returned the squeeze and asked, "Can I treat you to a coffee and breakfast sandwich?"

"Of course. I'm starving." The trial consumed all his calories, and more.

Cheri interlaced her fingers in his hand and they strolled down the street together. The air was brisk. Adam didn't like the cold Chicago air and he didn't care for crowds very much either. He always wanted to move away and now that he was an adult, he could go wherever he wanted. As soon as the trial was complete he was gone. Just a few more months. Transient until content. Somewhere warm and sunny.

"Adam, you seem like you are in a daze. You haven't heard a word I said, have you?" Cheri challenged him and stopped walking.

"Sorry. What did I miss, please repeat it. You have my undivided attention. I promise," he pleaded.

"I asked if you have seen God yet."

"That's not what you asked," Adam knew she was mad by her sarcasm.

Cheri said, "I asked how the trial is going. I am concerned about you Adam. You seem more withdrawn and I can tell you are losing weight. You are not sleeping good or eating right. Your foster parents call me all the time to ask how you are doing. Why don't you go home and speak with them?"

"I am done with them. They served their purpose."

"ADAM!" Cheri screeched with a gasp, "How could you say something like that?" She let go of his hand and stepped away.

Adam felt scared. He didn't know where those thoughts came from. He didn't mean to say it. It was freaking him out and now it was freaking out Cheri. He had to think of something to say or Cheri might run off again, this time never to return.

"I was just kidding. I plan on going there this afternoon and spending some time with them," he grinned as he said it hoping she would accept his response.

"That's not funny. They really do care about you. Are you really going there?"

"Yes, absolutely," he lied.

"Great! What time? I'll go with you," she offered. Cheri wanted to believe him and hoped he wasn't bluffing.

"Around five o'clock."

"Ok Adam, I'll meet you there at five. Let's go eat," she said as she grabbed his hand and started back down the sidewalk toward the restaurant.

Doris was sitting in the kitchen rifling through the mail when the knock at the back door startled her. She looked up at the clock and it was five after five. She wondered who it could be when the knocking began again.

"Are you going to answer that?" Chuck hollered from his chair in the other room.

Doris opened the door and was greeted by Adam's girlfriend, Cheri, "Hi is Adam here?"

"I am sorry, he hasn't been here for weeks, you know that," Doris replied.

"Um, he was supposed to meet me here at five. Can I come in?" Cheri asked. She tried not to let her disappointment show. She came a few minutes late so she wouldn't be there before Adam. But that obviously didn't work. Now she was alone with gossip girl.

"Yes of course, come on in," Doris held the door open and stepped aside for Cheri to pass through.

"Who is it?" Chuck yelled from the other room.

"It's Cheri, dear."

"Cheri who?" Chuck asked. He didn't pay much attention to details and it saddened Doris to think he didn't remember something that would be important to Adam. No wonder Adam hadn't been around.

"Adam's friend," Doris replied and shook her head.

Chuck went back to reading the newspaper. He knew who Cheri was; he just didn't want to get out of his chair to go and greet her. Deep down, it bothered him that Adam had walked away from them like he did. It hurt him that Adam could do that to Doris. Doris really cared about Adam. Chuck turned inward.

The front door slung open startling Chuck out of his inward trance. Adam quickly stepped inside and closed the door behind him. Chuck couldn't hold back his frustration when he blurted out, "Where have you been Adam?"

"Good to see you too Chuck," Adam shot back.

That remark stung because Adam always referred to Chuck as 'dad'. Chuck shifted in his chair. The air was thick with tension. The situation could turn either direction depending on what was said next. Chuck wanted Adam to stay so he thought hard about the right words to say next.

Cheri turned the corner from the kitchen and broke up the squabble, "Hi Adam."

"Doris, come quick, Adam's home," Chuck expressed enthusiasm as he yelled to the kitchen.

Doris wiped the tears from her eyes and regained her composure before stepping into the living room to join the others.

"Hi mom," Adam barely got the words out as Doris wrapped her arms around his shoulders and kissed his neck.

"I am so happy to see you. Can I get you something to eat, you looked starved? Dinner will be ready shortly. Will you join us?" Doris asked.

"I'd love to join you. Can Cheri too?" Adam asked because he didn't want to go alone through the twenty questions test he was about to receive.

"Yes, of course," Doris said and smiled at Cheri.

Adam decided before he went home that he was not going to tell them about the clinical trial. He needed to let Cheri know his intentions so the topic could be avoided completely so he said, "Cheri and I will go wash up for dinner," Adam tilted his head in gesture for Cheri to follow him out of the room.

Adam whispered in Cheri's ear, "We are not discussing the trial."

"What are you going to tell them then?" Cheri whispered

"I haven't thought about that yet?"

"I cannot be a party to any lies."

Adam felt a knot in his gut. He didn't want to lie either, but Doris could not handle the truth in this situation. She would be frantic and anxious and out of control if she knew what he was up to. Chuck wouldn't care. Or if he did, he wouldn't say anything.

"Let's get on with it then," Adam said.

"The truth is always best Adam," Cheri replied with a smirk.

As soon as they walked back into the living room Doris was standing stiff and upright with a serious expression as she said, "Tell us about your scar Adam."

CHAPTER 7

"I can't believe we got out of there without having to discuss the trial. Your slip up about the scar was a blessing in disguise!" Adam let out a in joyous sigh of relief, "And it was brilliant that you diverted Doris' attention by asking her for the recipe from dinner and then asking me to take you home right away after dinner."

Cheri was happy they didn't have to discuss the scar, but she did wish Adam would tell his parents about the trial. She couldn't stop thinking about what she learned at camp and that Adam was possibly being deceived by a dark force. Something unseen yet present, unspoken yet heard, surreal yet real.

"Adam, when will the trial be over?" Cheri asked with distraught concern. She also wanted to know about that scar, but felt it was better to wait to discuss.

"When I go all the way back through every genetic memory locked away inside my brain, my DNA, my genetic code. I want to know everything. I want to see everything; I want to experience it all!" He exclaimed.

Adam's eyes were wide open and he was staring right through Cheri and into some other place. He wished she would be more reassuring of his quest for knowledge and understanding. She wanted to be supportive, but had a notion of dark and fallen angels talking to him.

As if she read his mind Cheri said, "I will support you through this as long as you let me check in on you regularly since there are side effects with any chemical alteration to the human body."

"Deal."

"Not so fast. And that you will trust me if I tell you it is having a bad effect on you and that you promise to stop if it has any negative effects on your mind, body or soul."

Adam questioned, "Soul?"

"Yes Adam, soul. The angel you said you saw could be an angel of darkness."

"Deal." Adam said with a squint in his eyes. He didn't like what Cheri implied again but he wanted and he needed her support.

"Ok, then. Deal," Cheri agreed with a smile.

Adam liked it when she smiled. Her eyes smiled also. She glowed. She was the girlfriend every guy would imagine. Strong character, smart, intuitive and pretty. He noticed that sometimes there were slight variations to the way she looked and acted. Changes in eye color, skin tone, the way her face looked and her voice inflection, but it was always Cheri.

"I have an idea. Why don't you come with me to the clinic tonight and stay with me while I sleep. That should ease any concerns you have about the trial," Adam suggested with a hint of excitement.

"I have to work in the morning." Cheri worked at the local grocer stocking shelves, running the register or whatever else Mr. Martin, the store owner asked her to do.

"I'll ask Amy to make sure she wakes you up in time tomorrow."

"Amy?" Cheri questioned with jealousy.

"She's the technician that stays with me every night. If you come you'll get to meet her."

"Maybe you should get clearance for me being there, first."

"They don't get to decide. If they want me in the trial, they need to let you come along."

"I thought you were the one that wanted the trial."

"I am, they just don't need to know it," Adam said with a grin.

"Okay. And since my job is only part time and Mr. Martin is very flexible, I'll talk to him about it going forward too," she replied.

They had a plan to go through it together. Adam was very happy. Cheri wanted to do some research on memories. Anxious excitement left them both speechless.

Amy and Sondra were at the clinic preparing the room for Adam. The sun was setting and a red glow hovered over the bed that sent colored lights dancing off the reflection of the stainless steel bedside tray. Amy wheeled in an extra piece of diagnostic equipment to monitor Adam's heart rate and blood pressure. Sondra wanted to match the EEG fluctuations with other vital signs.

"I can't believe he just up and walked out of here this morning without telling us anything," Amy expressed her frustration to Sondra.

"Don't worry, he won't be doing that again."

"How do you plan on making him tell us what he refuses to disclose?" Amy asked. Half her face was squinting as she tried to comprehend.

"You are going to up the dose and add a little Valium. He'll be too groggy to rush out of here. We'll get him talking."

Amy shook her head and said, "You would do that to your own son?"

Sondra whipped her head around and froze. Her eyes were wide open, pupils dilated, jaw clenched, teeth gritted, face bright red, holding her breath, she finally let out a burst of air with the words, "What did you just say?" Sondra stepped toward Amy almost pinning her against the wall by imposing deep into her personal space.

"He's your son, Sondra," Amy was almost pleading.

"Don't ever say that again. To me, to anyone. Do you hear me?"

Amy stood silent and Sondra screamed, "DO YOU HEAR ME?"

"Yes I hear you," Amy replied and bumped her shoulder into Sondra's chest as she walked past. Sondra grabbed Amy's wrist and twisted it, "Ouch. What the heck is wrong with you," Amy ripped her hand free and backed away.

"Don't forget who you work for."

"Whatever mom," Amy said and slammed the door behind her. Amy stood outside the door for a brief moment and whispered under her breath, "Bitch. Psycho bitch."

Adam opened the door and climbed into the front seat of Cheri's dad's car and said, "Nice ride."

"I told my dad I was staying with you at the clinic tonight and was riding the bus there and back to work and he tossed me the keys to his car. Cool Huh?"

"Wait. You told your dad about my clinical trial?" Adam asked. He started rocking back and forth in the passenger seat.

"It's okay Adam...,"

"It's not okay Cheri. What exactly did you tell him?"

"I told him you were having trouble sleeping and it could be apnea or something else and they were monitoring you and trying some new all natural vitamins to see if it would help."

"And besides, I don't tell him everything. He doesn't know which clinic and he still thinks your name is Skip."

Adam sat silent during the ride over to the clinic. Cheri was talking the whole time and Adam responded with a few grunts and nods to lead her to believe he was actually paying attention. His mind was wandering deep into thought and he dozed off to the high pitched hum of Cheri's voice.

As their vehicle approached the intersection leading to the entrance of the clinic, a rusty old blue pickup truck raced through the red stoplight and Cheri slammed the brakes, swerved to the left jumping the curb and resting to a halt just inches from a pole.

She put the car in reverse and drove the last hundred feet into the clinic's parking lot. Adam's eyes were wide open and staring at the windshield, into the glass as if he was a part of each piece of melted sand.

"What just happened?" Adam whispered.

The world turned and life went on around them. Traffic resumed. Pedestrians kept walking. No concern or care from the humanity around them.

"I just avoided getting hit by a truck. Actually, you would have been hit because it came from your side. How did you sleep through that?" her words rumbled. Cheri was still shaking from the adrenaline rush, "I suppose you were dreaming of some adventure while I kept us from getting killed!"

"He handed me a watch," Adam was still staring into the glass as he spoke.

"Who gave you a watch?" Cheri started to calm down as her anxiety turned into concern for Adam. She wasn't sure if he hit his head or what might have happened because she was focused on avoiding the crash.

Adam continued, "It was a bit worn, smudged."

"Adam are you alright?"

"Yeah. I'm fine. I almost ate a truck and we almost died, I heard you."

Cheri's hands were white knuckle clenched to the steering wheel. She peeled them back from the wheel and there were moisture lines from the sweat of her fingers. She was looking straight ahead when she asked, "You dreamt someone gave you a worn out smudged up watch?"

"Just as I felt the rush of the vehicle swerving," Adam responded to the image in the windshield. He was alone in the glass, trapped by the profoundness of his own thoughts, *If the glass was shattered then there would be a puzzle. There is no puzzle, it is all so clear.*

Cheri was so perplexed her heart rate was almost back to normal. It was surreal. She was wondering if it really happened.

She was looking at Adam as he glared into the glass. Sirens were wailing in the distance. Fire engine horns were blaring from the direction the truck was traveling.

Adam turned to her, locked his eyes onto hers and said, "He was handing me time."

Inside the clinic, Amy was preparing the room's monitors and equipment for tonight's experiment with Adam. She gave up on being angry with Sondra. All it ever did was eat at her and never seemed to faze her mother. Her final thought on the subject was, *'How can that woman be so cold?'*

"Is everything prepped and ready?" Sondra asked from the entrance to the room.

Amy snidely replied, "Yes mother."

"You are to address me as Sondra or I will find a new assistant."

"Ok, Sondra," then Amy said under her breath, "Whatever."

"He has someone with him today. They are out in the parking lot. Looks like his little girly friend," Sondra stated with disgust.

"What is your problem? Is it that you hate the kid because he looks like his father or love him so much you want him only for yourself and your twisted little experiment?" Amy's voice was cracking.

"Enough! They will be in here any minute. And to answer your question, I loved his father. Now go let them in"

"That doesn't answer my question," Amy said as she stormed out of the room.

Adam and Cheri were approaching the entrance when Amy turned the deadbolt on the glass door so they could enter.

"Hi Amy. This is my girlfriend, Cheri," Adam smiled as he introduced them.

"Hello Cheri. Nice to meet you," Amy replied as she thought, *'Dang she's cute. No surprise, Adam is a handsome young man himself.'*

"Nice to meet you too," Cheri felt a little jealousy knowing Adam was spending all his time with another pretty girl their age, "You wouldn't believe..." Cheri was abruptly interrupted by Adam..., "Traffic. It took us forever to get here," Adam finished her sentence. He didn't want any drama carried into the clinic. He wanted these people to know as little as possible about his life. Yet here he was with his girlfriend. That was enough.

As they walked down the hall toward the room where Adam slept Cheri whispered in his ear, "What happened out there on the street with us and the truck?"

He whispered back, "Death postponed."

CHAPTER 8

Cheri stayed by Adam's side the whole time he was in the clinic. Adam was in a deep sleep after about thirty minutes. She observed the whole preparation procedure and noticed they never administered any vitamins, no intravenous, nothing was ingested.

"Amy, doesn't Adam take some sort of vitamin for this trial?" Cheri asked.

"No."

"A drug?"

"Absolutely not. We simply watch and monitor his sleep patterns and brain waves." Amy talked Sondra out of giving Adam any Valium.

Cheri was a bit puzzled so she said, "Well, Adam told me it was some new sleep vitamin he was taking as part of a clinical trial. He answered an ad on television."

"We don't advertise and there is no vitamin," Amy responded assuredly.

"What are all the wires hooked up to his head?" Cheri asked. She was getting frustrated. *'Why would Adam lie to me? I never saw any ads on the television. Or is Amy lying now? What is going on?'*

"They monitor his brain activity while he sleeps. That's what all this equipment is for. Look. See the different screens? They display information about the various areas of his brain. We observe, take notes and print out the results."

"Then what?" Cheri was interested.

"Then we debrief with Adam about what he dreamt. We try to get him to recount the dreams from beginning to end and map them against the brain activity," Amy explained.

"So what?" Cheri sincerely asked.

"Excuse me?" Amy was taken aback.

"I mean, so what happens next? What does the data tell you? The lines go up and down more when he's dreaming, right?" Cheri kept digging. There had to be more to the story.

"It's very complex. Scientific and all. You probably wouldn't understand it," Amy sounded a bit condescending.

"Try me," Cheri quickly replied.

"Adam has some very unusual patterns, but has yet to share with us everything he is experiencing," Amy paused and took in a deep breath, "It's as if he is wide awake and active, yet even more so."

Amy pulled out Adam's chart and reviewed the different patterns with Cheri. There were comparisons of his brain waves when he was awake, sleeping, and actively dreaming in R.E.M. stage. The R.E.M. patterns were more active and precise than his waking patterns.

"What's he dream about?" Cheri asked.

"Like I said, he hasn't told us yet," Amy said disappointedly.

"Amy?"

"Yes?"

"Why did Adam tell me this is a clinical trial?"

"I am not sure. This is a sleep clinic."

Cheri questioned further, "Why did he tell me you pay him to do this?"

Amy replied, "Oh, we do pay a small stipend in Adam's case."

"What's so special about Adam's case?" Cheri asked.

Amy had just boxed herself in a corner. She said too much and needed to think of something fast. She didn't know if Cheri could be trusted. She seemed friendly enough and Adam really likes her, but Sondra would have a fit if she found out Amy said this much.

The door of Adam's room swung open and a quiet voice requested "Amy, may I have a word with you?" Sondra was standing there slightly tapping her left foot.

"I'll be right back," Amy said to Cheri. As Amy walked out of the room, the display screens began jumping with activity. The lines on the graphs looked like a seismograph during a massive earthquake.

Adam feels a warm breeze. His vision is blurry but clearing. He is standing on a hill looking down at a field with men in uniforms holding shields and swords. There is a chasm between two sets of soldiers from different armies. One army has significantly more men than the other.

He watches closely at their mannerisms and behavior. The gear that they are wearing is very rudimentary, unfamiliar. One of the armies' looks more polished, the other rugged and gruff. Shouts are coming from both sides. One side yells out and cheers, the other side chants, then laughs.

The army that is laughing seems to be trying to intimidate the other, smaller army. They are pointing at them. A few men in the front spit in their direction. Tension seems to be building.

Adam looks around where he is standing and a few other people are watching the events below along with him. He notices he is holding a shepherd's staff and the others around him begin speaking to him. Adam does not understand the language but it is familiar. They seem to be acting like Adam is their leader. The head shepherd.

Adam motions for the others to sit and watch by moving his hands toward the ground and pointing at the valley below. He uses the universal sign for quiet by placing his index finger to his mouth. They follow his command and quietly observe. Adam kneels along with them. He notices he is wearing a wool garment, a tunic, tied at the waste with a rope.

Looking on, Adam sees in in the distance, in the back of the antagonizing army, a giant human manlike creature coming forth. He is carrying a giant shield and sword. He is wearing so much armor that as he walks very slow. The sun is high in the sky and the sun's reflection off the giant's armor is blinding at times. He is pushing his way through the other soldiers and making his way to the front.

As he reaches the front, the smaller army backs away several feet. The others spit at them and mock them from behind their giant. The man stands above every other man by several feet. He looks to be nine feet tall. His hands are massive, larger than the head of any other soldier.

They are shouting and pointing at their giant. They are motioning for the opposing army to come forth, like a challenge to fight their giant. They are chanting "قاتل! قاتل قاتل!" As the smaller army retreats further, Adam stands up. He feels drawn to go down the hill and stand on the side of the smaller army. He feels a strength and peace about him.

Adam turns and runs down the slope of the hill, jumping over rocks and sliding along the steeper parts of the hill as he rapidly descends toward the bottom. At the base of the hill is a stream of water. He pauses and wipes his hands on his sides. He feels something on his right hip. Tucked into the rope attached to his tunic is a slingshot. He looks around and detects there are very smooth, sharp stones in the creek formed by the flowing water.

Adam picks up five of the stones and places them in a small sack hanging from his left hip. He hops from large rock to rock across the stream. The small army is still several hundred meters away, so he continues a steady jog to join them.

As Adam approaches, a man runs up to him and says, "ديفيد!"

Adam repeats what he heard, " ديفيد؟" The man chuckles and shakes his head and points at Adam.

"What did he just say?" Cheri questioned as Amy slid back into the room.

"It's Arabic for 'David'," Amy replied.

"He's speaking Arabic?"

"Yes. Arabic, Aramaic, Hebrew. Similar, with slight dialect differences. It's happened before," Amy nodded with the response.

"I need to wake him, so he still remembers the dream," Amy said and before she could get to the bed Cheri was gently shaking Adam's shoulder and whispering, "Wake up. Adam, wake up."

The man gives Adam a slap on the shoulder, grabs hold of it and pulls him in the direction of the others. Another man rushes toward him with a greeting and Adam keeps walking. Adam walks all the way to the front, looking past the soldiers to see the giant.

The two men that greeted him shake his shoulder and begin speaking rapidly. They try to stop him from going toward the giant but Adam simply points to the heavens and removes the slingshot from his hip. He places one of the stones in the hand catapult and swings it in preparation for launching at the giant.

The giant approaches and looks confused as he towers over Adam's small stature. He pauses and his massive finger points at Adam as he roars with laughter. Each step the giant takes shakes the ground below Adam's feet.

The men in the army behind Adam begin shouting and the army behind the giant is chanting. The noise is deafening. The giant yells out and holds his sword above his towering nine foot frame. The sound rumbles in Adam's ears, "Wake up!"

Adam's vision is blurry. He sees a female's face looking at him. His eyes clear and the noises subside. There is a moment of silence and he recognizes Cheri's face and voice, "Good morning. Tell us about your dream."

"I need some water," Adam's voice was dry and cracked. He was still trying to make the transition from sleep to awake. He wasn't sure if he should share the dream, but Cheri's voice was so soft and comforting. Then he looked over and saw Amy standing over him and smiling. She could be so annoying some times.

He took a sip of water and suddenly Adam felt ill. He turned to his side and vomited. He began shaking and felt ice cold. Amy yanked the wires off his head and he immediately calmed down. Cheri noticed his eye sockets were sunken and swollen. Adam looked drawn and wasted. She never saw him like that before.

Adam felt a little fear. He decided to talk about the dream. He told them everything. Amy was frantically taking notes, even though the conversation was being recorded. Sondra entered the room with a printout of his EEG so Amy could try to correspond the timing of events with the brain activity.

Cheri stood frozen with her jaw hanging down, her lungs silently gasped during Adam's recap of the vision. He described it in such detail that she believed he was actually there. Cheri knew from her bible readings that Adam was in the place of young King David, before he was king, standing before Goliath and ready to do battle.

Adam finished his story at the point of the giant's taunting. He explained it was the last thing he remembered. He leaned over, took a cup from the steel table and drank more water. Amy refilled the glass and Cheri wiped the cold sweat from Adam's forehead.

"You went back in time several thousand years, Adam," Cheri explained.

"I know. Too far too fast. It made me sick. My body I mean. I feel awful," he replied.

"We need to run some tests before we let you proceed any further," Amy said.

Sondra piped in, "He'll be just fine. Here's twenty bucks, go get you and your girly friend a hamburger and a shake and we'll see you back here later."

Sondra turned and marched out of the room. Adam whipped his legs to the edge of the bed and hopped onto the floor and said, "I feel better already."

The room started spinning and Adam fell back onto the bed and Amy and Cheri each grabbed an arm to make sure he didn't hit the floor instead.

"Not so fast King David," Amy teased.

"Ok. Give me another drink of water, I'll get my bearings straight and we'll go get that cheeseburger. Want to come Amy?" Adam asked.

Cheri glared at him without even realizing it. Why was she so important all of a sudden? The jealousy twisted her gut. She never realized how much she really liked Adam.

"No I can't. I have to finish up here with my notes and report. You guys go have a good time and I'll see you later tonight."

"And Adam, please take it easy and drink lots of fluids," Amy instructed.

"Yes doctor," he smiled the response, took Cheri's hand and left the clinic.

Inside the clinic, Amy stood in silence before Sondra as she received her daily lecture about the experiment and data analysis, how important it was and blah, blah, blah.

"When are we going to tell him, Mother?" Amy asked Sondra.

"We're not."

"You told me we would tell him when the time was right. It's the only reason I agreed to support this whole effort," Amy's voice cracked and her eyes welled up with tears.

"Toughen up Amy," Sondra's words sent a chill through the air. She snarled when she spoke.

Amy was concerned about Adam. He didn't look good and his girlfriend was overtly jealous. She felt the time was right but her mother was a relentless control freak. She wondered if Sondra was the same way about Tom, if she was part of the reason Tom went insane. She decided not to respond but knew in her heart she would defy her mother's wishes if it meant Adam's health and well-being.

Amy hoped that eventually, soon, Adam's episodic memory would open the window into his biological family. If he figured it out and broached the subject first then she could tell him everything else and fill in the blanks for him.

Amy walked away, paused at the doorway, turned to Sondra and asked, "Why does Adam think he's taking vitamins?" and with her arm held high above her head displaying her middle finger she left the room.

CHAPTER 9

Adam let out a rumbling belch after he swallowed the last bite of his cheeseburger. Cheri was in the restroom splashing water on her face to wake herself up before she drove her father's car back home. It was cool and windy outside and neither of them were dressed for the weather. She would drop Adam off at his parent's house and meet up with him before he went back to the clinic. She didn't think her father would let her take the car every night, nor want her to stay with Adam every night so she would have to spread out her visits to the clinic.

"Let's go. I've got to get the car back home before 10:00," Cheri stood over Adam as he wiped mustard from his face and slid off the chair to leave.

Adam reached over and took Cheri's hand and tugged her close to him. Their faces were inches apart. They could feel the warmth of each other's breath.

"Thank you, Cheri. For being there with me. For being my friend. For..."

Cheri interrupted his words with a kiss. She wrapped her arms around his neck and squeezed. Adam returned the kiss and hug. They held each other for a moment. Hand in hand they walked to the car. It was silent the rest of the ride. Cheri stopped in front of the house and Adam opened the door, stepped onto the street, leaned in and said, "See you soon."

Cheri drove off. Adam could see her smile in the rearview mirror as she pulled away. Everything seemed right. Almost everything. Cheri was concerned about Adam. *'Why does he think he's taking vitamins for the sleep study?'*

Adam went into the house and rummaged through his dresser until he found it. His journal. He had not logged an entry in it for some time. It was time to start writing again. It helped him make sense of it all. Or at least try to. He picked up a pen off the floor next to his desk and began writing;

I have stepped back into my memories. It is my desire to travel backward to the beginning. I have thought about all of my memories and tried to piece it together. It has never been clear to me but last night's dream memory combined with the dream of the angel have convinced me that I am of the formal bloodline to the creation. Sondra and Amy seem like they are more than just scientists. They know something they are not telling me. Sondra is hard to read, but Amy, Amy knows me. I am not sure how or why, but I feel a connection. Maybe I can confide in her, tell her more and she will open up to me. Maybe tonight.

Adam placed the journal in his middle dresser drawer under his tee shirts. He sat down on his bed, thought for a moment and then decided to get the journal and place it under his mattress.

The afternoon sun was shining through his bedroom window so he pulled the curtains closed and for a moment everything turned pitch black. A gravitational rush pulled Adam downward and as his body descended he felt like he was spinning into a dark abyss.

Back at the clinic, Sondra was reading Amy's data set on the past few nights of Adam's tests. It was showing more relevance to genetic memory than she ever imagined. Adam would be back soon and she hadn't eaten anything all day. She walked down the hall to Amy's office to see if Amy would be interested in joining her for a bite to eat.

"Hey. Let's get out of this place for a couple hours and go get some real food. Whatta ya say? Huh?" Sondra asked.

Amy looked up and thought, *'I just can't get away from this woman'*, and then she replied out loud, "Sounds great. I could use the fresh air. Can we agree to not talk shop for those two hours?"

"Well, I guess. What else would we talk about?"

Amy shook her head thinking, *'Maybe you could get to know me,'* and then the words followed, "Maybe you could get to know me."

"I do know you. You are my daughter. We work together; I am around you all day. Is there something I need to know?" Sondra asked. For a moment Amy thought Sondra actually seemed to care.

"Let's talk over dinner," Amy replied.

"Alright, let's get out of here."

Cheri's dad was visibly upset when she asked him if she could spend the night at the clinic again with Skip (she never referred to him as Adam to her parents) and he asked, "Where is this place again? The Milton? Sounds like you made it up and you are meeting him at a hotel by a similar name!"

"Father!" Cheri cried out, "How could you say something like that?" She left the house and slammed the door behind her.

Her little tirade worked. Her dad ran after her and apologized handing over the keys to the car, and saying, "Tonight, but no more for a while. I am just being a protective father and all. Be safe. Leave me the name, address and phone number of the clinic so I can track you down if you do not respond on your smartphone."

"Here you go," she handed him a pamphlet she picked up in the lobby the night before. It had more than enough information for him.

He looked it over, gave her a hug and said, "Send me a message later letting me know you're safe."

"Will do," Cheri replied, "And thanks Dad."

She hopped in the car, sent Adam a text message from her phone and carefully drove off toward his house, until she was out of her father's sight, then she gave the engine a little more gas.

Sondra swallowed a bite of her sandwich and said, "Tom was receiving injections of the vitamin during his trial with Doctor Skinner. Adam is simply remembering Tom's experience. He's blending memories from Tom's life with infomercials that played in the background on his television while he was sleeping. That's why he thinks he's taking vitamins, and that's why he thinks he called a toll free number for the clinical trial."

"Sorry I gave you the finger before," was the only thing Amy could come up with for a response.

"Fair enough. You are in this as much as I am, so from now on you'll receive my analysis as soon as I finish each discovery," Sondra countered.

"You told me you bumped into him at a coffee shop. How come Adam doesn't remember that?" Amy inquired.

"He is having a hard time discerning his memories from Tom's," Sondra answered. She didn't want Amy to know she had been tracking Adam his whole life and began following him shortly before he turned eighteen. She had to wait until he was an adult before she could approach him with coming to the clinic and not worry about any foster parent intervention.

His name change added more complexity to the situation than necessary, but she had help dealing with that as a side project. For now she was focused on the experiments.

Amy was flustered, "Can we stop calling him Tom when it's just the two of us talking? He was my father."

"And if Adam is mixed up then we need to tell him. How do we help him so he doesn't go insane like Dad?" Amy enquired.

"We can't..."

"We can't what?" Amy interrupted, "We can't tell him or we can't help him?"

"Both. We tell him, it would scare and confuse him. And we can't help him, yet."

"What do you mean yet?"

"We need more data. We need to do blood work. DNA, chromosome and genetic mapping."

"More tests?" Amy was shaking her head, "No, mom, please. Don't make him a lab rat."

"How else are we supposed to help him if we do not know what to do!" Sondra was insistent, "Besides I have a plan for next steps."

Cheri pulled up in front of Adam's house and tapped the horn twice. The front door flung open and Adam came jogging toward the vehicle.

"Hey."

"Hey you," Cheri replied.

"You don't have to stay with me every night you know. Don't get me wrong, I really appreciate it and love that you care and all."

"No worries. My dad said no more for a while after tonight."

"Oh," Adam sighed, "Is this a dream?"

"OUCH!" Adam yelped, "Why did you pinch me?"

"I guess you're not dreaming if you felt that."

"Ha ha, but thanks I guess. Your message about picking me up snapped me out of a weird place."

Cheri pulled the car over to the side of the road, looked at Adam and asked, "What do you mean?"

"It was dark. I was frozen in time. Then tiny little lights started blinking all around me. They were very distant, like stars, and there was dimension to them. In the center of everything was a dim blue light. The blue light was getting brighter and I felt a peace inside, and then my phone vibrated."

Cheri responded, "Sounds like a nice place, not a weird place." She wanted to be positive even though it kind of scared her and she knew it was really scaring Adam. He was pale.

She put the car in drive and said, "You just need some rest tonight."

Adam was second guessing going to the clinic but Cheri seemed ok with it. Maybe he just needed a good night's sleep. One without so many dreams and memories. One night without going back in time. A night without battles. A night of just the blue light. *'What is the blue light? Why is it so peaceful there? Am I dying?'*

"We're here," Cheri interrupted Adam's thoughts.

Sondra and Amy were waiting in the clinic when Adam arrived. Sondra looked Cheri up and down with a hint of disgust. Amy noticed and spoke to break the tension, "Good to see you guys again. Cheri, are you joining us again tonight?"

"Yes, but then he's on his own for a while. But I know he's in good hands with you two." She really didn't mean it, but she wanted Adam to feel secure and not afraid.

The clinic felt colder to Adam than usual. He walked with Amy to his room and noticed a syringe and several tubes on a stainless steel table next to a chair. Cheri saw Adam looking at the table and she started to get a shiver in her spine. Adam was losing his color again and sweat was beading up on his brow.

"What the heck is that?" Adam's voice was loud and coarse.

"We want to do some blood work," Amy responded. She and Sondra got their story aligned on the way back from dinner, "We are concerned about your blood sugars and you appear anemic. Sondra wants to adjust your diet based on the results, which means your stipend just doubled!" She hoped he bought it. There was silence for a few seconds.

Cheri wasn't buying it and she glared at Amy. Amy smiled back which made Cheri even more frustrated. *'What are these two up to? Is this even legal?'* Cheri was going to observe one more night and then convince Adam in the morning to stop for a while. He seemed a bit delusional lately and this wasn't helping.

Adam relaxed his shoulders and he walked over to the chair, "Let's get it over with then."

After they drew blood Adam lay back on the bed and closed his eyes. He was extremely tired. His breathing was shallow. The ringing in his ears dissipated. He drifted away.

"Adam, wake up. I have to go, "Cheri whispered in his right ear. Sondra and Amy were standing behind Cheri. Sondra was tapping her foot with impatience.

Adam sat up, took a drink of water and said, "I don't remember anything. That was awesome."

Sondra handed Adam an mp3 device and said, "Listen to this every day for at least two hours. You need to learn Hebrew and Arabic. It'll help when you are hearing the language in your dreams. You'll know what's happening and where you are."

Cheri rushed Adam out of the clinic and during the drive back to his house she tried to convince him to take a break from the clinic, "I am concerned about you."

"You didn't seem concerned yesterday," he replied.

"Promise me you'll at least think about it."

As he was getting out of the car he answered, "Ok."

He went inside the house and poured himself a large glass of milk. He felt very thirsty. He poured himself a second glass and took it to his bedroom. He sat on his bed and put the earphones in his ears and turned on the mp3 player. He laid back plopped his on his pillow, closed his eyes and listened.

Everything is blurry. A warm breeze washes over Adam's body. He is whirling something over his head. A slingshot. A large silhouette is within fifteen meters. He sees the person approaching. It is the giant. The colossal man is swinging a sword and the force pushes warm air into Adam's body. The only sound is of the swoosh, swoosh of the giant's sword. *'Goliath'*.

A stone flies from Adam's slingshot and hits the giant squarely between his eyes. The beast of a man takes two more steps forward and is within a few meters of Adam. The sword is above his head. The giant drops to his knees, his hands fall to his side, the sword is in his hand and lands with the point skyward. He falls forward, face first, onto his own sword.

Adam hears a gurgle and a cracking sound followed by a sucking noise, like a plunger, as the giant's weapon pierces his stomach and exits his back. A death moan bellows from the core of the giant as he takes his final breath.

Thousands of men are running around, yelling, jumping up and down, celebrating. The two men that greeted him before are slapping him on the back and hugging his shoulders. They are yelling in his ears. Adam understands what they are saying.

Adam saunters over to the fallen body, kicks the body to its side and with both hands he grabs ahold of the giant's own sword. He pulls it out of the man's chest and swings it high in the air bringing it down with the force of a warrior. With a single slice the giant's body is separated. Adam grab's the giant's head by its hair and holds it high above him for everyone to see. Blood drips somberly to the ground as the reverberation of cheering explodes in the air. It echoes through the valley and the hills. The men begin disembodying the giant.

Adam knows who he is.

CHAPTER 10

"Where have you been all week? We've been trying to get a hold of you. We have your test results from the blood work," Sondra's irritation with Adam was not hidden very well.

"And?" Adam asked.

"Cholesterol is fine, no thyroid issues, no indication of diabetes, but your red blood cell count is low."

"And?"

"And, you need to eat more red meat, lean of course, and spinach. Also, egg yolks, raisins and liver."

"I'll pass on the liver," Adam said with a snarl as if he could taste it. He looked Sondra in the eyes and stated, "And, to answer your question, I was learning the two languages you told me to study."

"How far along are you?"

"I finished both."

She knew Adam had almost genius IQ but never thought he'd learn two languages in one week. She decided to test him with something from the Old Testament Bible. To be fair she would speak it slowly.

"Well then, גוליית הרג הדוד," Sondra said softly.

"How did you know?" Adam questioned her.

"Know what?"

"That I killed him?"

"Oh my gosh, who did you kill Adam?"

"In my dreams. I slew Goliath."

"When did you have that memory?" Sondra sounded perturbed because he wasn't at the clinic all week and they weren't able to monitor his brain activity and vitals.

"When I fell asleep listening to the lesson in Hebrew."

"What other memories have you had in the past week Adam?"

He was getting agitated by the inquisition. What did it matter if he missed a week? He was feeling better and stronger than he did a week ago. Adam decided before he went back to the clinic that he wasn't going to take any crap from Sondra so he said, "You know, I have better things to do than sit around and be badgered by you."

Sondra was enraged. She did not like being talked back to by anyone. She was a strong woman, used to being in control and the one telling people how it is. The silence in the room was being drowned out by the snorts of air bursting through her nostrils.

Adam appeared to be enjoying his new found position of strength. She was showing her cards more and more and he was beginning to realize that she wanted him there more than he wanted to be there.

There was a blinking light in the corner of the room. Adam hadn't noticed it before. Upon closer examination he determined it was a camera. He knew they were recording him, because he authorized it, but why a second camera?

Sondra anticipated what he was thinking and answered, "We installed a second camera to give us another view, another angle."

"Why. All I am doing is sleeping."

"Not always. Sometimes you move around. Once you stood up for a moment. If you begin sleep walking we want to match your actions with the memories you play back for us when you wake up," Sondra explained.

Amy entered the room, "Hello Adam. You ready for a fun filled night of adventure?"

"Hi Amy. Hook me up and let's get started," Adam replied as he lay on the bed. He trusted Amy and relaxed in her presence.

Amy placed the leads on his head and chest, attached the pulse clip on his finger and adjusted all the monitors. Adam was hooked up and ready to go. Everything was in place. Cameras were rolling and Amy settled in the recliner chair in the corner of the room to observe and take notes. She sipped her coffee and gave him a wink of assurance.

Adam turned his head to one side and the lights from the monitor were reflecting off the EEG leads. Amy stared at the twinkling, pulsating sparkles of light. She noticed something she had never seen before. The way that Adam's hair was parted and the wires and leads pushing the rest of his hair to one side exposed something on his skull. Amy thought, *'Is that a scar?'*

There is an icy chill in the air accompanied by a stench that Adam has never experienced. Large stone structures surround him. The brick is new, yet covered in dampness. A horse and carriage is off in the distance. The ground beneath Adam's feet is made of packed dirt and patches of stone. Very medieval.

His vision clears and he hears a voice crying out, "My baby, oh my precious darling. Why? Why?" Sobbing echoes through the street. The voice is coming from above him.

He sees a woman holding a small child to her chest. More sobbing. Cries and screams are rising up all around him. The words are in English with a European accent. The odor in the air is so strong he can taste it.

Adam sees people standing, walking, sitting and lying in the streets. A man stumbles and falls to the ground. Adam rushes over to assist him. As he reaches his hand to the man, their eyes meet. The man's sockets look dark, lucid, empty. Open sores are oozing blood and puss cover his exposed skin. He coughs up a green fluid and gasps his last breath.

Terror grips Adam's core, *'Where 'am I?* He hears a man's voice from above, "We must be rid of the body. Now!" He sees the woman clutching the child and the man tugging it from her grip.

"Noooo," the woman screams.

The man walks to the window opening and drops the body to the street below and says, "We will all die. It must be."

'This is a nightmare. I have to wake from this,' Adam's mind is racing for ideas to escape. The stench grows stronger and the cries echo louder. More people drop to their knees, to their backs and bellies, then perish. *'What disease has taken hold of these people?'*

Adam's thoughts are interrupted by a squeaking and scratching sound. Something is rubbing on his leg. He looks at his feet and a black rat the size of a bowling ball is scratching at his pants. He kicks at the hideous mammal and it bares its teeth. Adam screams but there is no sound. He screams again and still no sound. He closes his eyes and holds his breath, *'Please make it stop.'*

Adam feels a warm breeze and the stench is gone. He opens his eyes to the sound of music with thousands of people talking and singing. His vision clears and he realizes he is seated in a coliseum. A beautifully architected structure garnished by pillars and carvings of art above each entry to the seating. Below the circle of seating is a floor of dirt. Men with chains around their feet are tending to the dirt bowl, kicking up dust as they rake it level and remove objects that are scattered about.

Across the stadium from him sits and empty throne with a woman on one side and a young boy on the other. They are dressed differently than everyone else. Their garments are clean and adorned with jewels and gold. They are holding silver goblets and eating fresh fruit. The people in the stadium are all dressed different from one another. Every socioeconomic class was represented from the raged to the richest.

The assembly stops moving and silence consumes the air. Every person is standing and looking toward the empty throne. Trumpets sound. Men wearing armor and carrying flags enter the stadium floor and stand below the throne. A large man dressed like an emperor or Pharaoh enters from the left of the throne and the coliseum erupts in cheers. He is wearing headgear, a crown, twice the size of his head, made of gold and jewels.

The emperor holds his hands in the air, the crowd silences and he shouts, "Sit ludos incipiunt!"

The crowd bursts forth in cheers and chants and is jumping up and down. It reminds Adam of an American football game except there are no lines on the field below, only dirt. A gate with bars opens to the field and two more soldiers appear and step onto the field. One of them has a shield and sword the other has a large knife and a spiked ball attached to a chain. They stand at each side of the gate.

A man and woman covered in dirt and wearing rags are thrust out of the gate and dragged to the center of the field below. The soldiers all exit through the gate and it closes. Another gate opens on the opposite end and three lions come racing out toward the man and woman.

The woman drops to her knees and carves a cross in the dirt. The man puts his hand on her shoulder, looks to the skies, lets out a howl and runs toward the lions. The woman stays on her knees bowing before the cross.

Two of the lions leap on the man knocking him to the ground. One of them rips off an arm, the other beast bites into the belly of their victim. The multitude is going berserk and chanting as the third lion descends upon the woman. Adam closes his eyes as the lion leaps toward the woman. Bones cracking, fluids spilling, smell emanating, and the thickness of the dusty air in his mouth, Adam gags.

Adam is glued to his seat wishing the horror would end. His head drops to his chest. He slows his breathing. All sound is muffled and slow, slower, quieter, gone. Adam hears nothing, sees nothing, smells nothing, tastes nothing and feels nothing. *'Am I ceasing to exist?'*

Adam's breathing becomes normal again. He opens his eyes and he is standing on a hillside. No people around him, no coliseum, no lions, no soldiers, no evil emperor. No evil people cheering for the wicked emperor and chanting for more cruel violence.

Images begin to form around him. Timbres of a man's screech of terror bounce off the hills. Adam's body jerks as he turns around and looks to the valley below. He hears a banging noise but cannot see where it originates. There is another hill beyond the valley. A few people are milling about and two men, soldiers, are swinging objects into something on the ground. A woman cries out, "פיטר." *'Peter'?*

The shrilling screams and cries cease and the soldiers are hoisting up a large object. A man is hanging upside down from it. It is shaped like a cross. The soldiers slap the man's head several times, pick up their weapons and walk down the hill. Everyone else slowly walks away and leaves him hanging there, alone.

The hill beyond the valley slowly moves toward Adam. The image is getting larger with more clarity. He can see the spikes in the man's arms and legs. *'Peter.'* Blood is dripping from Peter's eyes forming a puddle on the dirt beneath his head. His chest rises and falls. A long pause and his chest rises and falls again, but no more.

Adam feels warmth on his face and goose bumps form upon the skin of his neck. A sound is vibrating in his ear. He turns to look. A blurry haze of movement, double vision comes together and clarity of sight ensues.

"Are you with us?" Amy is whispering in Adam's ear.

He breathes deep contemplating where he is. He can still see the outline of Peter hanging upside down from a cross. A rush pushes his body deep into the mattress. Coolness escapes from his pores and he shivers. Beads of cold sweat form on his brow. Wavy flashes of red, blue, white and yellow splash across his mind. *'Where am I now?'*

He sees Amy. He recognizes her face and voice. He sees another person standing behind her. *'Mom?'* Adam is confused.

'Am I dreaming? Who is that other woman?' He sits up and lowers his head trying to remember her name. He puts his hands over his ears trying to muffle his own racing thoughts. *'Sondra. That's it. It's Sondra.'* He is waking up this time, for real.

Adam blinked his eye several times and took another deep breath before he responded, "I have heard that before you die your life flashes before your eyes. What does it mean when someone else's life flashes before your eyes?"

CHAPTER 11

Adam purchased a Hebrew bible and spent hours reading it. He had skipped a week at the clinic after the last barrage of memories. It seemed like the rapid randomness of thoughts only happened at the clinic. His computer and the internet became his newest best friend as he researched historical events and characters to piece together his memories. He fine-tuned his foreign language skills.

He had experienced killing a giant Philistine, observed the black plague wipe out the population in Europe and sat in a stadium to watch Christians being fed to lions. Events were jumping around. He needed to control the sequence because it was too confusing as it was occurring.

Cheri hadn't seen Adam for a week. They spoke on the phone every day, but he wanted time alone to study and learn. She encouraged it. Cheri preferred he didn't go to the clinic for a while. He seemed happier, healthier, when he was away from those other two women. She was also happy he was studying the bible. She wanted to see him in person to know he looked as good as he sounded, so Adam relented and agreed to meet her for coffee. ·

"You look great, Adam."

"I feel really good. I still do exercises every morning." He had done hundreds of push-ups and sit-ups every day as long as Cheri had known him. He claimed he has never missed since he was twelve years old.

"I've learned a lot about God and history over the past week," Adam said enthusiastically.

"Tell me what you learned, Cheri inquired.

"God is real. He made us. He made, I should say created everything, and I believe it."

"Why do you believe it?"

"I have memories of the events. I've seen it," Adam was resolute.

"Would you believe if you had not seen it?" Cheri was being authentic.

"I am not sure. How do you believe?" Adam asked.

"His presence is everywhere. We are without excuse. Faith is in the unseen, the hope for what is unknown and yet to come. His word is real, you just said so yourself."

"I've seen him," Adam said.

"Who? Who have you seen Adam?"

"When I was younger, I had a dream memory of him. It is the first historical event I remember. I was standing at the foot of a cross next to other people. He hung there with a man hanging next to him on each side. Three of them, he was in the middle. There was a sign above his head. I didn't know what it said at the time but I know now," Adam explained.

"What did the sign say?" Cheri asked.

"King of the Jews."

Cheri was speechless. She always wanted to believe Adam, but this was a lot to take in. *He observed the crucifixion of Jesus Christ?* She was thinking of how to respond to Adam and a voice spoke through her, "Who do you say that he is?"

Adam thought in silence for a minute before he answered Cheri. Adam knew what other people said about Jesus, he never really thought about who he would say Jesus was, is. He looked like a man, but people say he is God's son. That's all he really knew.

"I don't know who he is, if he is what people say. He hung there and died like any man would."

Cheri gently asked, "Did you see what happened after he died?"

"No, well, one other thing, a soldier pierced His side with a spear and blood and water spilled out of Him and onto the ground. That's all I remember," Adam responded, but he left out the fact that he followed the soldier to his tent and stole the spear while the man slept. He also didn't mention that right after he acquired the spear he was surrounded by other beings that taunted him, followed him, yet feared him. The spear had power.

"I meant, did you see him after he was crucified?" Cheri clarified her question.

"I saw him again, but he looked different. It didn't make any sense because I knew he had died," Adam's response was soft and tender. His eyes were blank, his mind turned inward, remembering.

"He conquered death. That is our hope Adam."

"Who, what?" Adam was trapped in his thoughts trying to remember.

"Jesus conquered death and is alive today," Cheri assured him.

Adam remembered seeing the joy on people's faces. They talked about an empty grave. They spoke of walking with him and eating with him. Many believed. They celebrated.

"Yes, of course," Adam replied as he disembarked from his memory and back to the present to look Cheri in the eyes, "I remember it like it just happened yesterday."

Sondra and Amy were on their way to the clinic to prep for Adam's return. The roads were slick from a light freezing rain and traffic was moving slower than normal. Sondra was anxious to get the experiment started again. Everyone else thought it was a trial except Sondra, and well maybe Amy was on to her, but none the less, a week in between session felt like a lifetime. A week in the dream world is a lifetime, or two.

"I was looking through old files for some correlation data for Adam's trial and found your Ph.D. Thesis," Amy stated.

"Did you read it?"

"I just found it, so no, but I found the title very interesting," Amy was hoping for an explanation but Sondra didn't respond.

Amy tried further, "Cellular Programming and the Genetic Code?"

Sondra released a whisper of air through her nostrils, not even a full-fledged sigh. Amy was getting frustrated at her mother's indifference. Normally, she would have expected an outburst from Sondra accusing her of snooping around, but not this time, which made it even more unsettling.

Amy went for the sucker punch, "What is the scar on Adam's head?"

"My research was conducted and sponsored by Milton Medical Institute with three male test subjects named John, Billy and Tom. My sampling was small because we were breaking new ground and, well, to be honest, kept it very much under the radar. It was a very unconventional study. Initially I thought I would use the data to write my thesis however I never submitted it to the University. Only Dr. Skinner knew about it. He funded it," Sondra finally replied to the original question.

"What does that have to do with the scar on Adam's head?" Amy pressed for an answer.

Sondra acted indifferent again. She was lost in her own thoughts and mumbled, "I had nothing to do with expanding the program to include the other twenty-two test subject, I mean students."

Amy didn't hear anything more than a grumbling of sound coming from Sondra and thought she was avoiding the issue by cursing under her breath.

"Mom, you are such a bitch! Why can't you answer me?"

"That's no way to speak to your mother. And be careful what you wish for. Knowledge isn't always power," Sondra snickered as she snapped out of her thoughts of the research with Doctor Skinner.

As she parked the car in the clinic lot Sondra looked over at Amy and said, "We are at work now, so don't forget to address me as Sondra. And about that scar. Please keep the electrodes away from it, especially the red and white striped one."

"Why? Why should it matter? What is the scar from?"

Sondra shushed her as they walked into the building, "You ask too many questions."

"Hello Dr. Melvin," Sondra said with a smile as they passed the clinic's new Executive Director. Dr. Melvin came over from the Cleveland Clinic and was very hands off when it came to the day to day operations. He trusted his staff. That bode well for Sondra. She told him only what he needed to know.

Amy closed the door to Adam's room behind them, "What is the scar? Tell me or I'll walk. I don't need this bullshit, this is my brother."

Sondra reached for Amy's head and Amy pulled back with a jerk. Amy wanted to deck her and believed she could. Sondra was in good shape, but more than twice her age and Amy was on her fourth round of high intensity training. Work and exercise was her life and this experiment was making her a bit irritable.

"Relax, I want to show you something," Sondra said as she slowly reached for Amy's head again. Amy stood still while Sondra ran her fingers along her scalp and methodically parted through her hair.

"Ok, this is creepy. I don't have lice, what are you..."

Sondra interrupted as she held her finger on a small bump on Amy's skull, "Here, put your finger here and gently feel this spot on your head."

"Yeah, so? What am I feeling exactly?" Amy lips and cheek rolled up on her left side into a squint of confusion.

"Your scar," Sondra replied, "You and Adam are conjoined twins but only to the extent of your heads being attached in this one tiny spot. That's what the scar is."

Amy's jaw dropped and she fell back into the chair in the corner of the room. She shook her head in a loss for words.

Her thoughts were swirling. *'This woman is out of her mind. She makes it up as she goes. I have to watch her closely. She is sneaky, self-centered and dangerous. How do I get me and my brother far away from her?'*

"I told you to be careful what you wished for," Sondra sneered and walked out of the room.

Adam walked into the clinic a few minutes later than his scheduled time and was greeted by a very irritable Sondra Farber, "Glad you could make it Adam. You're late."

He was not going to let her control him so he responded confidently, "I can leave if you'd like and come back another time, or not at all."

Sondra didn't take the bait and said, "Amy's waiting in your usual room. Sweet dreams tonight Adam."

Amy was sitting in the lounger when Adam walked in. She looked frazzled. Her hair was a bit ruffled and she was rubbing her finger on the side of her head near her temple.

"Hi Adam," She greeted him and stood up. There was an awkward silence as her thoughts moved inward, *'I want to tell him I am his sister. He's going to hate me for not telling him sooner. I feel like I am a liar. I hate the deception. I don't know what to do. I'll protect him for now and when the time is right'*...

"Amy?" Adam was waving his hand in front of her eyes.

"Oh, sorry, I was just thinking about something. We can get started."

Adam lay on the bed and Amy hooked up all the equipment, the ECG leads, the pulse meter, blood pressure cuff and the EEG electrodes. The electrodes. Why did Sondra tell her to keep them away from the scar? Amy rubbed her finger on her scar. *'The right side of my head. The hippocampus! Memory. Adam's scar is on his right side also. How could we be attached facing each other? She cannot be trusted. It doesn't make sense.'*

The words came out loud, "She's such a liar!"

Just as Sondra entered the room Adam tilted his head with a puzzled look and asked, "Who is such a liar?"

Sondra stood behind Adam and glared at Amy.

"Oh, I was just thinking about something my friend said to me earlier today. Just girl stuff. No worries," Amy was back peddling in Sondra's presence. The woman was so powerful. She instilled fear in people. Amy was trapped in a vice of manipulation.

Sondra asked, "Can I help hook up those electrodes tonight?"

"No thanks, I have it covered, see," Amy replied.

Amy completed the task of prepping Adam for his evening's sleep. Everything was hooked up and ready to go. Satisfied, Sondra exited the room.

Amy picked up a magazine off the nightstand, turned off all the lights except for her reading light, sat in the lounger and said, "Good night Adam."

In the darkness Adam can only hear the sounds unleashed from the deep crevices of his inner psyche. A deafening silence complemented by screeches, like seagulls, rumbling like ocean waves against the shore, rustling like wind brushing through trees and the dull hum of people's voices.

Light creeps in. Blue light. Always blue within the darkness. Calming, peaceful, serene, it washes away the silent noises. Each sound separates, disperses, dissipates, disappears. Only the warm glow of the blue light. A fullness, completeness. A silhouette is in the midst of the light. Energy. Love. It is calling him.

Amy quietly opened the room's cabinet and pulled out the manual to the EEG equipment. She didn't recall a red and white striped electrode on the equipment she used in class during her labs. Sondra had trained her and always set it up with her using their 'new' equipment. It was new so Amy just assumed it would come with new procedures. She was finally verifying the electrode placement.

As she rifled through the pages she realized nothing matched the placement Sondra had taught her. There was no striped electrode listed in the manual. Amy looked over at Adam and he was sleeping peacefully. He was smiling. She checked the monitors and his heart rate was fifty five and slowing. His breathing was slow but deliberate and oxygen looked fine.

Amy walked over to his bedside and stood above him examining the electrode lead placements on his head. *'Move the striped one,'* she thought. *'No. Sondra said no.'* then, *'Try it,'* and *'No.'* She rolled her head, *'What's the worst that could happen?'*

Amy gently reached for the red and white wire and slid the pad directly over the scar on Adam's skull. As she pressed it into place she felt a little shock on her fingertip. That's when it all began.

CHAPTER 12

Adam jumped from the bed and burst into a rant around the room. All the wires were still attached to his body and the force of his bluster yanked the equipment from its stands. Monitors crashed to the floor, sparks flew as led displays shattered. The clanging and scraping of the metal stands thundered in the room as they slammed into each other and the walls.

As Adam moved so did the items still attached to him. His arms were flailing while electrode pads and leads were popping off his skin. Amy ducked for cover in the corner of the room behind the lounger, wrapping her arms around her head, hoping the chaos would end soon. What was only a matter of seconds seemed like hours.

There are thousands of them this time. The hideous beings he battled his entire childhood. They are back. They were gone for so long and now they are here again, everywhere, as far as he can see in every direction, unfettered shadows, unattached. Vultures, '*Angels of darkness, who is their prey?*'. Adam is alone and surrounded.

He feels energy and strength flowing from his right hand and into his entire spirit. He is holding the spear. The blade, covered with the blood reflects flashes of light off the exposed parts of the metal and the rays release an energy onto the adversaries that encircle him.

Each time the light passes across them it cuts them down, their faces display terror and anguish, their mouths open to scream out the pain but they vanquish without sound.

Those that remain approach Adam with caution, then step away as their comrades perish. One step forward, two steps back. Adam realizes what is happening and he spins the spear, twirling it so sparkles and flashes of destructive, cleansing, redemptive power burns into and through the limitless evil that pursues him.

While twirling the spear above his head Adam runs in the pattern of a figure eight. The infinity loop. He feels lighter, above the pull of gravity. The creatures, one by one, are ceasing to exist in this realm. They all look different, yet the same. He is sending them somewhere, away from here, never to be seen again, yet they all looked so familiar. Familiar yet strange. Oddly impure, divinely unique, wholesomely separated.

Adam hears a distinctive voice, "You are alive, so live!"

In the midst of the chaos inside the room Amy lifted her head enough to sneak a peek at Adam, *'Is he floating?'* She stared as Adam moved effortlessly around the room in circles, arms flailing, his eyes open, determined and in control.

Just then Sondra burst into the room and moved toward Adam. She quickly assessed the situation and noticed the red and white wire dangling from Adam's head so she wrenched it from his skull.

Adam sees a white light moving toward him. The light passes through other objects and grows larger and brighter as it moves closer. There is a blinding flash and pop like a giant light bulb just burnt out. Adam feels a tingling sensation on the side of his head. All the entities that encircled him dissolve and there are only blurring colors left in their place.

Amy watched as her mother took control over the situation. Amy had grown up under that same control. The hand-picked private schools, home schooling, private university. The way she dressed, what she ate, the books she read, on and on, all at the beset of dear mom. While she cowered in the corner the almighty Sondra stepped in to save the day.

The same almighty Sondra that let her son grow up in foster homes around the state. *'She separated us at birth.'* Amy yelled out, "WHY?" and Sondra turned, raised her right hand and slapped her square on the cheek.

"Get a hold of yourself kid," Sondra scolded her daughter.

It was a pathetically embarrassing feeling, for both of them.

Adam was leaning against the wall furthest away from the two of them. He was beginning to regain consciousness. He saw the outline of two figures. Sound was distant but gaining clarity. He recognized the voices. He could make out the images. Sondra and Amy.

Amy was holding her hand against her jaw and Sondra was holding a red and white wire in her left hand. Both of them were staring at him. The room was a shambles. Busted glass and broken equipment was sprawled across the floor. The bed was overturned and the three of them simply stood silently gazing at each other.

Sondra summoned Amy, "In my office, now!"

"Yes mam," Amy wanted to say Mom.

"Adam, go home. Take the day off. Here is two day's pay. We'll clean up the mess," Sondra said as she handed him a stack of cash.

"What the hell happened?" Adam had a puzzled look on his face. He was distraught and attempting to recall his dream. Then he remembered. He was about to speak, paused, stepped quietly over and around the mess and left.

Amy followed Sondra to her office. Sondra closed the door, walked behind her desk and sat down. Her desk was cluttered with books, papers, stacks of files, pens...a complete unorganized mess.

Some genius' are disorganized externally because they don't focus on one thing at a time. Multi-tasking is a way to help them control the chaos in their brilliant minds and Sondra was a genius, borderline Autistic Savant, apparent by her lack of substantive emotion.

Sondra started the discussion, "Let's get it all out on the table, Amy. I know you are concerned about Adam. So am I. Also, I know you want to tell him you are his sister. So do I. And I suspect you have had thoughts about taking him and getting far away from this clinic and from me. That's not possible."

"How would you know..."

"Let me finish Amy. I have only told you what you needed to know up until this point. You are about to hear the whole story, so sit down, we are going to be here awhile."

Amy sat down and with cautious optimism said, "I am ready, I need to know. But what about Adam. What the heck happened in there? We need to talk to him."

"He'll be back tomorrow. He needs time to sort it out, then he'll be back with answers. And questions. That's why we need to talk."

When Adam returned to his foster parents house, no one was home. He grabbed a snack bar from the cupboard and went to his bedroom. The room had a musty, unkempt odor to it. His mom must have given up on keeping it clean for him. He couldn't blame her, he was never around.

When he did see them it was brief and in passing. He was surprised they hadn't asked him to leave. He was glad they didn't. It was the first place in a long time that kind of felt like home to him. He wondered how the old man was holding up. He knew Chuck had some health issues, *'Maybe that's why no one is here?'*.

Adam went to his dresser to retrieve his journal out of the drawer. It wasn't there. Then he recalled placing under his mattress. He sighed in relief. It was more like a diary, but he preferred to call it his journal. He believed diaries were for girls. *'I wonder if Amy has a diary?'* He felt like he knew Amy and didn't know why.

With no one else home, Adam used the opportunity to silently reflect on what had been occurring. After writing the words he re-read them to himself.

'So far in the past few months my memories have been scattered and a bit jumbled. Too random to fully appreciate their individual contribution to the significance as a whole.'

'I've met an angel that told me I could see God. I observed the Black Plague in Europe and watched a Roman Emperor, Nero I think, in a fit of megalomania. I bounced into the era where Christians were being fed to lions before a raging crowd of lunatics.'

'Another time the Apostle Peter was crucified upside down. I re-visited the crucifixion of Christ and most recently battled the demons of my childhood.'

'My understanding of Hebrew and Arabic languages has increased exponentially to the point where I have been able to read the Hebrew version of the Bible. I now understand most all of the languages of the Middle East as well as their various dialects. Also, my Greek is improving and my awareness of God has transcended the mere physical human understanding I once clung to.'

'I believe if I slow down and focus, I can travel through my genetic memories in a serial and organized manner, which will take me back to my origin, mankind's origin, and there I will see God face to face.'

'I am seeing history through the eyes and lives of the men who lived it. I was them. I am them. Finding the right place in my memory to begin moving backward in time might help me gain control over the sequencing.'

Adam set the journal back beneath the mattress, the very place he slept, laid back on the bed, stared at nothing in particular then picked up his English version of the New Testament Bible. To better understand who he is and where he is going, Adam needed to dig deeper into scripture. And if he truly was going to see God, he should at least know what to look for.

Adam finished reading Matthew, chapter one, rested the book on his chest and said out loud, "Joseph," then closed his eyes.

A voice," יֵשׁוּ לוֹ לִקְרוֹא אַתָּה," Adam is translating it to be, *'you will call him Jesus.'*

He is lying next to a young lady, a very pregnant, very young lady. She is glowing of innocence and purity. She is plain, yet beautiful. An inner beauty emanating through her eyes and smile. She is holding his hand and slightly nods her head in the affirmative as if she heard the same voice. No words need to be exchanged because they are one in purpose now and they both know it.

Adam asks in Hebrew, "Mary?"

The young lady responds in the same language, "Yes Joseph."

Adam smiles at Mary. Mary smiles at Joseph.

'Buzzz. Buzzzz.' Adam's phone is vibrating on top of his nightstand. He sits upright, looks around his room and realizes he had dozed off. He grabbed his phone and the screen display said, 'Cheri'.

"Hey," Adam answered the call.

"Hey back," it was Cheri's voice on the other end.

"Sup?"

"Sup with you Adam?"

"Want to come over?"

"Thought you'd never ask," Cheri sounded delighted.

Adam paused, then said, "I have some things I want to tell you."

"Can't wait." *'Click.'* Cheri hung up and headed out the door.

CHAPTER 13

Sondra began the conversation with, "You know that you and Adam are siblings, twins. Tom Dory is your father. What you don't know is that it was a planned mid-wife birth so we could separate you and Adam. "

"Why did you need to separate us?" Amy asked.

"Dr. Skinner's experiment, based on my research, only affected the male genes. It was disruptive to the female genes and potentially lethal for you. The government started snooping around our work. We needed to protect Adam from them and keep you monitored closely. When they learned that only a girl was born they backed off, disappeared."

"Only a girl," Amy response was wrought with disgust.

"I didn't mean it that way. They were looking for a boy. The research and the experimental gene therapy was all geared toward males," Sondra spoke softly now.

"Why boys?" Amy inquired.

"It was easiest to track through the male seed and the techniques we were using only passed on through the male with a high efficacy. Female test results were only showing potential of less than 2% while the male results were above 90%, every time," Sondra was deep in her own thoughts as she spoke.

"Tell me about the research. Explain the experiments to me. What the hell were you people up to and why?" Amy demanded.

"Easy girl. I'm getting there. And before I proceed, you need to stop being so accusatory of our intentions. He's my son. Tom was my husband," Sondra stated emphatically.

"And I'm *NOTHING*?" Amy loudly questioned.

"You need to stop the pity party. I have kept you close to me. Watched over you. Protected you. Loved you..."

"Controlled me!" Amy finished Sondra's sentence.

"Enough!" Sondra yelled as she opened a drawer on her desk, reached her left hand inside and quickly removed it, "You have no idea, and I am trying to clue you in. So sit back, shut your mouth and listen or this conversation is over."

Amy instantly complied. There was a long awkward silence in the room. Amy felt short of breath and had a hard time taking in complete lungs full of air. A crescent shape of sparkling dots flashed colors across her right eye disrupting her vision, her thoughts, her psyche. She began to sweat. She felt like vomiting. Nothing seemed right.

"I need a drink of water," Amy's voice cracked and trembled.

Sondra turned in her chair and opened the small office refrigerator and retrieved a bottle of water.

"Here, it's cold."

"Thanks mom," Amy said as she unconsciously rubbed the scar on the side of her skull.

Adam opened the door to greet Cheri before she could even knock, "Greetings."

"Hello Adam," Cheri said it in a more intimate tone than ever before. Their eyes locked and Adam pulled her toward his body, then released her as he closed the door behind her.

Cheri liked the emotions she was feeling. She liked that Adam pulled her close and held her there just long enough to show his feelings were growing stronger also without compromising her space or violating her body. Cheri also liked that Adam was growing closer to God.

"I think I figured it out," Adam started right in, "I think I know how to manage a serial regression in genetic memories that will walk me through history and to the origin of humankind."

"I was reading the bible and I fell into a memory. I thought I dozed off and was dreaming, but it was a conscious experience. More like a daydream, yet so real. I was there."

"Where Adam?"

"With Mary."

"Mary who?" Cheri wasn't sure if she should be jealous.

"I was Joseph."

"Joseph and Mary, Joseph? Like Jesus' parents?" Cheri's eyes were wide open.

"Yes. And after reading the genealogy listed in the book of Matthew it is clear that I am a descendant of the first man and woman in recorded history," Adam's voice was clear and confident. He was believable.

Cheri was a few steps behind in getting her head around what Adam was saying, "You were Joseph?"

"Yes."

"What happened in the daydream?" Cheri was truly captivated.

"I heard the Angel's voice."

"Who else have you told this to Adam?" Cheri asked. She knew that anyone else would think he was a lunatic.

"No one. Just you."

Cheri sighed in relief, turned her back to Adam and stared out the window. They were still standing in the front foyer of his foster parents home. She felt like she was standing there for an hour. Time crawled.

"Is your mind tricking you? Did you think it because you read it?" Cheri was questioning the validity of his story.

Adam put his hands on her shoulders and turned her towards him and said, "I thought the same thing at first but then I thought about the other memories. The ones about the crucifixions. I never read about those. Never heard about those until after the memories. I told you about the first time I stood before the cross. I was just a boy. I didn't understand it then, but I am beginning to now. I believe."

The air was still at the Milton Clinic. Amy finished drinking the bottle of water before she spoke, "What happened with the experiments mom?"

"Let me start by explaining the hypothesis. Dr. Skinner and I both believed that humans possess Genetic Memory. What I mean by that, in our definition, is the ability to remember people, events and ideas that took place anywhere along the continuum of that individuals genealogy. We also believed that those memories are fragmented and corrupted by other internal and external influences on the brain."

"The whole idea started when I read an article about Flatworms," Sondra expounded.

"Flatworms?" Amy wasn't seeing the connection.

"Yes. Let me explain. They are an amazing invertebrate that perform epimorphic regeneration. In other words the worm has the ability to separate and then regenerate the missing parts."

"I presented the idea to Dr. Skinner that if a worm could do it, why not memory genes. Why couldn't we find a way to regenerate the gaps in memory, or at least expose them by relinking them," Sondra was sitting on the edge of her chair and excitement was threaded in her speech. She complimented her words with arm and hand movement that had Amy fully engaged and intrigued.

"What does this have to do with Adam? Are we trying to regenerate his memories?" Amy probed.

"Not really," Sondra responded, "The regeneration experiments were done on your father, Tom. But as you know, he died before we finished. We still believed that the experiment worked and that the memories are actually intact inside of Adams genes."

"I feel unusually thirsty right now," Amy gently ran her finger across the scar on her scalp and requested another bottle of water. It was warm in the office and the air tasted stale in Amy's mouth.

Sondra handed her a fresh bottle and joined her by opening her own and pausing for a minute to drink down half of the pint, "Ahhh, so where was I?"

"How did you regenerate dad's memories?" Amy kept her on track.

"Oh, yes. Well, Dr. Skinner devised a mixture of a couple simple ingredients and started testing the reaction of DNA and genes when they were enhanced by his vitamin potion."

"What was in it?"

"Ginkgo and Mescaline were the two main ingredients. Most of the others were used as binding agents or fillers to support absorption and sustainability. The theory was that the Mescaline would free the mind and the Ginkgo would enhance the memory."

"It started in the lab, advanced to rats and then we went to clinical trial with humans. It worked well on the rats because we could test it rapidly due to their gestation period being only twenty two days. It enabled us to do multi-generational studies within months."

Amy looked a little lost so Sondra clarified, "We observed the untrained third and fourth generation rats replicating the exact behaviors of the primary subject. It was amazing. We went to human testing very quickly. We were excited to be able to talk to the test subjects and actually record result patterns. You can't talk to rats, so we were limited on the ability to fully prove our hypothesis."

Amy put her hand up in order to get Sondra to pause. Amy asked with great consternation, "What happened to my father?"

She leapt from her chair, slammed her fist on the Sondra's desk with one hand, pointed at her head with the other hand and screamed out, "AND WHAT THE FUCK IS THIS SCAR ON MY HEAD?" Amy insisted with gritted teeth, "And none of your bullshit about being a Siamese twin either. What is it?"

Sondra slowly reached for her desk drawer and Amy lunged across the desk. Amy swept away Sondra's wrist, before it reached the drawer, and with her left hand used all her weight to slam the base of her right palm into Sondra's chest knocking her backwards and flipping Sondra and her chair on their back.

Amy quickly jumped over to Sondra's side of the desk and place her right foot across Sondra's throat. She pressed down slightly enough for Sondra to panic and grab Amy's ankle, struggling to remove it. Amy was in control for the first the time in her life, and she liked it. The surge of adrenaline gave her additional strength and her foot held firm over her mother's throat.

Amy slowly reached behind, opened the desk drawer and removed a small hand held device containing a single white button on it. She noticed it had a little sensor on it. It reminded Amy of the remote control device used on shock collars for dogs. Her eyes widened and she gasped.

Amy's burst of anxiety and fear were just enough for Sondra to force Amy's foot off her throat. Sondra pushed it away and then quickly punched the back of Amy's other knee dropping Amy to the floor next to her. Sondra rolled toward Amy and a cat fight ensued with slapping, kicking and scratching with neither woman gaining a dominant position.

Sondra tried to pry the remote from Amy's hand but Amy bit her hand then punched her hard in the nose knocking her backwards. Blood spurted from Sondra's nose and Amy was able to retreat several feet from her mother and get back on her feet. Sondra held one hand to her nose and her other hand in the air signaling for a truce. She was defeated. 'For now'.

Amy could sense victory. She knew she had to take a stance. This moment would shape their relationship for the future. Amy stood over her mother, grabbed a handful of hair, squeezed it and pulled Sondra's head back so she was looking straight into her eyes and said, "Don't ever mess with me again. Do you understand me?"

Sondra was physically no match for the younger woman. She knew it. She also knew she could not control her with the device anymore. She forced a tear and said, "Amy, I am so sorry."

At the house, Cheri took Adam's hands in hers. She smiled showing all her bright white teeth and said, "Praise God!" Just as she spoke the words the door swung open. Chuck and Doris were home.

Doris immediately chimed in, "What are we praising God about?" Doris and Chuck were not very 'religious' people but were not ignorant of religion either. Doris couldn't help sticking her nose into everything and she just blurted it out. Chuck grunted and gave her 'the look'.

Cheri started to say, "Adam and I were sharing some personal stories..." but Adam finished by stating, "And I told her I believed in God. And Jesus of course."

"Come on Doris, let's leave them be," Chuck said as he lightly tugged Doris' arm and walked the two of them past Adam and Cheri and into the main room of the house.

Chuck didn't want to get into a discussion about religion. He just wanted his recliner and his favorite television program. Doris complied for a few moments, then she peeked her head back into the other room and said, "I am happy for you Adam. Are you two staying for dinner? You could tell us all about it."

"Thanks mom, but we'll take a rain check. We were just leaving when you came home, that's why we were standing by the door."

Doris looked down at Adam's feet and asked, "Where were you going without any shoes on?" She knew he wasn't being totally honest with her so she continued, "I understand if you don't want to be around us. Well, not really I don't, but we need to sit down soon and talk this through. You are an adult now and we want to help but have no idea what you have going on."

Cheri gave Adam a puppy dog look and he knew that meant she wanted him to spend time with his foster parents so he replied, "What's for dinner mom?"

"Chuck, did you here that? Adam's joining us for dinner tonight."

"Yeah, I heard," Chuck grunted from his recliner.

"Come in and relax you two. We have some catching up to do," Doris was so excited that she could hardly contain herself.

CHAPTER 14

Sondra gathered herself, stood up, picked her chair off the floor and sat down. Amy stayed standing and said, "Tell me about the scar mother." Sondra broke down and began weeping. It was genuine and Amy could tell she had broken her. A few minutes passed and Sondra regained her composure before she began speaking.

"We were fascinated by the brain."

Amy was not going to let herself get caught in assumptions anymore so she interrupted, "Who is we?"

"Your father and I. In fact Tom was very instrumental in my research in more ways than being the test subject. The two of us spent countless hours doing research together. Long days and late nights of microwaving cold coffee to stay awake and talk and explore. We were unified in our purpose."

Amy could see the joy and regret seeping through Sondra's words and facial expressions as she spoke. A lump formed in Amy's throat as she thought about her parents being together and in love. Something she never witnessed. She never had a chance to know her father, and her mother had raised her in a lie.

Sondra continued, "We dove in head first, no pun intended, into studying the limbic structure of the brain. Tom believed the hippocampus was the key to unlocking trapped memories,"

Sondra sobbed, "He wanted to find a cure for Alzheimer's disease. His theory was that the memories never went away, but they would be blocked over time by the degeneration of the limbic system thereby trapping memories in the deeper recesses of the brain."

Amy asked, "Why did he want to find a cure for Alzheimer's? What was his motivation?"

"Your father witnessed first-hand the effects on a human. Someone he dearly loved that played a significant role in his life. He wanted to beat the disease and his passion was contagious. I jumped on the band wagon. Things were going so well and then..." Sondra paused and began weeping again. Her weeping changed into sobs and mini gasps, tears ran down her cheeks and her nose dripped.

Amy could see her mother was clearly distraught. A part of her quietly sneered in contempt, *'she deserves this'*, and the other part of her felt empathy for a broken woman. Amy backed away, sat down and let her mother cry it out.

Sondra took a tissue from the box on her desk, wiped her eyes and blew her nose. Then another sob and another tissue. Then with a deep breath she continued, "Then everything went so wrong."

Doris placed a hot casserole on the table for the four of them to begin eating. Chuck began piling food onto his plate when Adam said, "I'd like to pray before we eat."

Cheri's head slightly snapped in Adam's direction. She was tingly inside. She never heard Adam say that before. Chuck stopped spooning his food in mid-stream and Doris let out an uncomfortable sound.

"God, thank you for Chuck and Doris in my life. Thank you for my best friend Cheri. And thank you for this meal," Adam paused, took a deep breath and said, "In Jesus name, Amen."

In unison Cheri, Chuck and Doris all said, "Amen."

Food was passed and everyone began eating amidst an awkward silence. Doris was never one to let things be quiet for too long so she broke in with, "Did you really mean that Adam?" She began to whimper, "Are you thankful for us in your life?"

"Well, I did just say it to God, so yes, I really mean it. All of you. I've been thinking about my life and where would I be if the three of you didn't care about me. I am so blessed."

Doris burst out of the room in tears and Adam looked at Chuck and asked, "What did I say?"

"You said what she wanted to hear for a long time Adam. She'll be fine. And thank you," Chuck had a crackle of emotion in his voice.

Cheri reached her hand across the table and place it over Adam's hand. They looked into each other's eyes and smiled. Chuck stood up and patted Adam on the back, "I am going to go check on your mother."

Adam responded, "Okay," and began eating his dinner while it was still hot. He loved Doris' cooking. He missed eating at home. He knew he was where he belonged and thought, *The two crazy women at Milton will just have to wait until I am ready to go back there.*

Amy and Sondra were interrupted by a text message from Adam stating he would not be coming to the clinic and he wanted to spend time with his family. Amy was struck by the irony of his message. They were his family, not Chuck and Doris.

"I'll make some coffee. It's going to be a long night. We have a lot to discuss," Sondra stood up and walked out of her office.

Amy picked up the remote control device and looked it over. She found the battery compartment, removed the batteries and tossed them in the waste basket next to the desk. Then she placed the device on the floor and stomped on it. She kept stomping until it was in little pieces.

Sondra re-entered the office with two cups of coffee and walked past Amy while she continued to crush the remote control. Sondra was indifferent to the action and handed Amy one of the coffees. Amy made one final step on the broken pieces and with the ball of her foot she pressed and twisted the particles into the floor. Then she reached over and took the cup of coffee.

Amy started the conversation "So what went wrong?"

Sondra sipped her coffee, cleared her throat and continued where she left off, "When we went to human trial, we had limited approvals from the FDA. They made us classify it as a drug. We tried to avoid the FDA by getting it classified as a vitamin. During the trial we referred to it as a vitamin to each other and to the patients. To the general public it was a drug and the FDA placed enormous controls over us and the trial. The only reason we got it approved is because the government's defense department caught wind of what we were doing and suddenly it was fast tracked. Actually, I still believe Dr. Skinner provided the 'leak' to someone in the defense department so that we could get approvals."

"Because of all the oversight and undesirable press we had a difficult time finding test subjects. In fact months went by and no one signed up. No recruits, virtually no interest, so, so Tom and I were the first."

Amy's jaw dropped. Sondra wasn't sure if Amy was even listening, but that visual made it clear she was. Amy said, "So you and dad started taking this stuff? You took it? How long ago? Were you pregnant with us when you were taking it?"

Amy stood up and paced around in a small semi-circle in front of Sondra's desk. She set her coffee down and started rubbing her fingers through her hair on both sides of her head. She blurted out, "You two are freaks!" Spit sprayed from her mouth as she said it. She began sobbing, then screamed.

Sondra let her vent. Amy needed to get it out and it was late. Everyone else at the clinic had gone home for the evening. Amy had to experience and release all the emotions so they could get on with their work. Sondra needed Amy one hundred percent on board with everything going forward and she knew she was losing her the past few weeks. It was time to get it all out on the table.

Sondra was slow in her response to ensure she didn't come off as patronizing, "I don't blame you for feeling that way Amy. Let me continue."

"We were young and wanted to make a difference. We had no idea our decisions would have radical consequences. And I never should have agreed to let Johnny and Billy join the trial. Skinner insisted. I resisted. Tom wanted them in it. He had this crazy idea that he could find them in his dreams if they were all under the influence of the vitamin's effects at the same time."

Amy was shaking her head. Her eyes were bloodshot and dry. Sondra hesitated, wondering if Amy could take anymore this evening, then asked, "Should I keep going Amy? Or do you want to get some rest and pick it up in the morning?"

Amy took a tissue from the box on the desk, blew her nose, tossed the snotty rag into the trash and insisted, "Please carry on." She displayed a fresh composure.

Sondra explained, "I only took it once. The side effects were horrific. I spent sixteen hours in 'hallucination land' that felt like an eternity and even Skinner was concerned I may never come out of it. It must have been a supratherapeutic dose. I spent the following sixteen hours vomiting. Skinner had to feed me fluids intravenously to keep me from completely dehydrating."

Amy sat down and asked, "What do you mean by 'hallucination land'?"

"Oh, Amy, please don't take me there."

"Bullshit. You've taken *me* through bullshit. Tell me what happened."

"Skinner claimed that my mind experienced rapid fire genetic memory trips through my ancestry. It wasn't pretty. It was horrifying. My family of origin is riddled with psychotic behavior throughout the centuries."

Amy busted a chuckle, "There's a shocker. You didn't have to take the memory drug to know that," she laughed, "I could have told you you're psychotic."

Sondra gritted her teeth and glared at Amy. Amy thought, *'bring it bitch'*. Sondra sat back in her chair and took a few deep breaths to calm herself. She couldn't help but feel the exasperation of losing control for the first time in her life. Even so there was a sense of pride that Amy had finally stepped up and gotten tough. *'Like mother like daughter'*, Sondra thought, *'And look out if she is anything like me'*.

"Don't worry Amy it's hereditary," Sondra snickered back, "So you're certain to be just as freaking nuts as the rest of us."

"Whatever crazy woman. Just keep talking. I want to hear the whole story," Amy was dominant yet reserved as the conversation ensued.

While Chuck was checking on Doris, Cheri leaned over and whispered in Adam's ear, "Well it looks like you managed to avoid another conversation with your parents."

Adam raised an eyebrow and shifted back slightly, then smiled. He was about to respond, but decided he would just let it be. Cheri locked her gaze upon Adam. She was really falling for him, and it was okay. He was moving in the right direction. They had more in common every day. Adam believed the same way as her, but he also knew something Cheri didn't know…which also made them very different.

"Should we wait for your parents to come back in the room or do you want to say good bye and escape to the clinic," Cheri asked.

"Neither. I will poke my head in their room and tell them we are going to your house and thank them for dinner."

"Sounds like a plan."

Adam did as he said and Chuck waved him off and thanked him again. Doris asked when would they see him again and he told them he'd be back soon. They seemed content with that response so he took Cheri by the hand and left.

Chuck asked Doris, "Why are you afraid to confront him with your questions? It's all you talk about when he's not here."

"I can't. I just can't. I don't want to scare him away. He may actually come back and stay here."

Chuck shook his head, "Not too long ago you were ready to show him some tough love and bounce him out on his ear."

Doris sniffled, "I know. I know. I am just not as tough as I sound, am I?"

Chuck patted her on the thigh and said, "That's what I love about you Doris. And sometimes it's okay to just let time take care of things. He'll come around. When he's ready."

"I know but I am scared for him."

"He's a man. A young man but a man none the less. He'll be fine."

"Yeah. A tough guy just like you Chuck," Doris replied and pecked a kiss on his cheek.

"Besides," Chuck said, "His sleep walking episodes seemed to have subsided. Maybe he's outgrown them."

"Chuck, he hasn't been here. We don't know how often it happens. And he doesn't know that we know."

Doris looked down and Chuck pulled her close to his chest and gave her a long tight hug, "You know Doris, that we do need to get it all out on the table with him, soon."

Doris chuckled, "Ha. You mean the part where we tell him I am not really Doris and you are not really Chuck. I can't wait."

"Yes, that too. But I was referring to the part about his sleepwalking and, and his journal. That book he writes in that you call a diary. Diaries are for girls. Adam uses a journal. And we can't wait forever for him to step forward and open up to us when we already know everything."

Doris sighed, "We weren't supposed to grow attached to him. We were brought here to keep an eye on him and protect him."

"I know," Chuck reflected, "And we've done good. The kid does grow on you after a while." He gently rubbed Doris' back and asked, "What's this stuff about God all of a sudden? Where is that coming from?"

"The girl. His friend Cheri. I can tell he's really fond of her. We've got to watch that girl. I'm not going to make too much of it right now, but we do need to monitor it."

"I'll report it when I log in tonight," Chuck said as he stood up and walked out of the room.

CHAPTER 15

Adam and Cheri were sitting on the porch outside of Adam's house. Her parents were out to dinner, so she called them to see if she could hang out at Skip's house for a while. Her father said okay as long as they sat on the porch until Skip's parents came home. She probably would never tell her parents of Adam's name change.

Adam thought long and hard before he said, "I need to get into the clinic when Sondra and Amy are not around. I need to get into Skinner's old files."

Cheri felt anxiety creeping in and expressed her concerns, "Adam, Adam, Adam. That's like espionage..."

Adam burst out laughing, "Ha ha ha. Oh my gosh. that's hilarious. I guess it would be."

"It's not funny. I'm not kidding. You shouldn't be sneaking around that clinic Adam."

"I have to know what they are really up to."

"Who?"

"Sondra and Amy," Adam responded and looked at Cheri as if she was out of touch.

"Why not just stop that silly experiment?" She rebutted.

"It's a clinical trial."

"Yeah right. You don't believe that for a minute Adam."

"Doesn't matter. I've thought it through and I have a plan."

"What's your plan, secret agent man," Cheri chuckled.

"Seriously. I am going to do this. The next time I go in for the sleep study, I am going to pretend to leave. I'll have one of those pocket ponchos in my back pocket. I'll hide out in the men's bathroom stall until Sondra and Amy leave. Then I'll slip on the poncho so I cannot be identified by any video cameras and I'll jump onto the clinic's computer system and rifle through the files in Sondra's office."

"Won't the camera's show that you went into the bathroom and a guy in a poncho came out. I think they'll figure out it was you," Cheri challenged his plan.

"I checked. There are only four cameras, and they are all around the entrances and main hallways. Nothing in the hall by the restroom or Sondra's office."

"Okay," Cheri said, "Then they will know you never left."

"Hmm," Adam could feel his plan unraveling a bit.

"Wait. I have an idea. You will come with me to the clinic. There is a unisex bathroom in between the men's and women's rooms. I will go in there first and put my hoodie sweatshirt in a bag in the trash can. Then when it's time to leave you will go in there and put it on and leave. They will think I left the building."

"And, they will think *I* never did," Amy stated as she shook her head.

"They won't be looking for you. They are watching for me," Adam had some excitement in his voice. He was beginning to believe in his plan. "We will arrive a few minutes apart, and you'll pretend to leave a few minutes after me, so when they watch the tape, if they even watch the tape, they will see me leave and won't bother watching after that."

Cheri was shaking her head, "I don't like it. But I'll do it for you."

Adam smiled and said, "Thanks!"

Amy and Sondra were still going at it, "It's time to tell me about the scar mommy," Amy's tone was getting more intimidating by the minute. Sondra was used to tapping on the remote device and watching her daughter instantly submit. It was a bit concerning that Amy could suddenly be experiencing a 'rebound' effect.

"Dr. Skinner invented a biochemical, electromechanical device he referred to as 'The Memory Chip'. He had them surgically implanted into you and Adam the day you were born," as Sondra explained she slowly pushed her chair back away from her desk in anticipation of Amy attacking her physically again.

Amy's face flushed a burgundy color, her teeth were grinding and saliva was seeping through her teeth as she growled, "You let him do that to your babies?" She clenched her fists while she slowly stood up. Sondra braced herself.

Amy screamed and ran out of the office, down the hall and burst through the doors of the clinic continuing her run for almost a mile before she collapsed over her knees panting and sobbing.

Cheri and Adam kissed. Cheri stood up and said, I'm glad you are sleeping here tonight. I think Doris and Chuck will be happy also."

"Goodnight Cheri," Adam smiled and waved as he went back into the house.

Doris was standing inside waiting for Adam, "Can we talk now?" she asked.

"I'm really tired. Definitely in the morning though," Adam responded as he walked past Doris and into his bedroom.

Doris followed Adam and stood at his doorway with a stoic expression and whispered, "I think now would be a good time to talk Adam." She hollered down the hall, "CHUCK, come join us please."

"What's this all about?" Adam's voice crackled a bit. He was taken aback by Doris' seemingly more aggressive behavior. He had never seen that side of her before.

Chuck pushed his way past Doris and stood over Adam. His presence dominated the room and Adam thought to himself, *'I don't recall him being this big.'*

"We're not who you think we are Adam," Chuck's words came out slow and hollow like someone turned the speed dial down on the sound equalizer.

Adam took a few steps backward and sat back on his bed. Chuck and Doris moved in closer and it felt like the air was being sucked out of the room, "Adam? Are you ok?" Doris asked, "You look a little pale."

"Get him some water," Chuck barked out like a commanding officer.

'This is weird', Adam thought as he put his head in his hands. He concentrated on slowing down his breathing. He felt like he was dreaming. His mind was dancing on the fringe of consciousness.

"Oh my gosh, he fainted," Doris gasped, spilling water from the glass as she rushed back in the room, "I knew he wouldn't be ready for this discussion yet Chuck."

"When the hell are we going to tell him then?" Chuck growled back.

He is sitting inside a large building, blurry colors surround him. His eyesight clears and the colors become windows of stained glass. Adam is in a cathedral. He hears a single voice reverberating off the walls. A man is standing on a podium speaking to a large crowd. Adam is in the midst of the crowd.

The man is finishing up his speech, "In conclusion, in summary, we were created in his image for his purpose. We do not always fully understand that purpose. It is different for each of us. Most of us are still being fashioned for that purpose."

"Think of how mankind invents. For example, the lawnmower, as its being assembled, does not know its purpose will be to cut grass one day. We know what purpose it will serve us, just as God knows what purpose we will serve him. I am not saying we are lawn mowers," the crowd chuckles as the man continues, "Someday each of us will know our purpose. Until then we simply need to have faith."

Adam stands and steps in line with the crowd that methodically shuffles out of the building. The sun is bright and it makes him sneeze. An old woman hands him a tissue and smiles. Her teeth are yellow and crooked. She looks familiar, "Do I know you?" Adam asks.

The old woman shakes her head slightly, in disappointment rather than affirmation or denial. She turns and walks away. Adam follows her for a few steps until someone grabs his arm and begins shaking it. He feels a splash of cold water on his face.

"Adam, wake up. Adam are you there?" Doris is pleading as she flicks drops of water onto his face and Chuck is attempting to shake him awake.

The old woman turns to Adam and with the voice of a little girl says, "He was our sacrificial goat and our scapegoat. You need to understand that the true suffering came with death and the spiritual suffering as the scapegoat for all of us. The time he spent separated from God, in hell, was more significant than anyone will ever understand."

"You are speaking of Jesus," Adam confirms.

Her eyes are shining like the eyes of a child absorbed in the eminence of the sun. Her voice is soft and precise, "Time is physical. Spiritually, a day could be like a thousand years. In order to pay for the iniquities of the whole world His time in the grave should not be observed or considered as merely days, but rather thousands of years. Eternal extrication, then resurrection and glory."

"Dang it Adam wake up," Chuck grouses in frustration. Doris is sobbing, "Are we losing him?"

In unison, Adam gasped and his eyes flashed open. He was coughing and puffing for air. He reached out and grabbed a hold of Chuck's arm. Chuck pulled him forward into a sitting position and Doris gently patted his back. Adam calmed down and gained his composure.

"What happened?" Adam asked shaking his head in disbelief, "Where am I?"

Doris assured him, "You are at home and everything is all right now. Here, drink some water. It seems you fainted."

"Fainted?" Adam was still snapping out of his catatonic state.

Chuck was wondering if his comments sent Adam reeling so he asked, "What's the last thing you remember?"

"The old woman. Her words. I understood them. I recognize her from somewhere but I cannot put my finger on it."

Chuck and Doris exchanged concerning glances. They each knew what the other was thinking. "Let's allow Adam to rest now Chuck," Doris said as she tugged at Chuck's shirt sleeve. They left his room and pulled the door behind them leaving it open just a crack.

'Where am I and who are these people?' Things are not what they seem to be', the voice speaking inside his head elucidated. He whispered aloud, "I've got to get back to Milton." Doris and Chuck were outside his room, listening.

CHAPTER 16

Adam is walking in a line of people chained to one another. The metal is cutting into his wrists. He is barefoot. His feet burn. They are walking on dirt, sand and stone. They are being led by soldiers in wagons, no, chariots, both. He is thirsty, dirty. There is another row of people in chains next to him. Men, women and children are in a line. The men are in chains. The children and most of the women are not in chains.

A woman in chains next to Adam leans over and susurrates something to him in Hebrew. Adam understands her words to say, "King Jeconiah. What will they do to us when we reach Babylon?" Adam simply shakes his head. The woman begins weeping.

A guard notices their exchange and he punches Adam in the face then kicks him in the chest, knocking him to the ground. The guard unchains the woman, strikes her in the head several times, picks up her limp body and tosses it into a ditch.

Another soldier grabs Adam's chain and pulls him up from the ground. The metal tears his skin and he is bleeding. It stings. The sun is hot. Shouts come from the front of the line and the procession continues.

Adam thinks about the story of king Jeconiah. He was cursed. Jeconiah and his people would be under the reign of

Nebuchadnezzar. He knew there was nothing he could do. He was a king in captivity. A young man the same age as Adam. He wondered what he looked like. He knew what he felt like. Defeated, beaten, hungry, thirsty, stripped of his kingdom and reviled by God.

Amy called into Sondra's office, "Come quick. A bruise is forming on Adam's cheekbone while he sleeps."

Sondra burst into the room and immediately went by Adam's bed, "What happened?"

Amy replied anxiously, "His head kind of snapped back and then I noticed a red mark, and since then it has been turning into what you see now."

Adam's cheekbone was swelling and turning a deeper red and blue. "He looks dirty," Sondra said, "I don't remember him coming in here looking like this." Sondra pulled his covers back.

"Mom! His feet. They are filthy and torn up. It looks like he's been walking in the desert or something!"

"We need to wake him, NOW!" Sondra screeched.

The soldier splashes water in Adam's face. It feels cool and refreshing. Adam licks a few drops from his face where his tongue can reach. Another soldier is shaking him, yelling and slapping his face.

Amy grabbed the cup of water off the stainless steel tray and flung the remaining water into Adam's face while Sondra shook him and pleaded, "Adam, wake up. Wake up."

Adam feels weak and his life is fading. Everything is blurry and sound is distant. He is numb to sight, sound and touch. He sees flashes of light and pulses of energy slam into his mind. His thoughts slow to a complete halt, momentarily. He is floating in a void. His vision clears and he is back with his people as their imprisoned king.

"Amy, get me the Adrenaline syringe, now!" Sondra pointed toward the door and Amy took off down the hall to retrieve the medicine. Adam's eyes were open in slits. Sondra could tell he was between two worlds, but didn't want him to eddy around, lost in the middle.

Adam's breathing was shallow, and the alarms on his vital monitors were all beeping, all registering in the danger zone. He started foaming at the mouth, convulsing as his heart beat went into a rapid arrhythmia and then dove into a slump of less than 40 beats per minute. *Where is Amy with that adrenaline?'* Sondra anxiously wondered.

Amy raced back into the room slamming her shoulder into the door frame on the way in but not slowing down while she held the large needle upright and squeezed a few drops of liquid into the air to clear any bubbles from the syringe.

Sondra ripped Adam's shirt open to expose his chest, grabbed the syringe from Amy and rose it in the air preparing to plunge it into Adam's chest cavity. Adam lunged upright gagging and gasping for air, arms flailing, knocking the syringe from Sondra's arm sending it spinning along the floor.

Amy dropped to her knees to retrieve the adrenaline syringe while Sondra pressed Adam back onto the bed, "You do it Amy while I hold him down."

"But wait, his heart rate is soaring now," Amy replied staring at the heart monitor which was registering 176 BPM.

Adam's eyes opened wide and he tossed Sondra aside like a small rag doll. He leapt from his bed and knocked Amy backwards into the monitoring equipment.

The soldiers are encircling him. He hears them speaking in ancient Aramaic and they call out his name in mockery,

"Jeconiah you fool. Try to trick us. We will now beat you near death and deliver you barely alive to King Nebudchenezzer."

Adam is in the fight of his life and is enduring pain like he has never felt before. They are punching and kicking him. His bowels and bladder release themselves of fluids and waste. He falls to the ground and curls up in the fetal position as the beating continues, until, darkness.

Adams lay in the corner of his room in the fetal position with a urine stained garment and a load of fecal matter pressed against his hind side.

"Where am I? Adam asked no one in particular.

Amy knelt beside him. That's when she noticed the cut above his left eye and the lump on his forehead. Dirt was embedded in his nostrils. His lower lip was split and the blood was mixed with sand. She smelled the mess and said, "We need to get you cleaned up."

Adam groaned and held his right side where he was kicked in the dream. He was trying to discern how he could be all banged up and lying on the floor at the Milton Medical Clinic, *I must have fallen while dreaming and the pains created the images of the beating I took in that dream'.*

As his eyesight cleared he noticed how dirty he was and begged the question to Amy, "What happened in here? Why am I such a mess?"

Sondra answered first, "That's exactly what we are trying to understand ourselves Adam. I've never seen anything like this before. Tom spoke of bringing things back from dreams and such, but never this dramatic or vivid or explicit." Then she said to herself, *This is freaking me out.'*

"Don't freak out. This has happened to me before. When I was young," Adam explained. Sondra pulled back in astonishment and thought, *He heard my thoughts'.*

"I did," Adam responded.

Amy laughed out loud and thought, *You better watch what you think around him Mother'.*

"Mother?" Adam had a puzzled look on his face, "Did you just call Sondra 'Mother'?"

Sondra's glare would have pierced a hole in the side of Amy's head if her eyes were laser beams. She quickly said, "Adam, are you ok? You are talking funny. You must be in a mild state of shock from whatever you just experienced in your dream."

"It wasn't a dream," he replied, "It was a memory, and I was there. It was real. I have the dirt and bruises to prove it."

"And by the way, I think I can hear your thoughts," Adam went on to say, "And I have a question for you two. If you know something is going to happen before it happens, then when did it actually happen?"

While things at Milton were unfolding, Doris and Chuck were debriefing the events that occurred with Adam during the week. He was beginning to realize and even better comprehend his journey and was getting closer to the truth. They wanted nothing more than to preserve the truth. Their assignment was clear, protect Adam at all costs.

"I'm not sure how just coming right out and telling him protects him," Doris shot back at Chuck.

"It's time. He needs to move on. We've brought him this far, we must reveal the facts to him and release him, set him free," was Chuck's retort.

"Oh yes," Doris disparaged, " And the truth will set him free."

"I will take it from here. You are no longer capable. You service your doubts and he cannot have that. He needs to get stronger. You should retract from him. Let him go, and quickly," Chuck was almost demanding.

Doris stared out the dining room window. It had just started to drizzle and tiny raindrops plinked across the window pane. She turned toward Chuck and a steady down pour of water was streaming behind her. Chuck looked past her, no, through her.

A flash of lights flickered through the glass. Doris began counting, one, two, three, four... the ground rumbled and the house shook from thunder. They looked into each other's eyes and exchanged smiles. Doris reached over and took Chucks hand in hers. It was dry and cracked from the weather and age.

"Isn't His power grand!" Doris announced.

"Yes it is," Chuck enthusiastically responded.

"Chuck, we both know Adam needs to be here and not at Milton," Doris didn't blink while her eyes pleaded for agreement.

"Agreed."

"He needs to finish it here in his own home, his own bed."

"Agreed."

"We'll do it your way Chuck," Doris stated.

"Again, I say, agreed."

"Chuck?"

"Yes Doris."

"What if a person's last thought is the one they spend eternity with?"

Chuck looked deep into her bright blue eyes. He noticed they had a silver outline this time. He smiled and said, "Then they'd better make it a good one."

CHAPTER 17

Cheri was racing down the street in her father's car on her way to Milton as fast as she could after she received the call from Adam. Her dad just happened to be in a good mood when she asked to borrow the car to go over and see Adam. She left out the part about Milton Medical and referred to him as Skip. Her dad was not too keen on her spending anymore nights over there, but he was beginning to grow fond of Skip. He even felt he could trust him alone with his daughter. Not for very long periods of time, but as young adults, he knew he had to give them some breathing room.

The car screeched to a halt and Adam grabbed the door handle, flung open the passenger door and jumped in the vehicle.

"Thanks for doing this. Get me out of here, " Adam implored and Cheri stepped on the gas.

"What happened tonight Adam? It's early and you always stay through till morning."

"Let's go someplace where we can grab some coffee and talk for a while," Adam said.

Cheri noticed his hands were trembling. He appeared visibly shaken, so she decided to wait until they stopped before asking anymore questions. There was a small diner up the road from

116

her house that Adam said he really liked once, so she headed in that direction.

Adam was rocking back and forth in the passenger seat and every few seconds he slapped his thighs in a drum roll. Cheri was getting annoyed but they were almost to the diner.

"I think she might be my mom," Adam whispered while staring out the windshield of the car.

Cheri thought she heard him, but wanted to be certain so she reflected back, "Who is your mom Adam?"

"She is. The woman doing the trial. Sondra. Sondra is my mom," Adam was mumbling the words and it was making Cheri nervous.

Cheri pulled into the parking lot of the small diner, put the car in park and turned off the engine. She took a deep breath and looked incessantly at Adam for almost a full minute, then reached for the door handle and said, "Let's go in and have a cup of coffee and you can tell me all about it."

"No," Adam grabbed her arm, "Let's talk here. Please."

Cheri hesitated and replied, "Sounds good to me." She was not sure how things were going to play out but knew that Adam needed to get it all out. She was also concerned he might be delusional from the dreams and maybe was having challenges discerning his dreams from his memories and both from reality.

"I have to get in there and get some answers," Adam stated firmly, "I need to know the truth and I just don't trust those two. I feel like my mind is in a constant struggle when I am around them. And then there is Doris and Chuck. I overheard them talking about protecting me. I have to sort this all out."

"Ok. Slow down, Cheri requested, "And let's take these one at a time so I can track with you."

"I need to get inside the clinic's files and computers to find records on Tom Dory."

"So we are going forward with your plan?"

"Yes."

"Do you mind if I ask what you are looking for?"

"Answers."

"To who your mom is?"

117

"And to what happened to Tom and why I am able to remember so much so clearly. And who Amy is. I think Amy is my sister."

Cheri tilted her head slightly and her eyebrows closed together in curiosity, "What makes you think that?"

"I don't think it. I heard it."

"They told you Sondra was your mom and Amy was your sister?"

"No. I heard them think it."

The last comment threw Cheri back in her seat in a jerking movement. She shook her head and wondered if she really heard him say it so she asked, "You read people's minds now?"

"Not now, but again."

"Ok, so you just pushed me into the 'Now I am freaking out' zone. Adam, are you being serious?"

"I haven't experienced it since I was a kid, but I know I can do it. I know I can hear people's thoughts. I am pretty sure it happened again tonight because of the way they were acting when I spoke their thoughts aloud."

"Let me take you home so you can get some rest Adam," Cheri suggested.

"You don't believe me. I knew I shouldn't have called you."

Adam decided in that moment he would be very selective in what he shared with Cheri. Or anyone else for that matter. No one believed him half the time and why would they. Normal people don't talk like that, don't talk about those things. Those thoughts are for science fiction novels.

"Can you hear what I'm thinking right now?" Cheri asked as she thought to herself, *What did they do to him at the clinic tonight?*

"They didn't do anything to me at the clinic tonight," Adam said aloud, "I slept like always, with all the wires hooked up to my head." Adam brushed his hair back as he said it and Cheri noticed something she hadn't seen before. The streetlight reflected off Adam's scalp and revealed a small scar. She reached over to brush his hair back where she noticed the scar and Adam pulled away.

"It's okay Adam. I think I see something on your head."

"I am sure it's just the glues from the electrode pads," he replied.

"Can I see?" Cheri softly requested.

Adam leaned away from Cheri and sat quietly for a moment. Cheri reflected on what occurred and realized, *'I think Adam heard my thoughts. He responded to my thought about the clinic. He really needs my support if this is actually happening.'*

"It is actually happening Cheri," Adam whispered as he dozed off in the passenger seat of Cheri's father's car.

Cheri gasped at his response as she watched Adam's eyes close and his mind fade into a catatonic state. No wires, no crazy women. Only her and Adam. She would watch and listen.

Adam is surrounded by people he doesn't recognize. He is sitting on a large chair. His vision clears and he sees beautiful women surrounding him. By their demeanor it appears they belong to him. The chair he sits on looks like a throne. Soldiers stand at each side of an archway in front of him.

He stands up and the room of people stills itself. The room is silent. A contingent of guards enter. They are followed by people dressed differently than everyone else. It appears as if they are from another land. Four men are escorting a woman toward Adam. She is adorned like a queen, with silk garments and jewels and a crown-like headpiece. She genuflects. Adam sits down.

Adam understands only bits and pieces of the language she is speaking. She greets him and refers to him as King. She has traveled to see him and brings him gifts. Two men step forward and open the chests they carry. They are full of gold and jewels. She smiles and bows and the men place them at Adam's feet. She tells him there is much more she brought for him and his kingdom.

"You are a deserved King," the queen expresses in Hebrew.

"You speak Hebrew," Adam replied.

"Of course. Anything less would be an insult to such a wise king," she states with an air of confidence, "Maybe you could escort me from Jerusalem in one of your fourteen hundred chariots." She winks and Adam feels a rush and tingle of lust. The other women that surround him look uneasy and their faces are expressionless, stoic. Jealous. They are his wives.

The windows of the car were fogging up so Cheri pressed the automatic control to lower her window and let some air inside the vehicle. The suction and pop of the window releasing from the rubber seal startled Adam. He shifted in his seat turned his body toward Cheri and rested his head on the headrest.

Cheri noticed an imprint on the passenger window where Adams head smeared the fogged glass. It was dissipating rapidly from the fresh air she allowed in from her window. It looked like words. She reached for her cell phone, turned on the camera app and took a picture. Adam huffed at the flash but remained asleep. The words were gone and the window was clear again.

The battery on her phone was low so she plugged in the car charger. Nothing. The car needed to be in auxiliary mode or running for the power to work. She didn't want to wake Adam with any more noise, but she wanted to see what showed up on the camera so she pressed the screen on her phone to get into the photo gallery.

She found the picture of the window and she could see something imprinted in the foggy glass. She spread her fingers across the screen to enlarge the picture but that just made it blurry. She would have to wait until later to download it to her computer and review it on a bigger screen.

There is a rumbling of horses and a flash of lightning. Adam is dressed in armor and leading a team of soldiers down a muddy dirt road in the pouring rain. He feels anger and coldness in his heart. Adam looks back at the army he leads and sees thousands of men, horses and chariots yet he feels distant and alone.

Adam wonders why he is hearing these thoughts, *'Where are your gods now? Wisdom and power, wealth, everything, yet you turn from me. You follow false gods, therefore you will lose your kingdom. Adversaries will rise up against you and overcome you. For the sake of your father, my servant, I will spare your son and leave a trace of your father's kingdom.'*

Adam halts his delegation and dismounts his horse. The raindrops are the size of large coins. The thunder shakes the ground as he drops to his knees and bows his head in humility. He sees light piercing through the dark clouds. It shines upon the ground behind him. The path ahead is dark and cold.

Adam's eyes flickered as he regained consciousness. He shivered from the cold air blowing in from Cheri's window. It was late and very dark outside.

He pondered what had occurred in his sleep, *'Another fallen king. Who was it? I am moving back in time through my memories. David's son. Yes. David will be next. I remember the giant. That memory preceded this one. If I return to the time of David, the memories are finally appearing in order of occurrence. No more randomness. Everything will be clearer and my enlightenment unassailable.*

"Welcome back," Cheri said to Adam, "I am beginning to believe there is something special about you, my little dreamer."

Adam smiled.

CHAPTER 18

Adam and Cheri were holding hands as they walked toward the doors of Milton Medical. She was with him so they could carry out his plan. She might be accessory to a crime if he got caught. She wasn't sure because he wasn't breaking in, only looking into their files. And she liked his idea that if they found him he would claim he was sleep walking. Although he would have to close out any computer files and put back all the paper files in their exact order for that idea to even remotely stand a chance.

"Are you ready for this?" Adam asked Cheri.

"I know my role. You have the tough part. Those two watch you like a hawk, but I'll do my best to distract them both."

Adam was nervous and second guessed himself dragging Cheri into this. It wasn't her problem. She was a good friend. She believed in him, and, believed him. Or she was humoring him and he was actually crazy. He decided to go with the fact she believed in him. It felt better than thinking he was nuts.

Something felt wrong about sneaking around and breaking into files and hacking the computers at Milton, yet it seemed trivial compared to what Adam might find in those records. He had to know. Sondra couldn't be trusted. Adam believed she had her own intentions. Self-serving intentions.

"I have to tell you something, before we go in there tonight," Cheri whispered.

"What is it?" Adam displayed a confused look.

"When you fell asleep in the car the other night, your hair brushed against the foggy window and left an imprint. I took a picture of it and then examined it on my computer the first chance I got."

"What? I what? You took a picture of some words on the window that my hair made?"

"I know it sounds weird, but yes."

"What did it say?"

"Good evening you two. I didn't realize you were bringing company tonight," Amy greeted them at the door, opening it for the two of them to enter. She had just left Sondra's office. Adam walked in first, smiled at her, then walked past her to the restroom. He would be able to get a better look at the layout one more time before they enacted their plan.

While waiting for Adam, Amy asked Cheri, "Will you be spending the night again?"

"Yes. He wants me to. He said the last time was a bit freaky."

"Really? What did he tell you exactly," Amy was concerned Adam told too much. She wanted to find out how close he had become to Cheri.

"That's all really. You know Adam, he's not much of a talker. Keeps a lot inside," Cheri explained in a coy manner. She didn't trust Amy as far as she could see her.

Adam exited the bathroom and walked up to the girls and said, "Ok. Let's do this," he gave Cheri a wink of confidence the plan would work.

Sondra was waiting in Adam's room. Amy proceeded to prep Adam by connecting him to all the wires and monitors. Cheri noticed that this time there was an IV stand with a bag of fluid attached. "What's that for," Cheri asked.

Adam followed Cheri's eyes to the IV stand and joined in the conversation, "That's not for me, is it?"

"It's just to keep you hydrated. We think that will help based on what occurred last time," Sondra explained.

Cheri knew what happened last time and was getting irritated. She didn't believe it was only for hydration, but rather sedation. Her and Adam exchanged glances and Adam spoke up first, "Not necessary. Ain't happening or I'm out of here."

Sondra gave a head nod to Amy to remove the device from the room and Amy complied. Amy really didn't like continuing to put on a show of subservience to Sondra since she was no longer bowing down to her mother's every whim, but for now, the show must go on.

"I've been thinking about my father," Adam said to anyone who felt like listening, "When someone dies, that person remains alive as long as they are not forgotten. I remember." Adam closed his eyes and fell asleep.

Adam is weak and cold. He shivers under layers of wool blankets. He lies on a giant bed too weak to move. A young woman enters the room and crawls into the bed to comfort him and keep him warm with her body. He feels the warmth of her skin on his side. She whispers in Hebrew. He listens but the words are faint. She repeats, "Stay warm my King."

His eyes are heavy and he struggles to keep them open. Another woman enters the room. She is pleading with him for her son to be the next king. A man walks into the room and joins the discussion. They ask him to make a judgment as to who will be their new ruler. Adam struggles to determine what is occurring.

The scene is so familiar. He hears the woman speak the name of her son, "Solomon." Adam realizes he is lying on David's death bed and the woman and prophet want him to make a decree for the heir to his kingdom.

Adam announces the heir to his kingdom will be Solomon. The people hurriedly leave him. Cold and alone. Life is so cruel. People are self-serving. There is a purpose and he knows the outcome. These people will not live to see the day he has seen. He closes his eyes. His breathing is light, shallow, faint.

"He's waking up," Cheri called down the hall to Amy. Amy had just stepped away to get some coffee for both of them because Adam's rest was uneventful. She came scurrying back to the room, without the coffees.

"Now there's a face I recognize," Adam said to Cheri a few moments after his eyes opened.

"Welcome back," Amy said from the doorway. It irritated Cheri that Amy had to butt in as soon as he woke up. That's what she gets for calling her back in the room. She should have let her finish getting the coffees so she could have had a couple minutes alone with Adam before *she* came back. The good news was that Sondra had left and Amy was in charge which meant Adam could move forward with his plan. She needed to find a way to distract Amy so Adam could slip into the restroom and appear as if he left with Cheri.

"Tell us about your dreams Adam," Amy sat down next to his bed with her notepad open and ready for scribing.

"Pretty uneventful actually. I was a king on his deathbed."

Cheri's jaw dropped and Amy did her best not to flinch as she replied, "Go on."

"That was it really."

"Which king were you?" Amy asked.

Adam thought for a few moments, looked at the ceiling and let his thoughts drift away before he answered, "David. They called me David."

"I was David and I named Solomon as the next King of Jerusalem. So far it's been Jeconiah, Solomon and David. . If I have my bible history correct, I should travel backwards again. I am obviously skipping a generation here and there but am definitely stepping back in time. I haven't bounced around. It's been linear for the past few weeks. I believe I am on track. It's awesome."

"On track for what?' Cheri inquired.

"To experience all the patriarchs of antiquity and to come into contact with the beginning," Adam answered. He took a deep breath and exhaled very slowly.

"The beginning?" Amy was questioning him this time, "The beginning of what, exactly?"

"I need to pee," Adam replied. That was the cue for Cheri to distract Amy when Adam went to the men's room.

Adam swung his legs around and hopped off the bed and walked out of the room and into the restroom.

"What do you say we go get those coffees?' Cheri suggested to Amy. It was the perfect distraction. It actually worked out well that Amy never made it to the coffee machine before.

"Let's do it," Amy said as she popped up from her chair and waved Cheri on to follow. Cheri smiled to herself. Game on. The rest was up to Adam.

What Amy didn't see was Cheri placing a note on the bed that Adam had written earlier before they came to the clinic. Amy would find it when they returned with the beverages. Cheri played it up and suggested they bring back a cup for Adam. That also would buy another minute waiting for the extra coffee.

Adam was in the restroom stall hiding out, waiting for Amy to leave so he could break into the files and find out what the heck his dad's life was all about. And who was his mother for that matter. All he knew were the foster homes. He was told his mother died giving birth and according to Sondra, his dad went insane before he was born. He didn't believe any of it.

When Amy and Cheri arrived back at the room Amy said, "He's not back yet…" and then she noticed the note on the bed.

'Sorry girls. I decided to get out of here and spend some alone time. See you both tomorrow. Adam.'

"I can't believe he left without me," Cheri sounded convincing.

"Does he do that often?" Amy asked.

"No. I wouldn't put up with that, Cheri chided.

"Of course not. I have to because Sondra wants the data for this trial," Amy responded, then asked, "Do you think he'll really come back tomorrow?

"Oh, yeah, I think he will. He probably felt like you were interrogating him," Cheri poked at Amy a bit.

"Excuse me?" Amy was taken aback.

"Listen, I've gotta run. Thanks for the coffee," Cheri said as she exited the clinic.

CHAPTER 19

Amy walked past the men's room and noticed the light was still on. It had a back-up motion sensor that would keep the light on as long as someone was inside. *'Adam never left,'* she thought. *'Oh, crap, I wonder if he heard me think that?'*

Amy pretended to lock up for the night, but she deliberately unlocked the door to Sondra's office. She had a master key. Ripped it off the maintenance guy a year ago, Sondra never knew. She never used it before this night, but suspected Adam must be desiring access if he was willing to hang out in the bathroom for over an hour.

After closing the door behind her and locking it, Amy went to her car to fulfill the guise. She drove away but parked just down the street so she could walk back and quietly sneak up on Adam to determine his intentions. *'He is going to have some explaining to do. Actually, no, I will. I need to tell him tonight. Everything. I need to help him get the information he's so desperately looking for. He's my brother.'*

Just as she suspected, when Amy came back into the clinic she found Adam behind Sondra's desk hacking away at her computer.

"You could have just asked!" Amy said loudly to deliberately startle Adam. He visibly jumped backwards from the chair and knocked over the plant stand behind him.

"You scared the crap out of me Amy," Adam yelled at her. Then he quickly realized that his story was supposed to be that he was sleep walking. Too late. Amy was on his side of the desk looking at the computer screen.

"What have we here?" Amy reproached, "Didn't get very far now did you."

"You knew?" Adam asked surprised.

"I suspected. It's time. You need to know."

"Time? To know what?" Adam had a seriously puzzled look on his face. He hardly knew this girl and she acted like she was his path to enlightenment.

"Well my twin brother, there is a lot you don't know," Amy cynically responded to his arrogant questioning of her knowledge.

Adam growled, "What the…?"

Adam didn't get the last word out and Amy interrupted with, "And the witch is our mother!"

"Sondra?" He was shaking his head in confusion and disbelief.

"None other," Amy giggled, "It's funny you knew who I was referring to."

Adam blurted out, "She is a witch. I don't trust her for a moment."

"Don't," Amy validated, "And frankly I can't stand the woman. You'll like her even less once I tell you what I know."

"How long have you known," the anger was evident in his voice. He wasn't sure he believed any of this nor if Amy could be trusted. He wished Cheri was there. Cheri was a good judge of character.

Taciturnity hung in the air as they each waited for the other to speak first. Amy knew they were at a critical point in the relationship and didn't blame him for any distrust. She also knew she had to answer him completely and honestly so she decided to break the silence.

"Sondra, our mom, told me you were my brother before we started the trial. She convinced me that it would be best to withhold that information from you. It was to protect you. She lead me to believe that you wouldn't be able to handle it. She was going to determine the time and place if and when she told you."

"And you played right along?"

"She had a hold on me, but not anymore."

"A hold on you?" His voice was visibly distressed.

Amy rubbed her fingers along the scar on her head and thought, *'Oh my gosh, the memory chip inside his head.'*

"I have a chip in my head?" Adam replied aloud to her thoughts as he ran his fingers along the side of his own head.

"How do you do that?" She asked.

"Do what?"

"Read my mind."

Adam paused and looked deep into Amy's eyes. The words were so clear and audible he was certain she spoke them. Why did she look so familiar. He would have never seen her before the trial began and she couldn't have been part of Tom's memory chain if Tom died before they were born. He descended deep into his own memory banks to find where he had seen her before.

"The womb. That's where I have seen you before," Adam announced.

"That was a random expression of thought," she exclaimed, you are certainly unusual... In a good way, of course."

He sat back down in the chair and resumed his hacking of the computer. His fingers were frantically clipping away at the keyboard when Amy grabbed hold of his left hand. He stopped typing and asked, "What are you doing?"

"Wouldn't it be easier if I just typed in the password? I've seen mom enter it a dozen times. It's all caps, all letters," Amy stated as she took control of the keyboard, typed SONDRASKINNER and hit enter.

"Jackpot!" Amy exclaimed joyfully.

Adam grabbed hold of both Amy's arms and stared at her with his teeth gritted, "That was too easy. How do I know this isn't a sham. How do I know I can trust you?"

"You really can't trust anyone Adam. But what do I have to gain by being here right now? Why would I waste my time and energy concocting a series of lies?"

"Money. People will do almost anything for money. Sondra or someone else could be paying you. This is crap. You could be taking me exactly where you want me to go, show me exactly what you want me to see."

"Scroll over some of the files, the .pdf's and you'll see the dates they were last modified. Some of those files are older than you. There's thousands of them. Who would have time to set up this kind of sham? And for what?"

Her story was making sense. Many of the files were dated years ago.

"So you've been in here before?" he questioned.

"Once, but only for a few minutes. I got out in time before Sondra noticed I was in there."

"Wait. Sondra Skinner?" He questioned, "Why Skinner?"

"What about it?" Amy wasn't following the line of questioning.

"The password. Sondra Skinner. Wouldn't her name be Sondra Dory if she was married to Tom?"

Amy replied, "I always thought she just used her first name and the Doctor's last name because they did the research together."

Adam sat back and contemplated before sharing, "What if her maiden name was Skinner? What if Ben Skinner was her father?"

"Adam, you really are unique. I would never have come up with that one. It's almost to absurd, yet so obvious," she gasped, "Hold on. He's our grandpa? What kind of family is this, does this kind of stuff?"

Adam sat forward in the chair and started to peruse the file system. Sondra kept everything orderly and by name. There was a folder with his name on it, a folder with Amy's name on it, there was also a folder with Tom Dory's name on it. Adam requested that Amy sit on the other side of the desk and let him peruse at his own leisure, "That will help with the trust issue. If I feel like you are guiding or leading me in a certain direction then I can't trust you."

Amy quietly complied. She had to empathize with her brother. It must be overwhelming. A crazy controlling mother, memory chips in your head, dreams that track the memories of your father. Traveling on a historical journey through genetic memories. It was a lot for anyone to get their head around.

The room was silent other than the sound of their breathing and the clicks from the computer keyboard. After scrolling up and down the folder names for a few minutes Adam decided to open the folder labeled BEN SKINNER.

CHAPTER 20

Adam looked up from the computer screen and asked Amy a question that she had been pondering herself, "How do I get this freaking thing out of my head?"

Amy wished she had an answer, but right now she was in the boat with him and hoped he could appreciate that and build trust based on their shared dilemma. She had thought about beating the answer out of Sondra, which was still up for consideration.

"I was hoping we would figure that out tonight while you scoured the files. The answers must be in there somewhere."

"There's thousands of files in here…"

"Do a search on 'memory chip'," she encouraged him.

The sound of clicking filled the room again. Adam did a search inside the Ben Skinner folder since he was the master mind behind this. Or maybe Sondra was, and Skinner was her puppet. He'd know soon enough.

"Got it. Seven hundred and thirteen hits," Adam said as he leaned forward to get a better look at the list.

"Start with the most recent," Amy reinforced.

Amy stood up to come around to the other side of the desk to get a look at the data. Adam gave her a sideways look that included some stink eye.

"You just suggested what I search for. You are leading me, aren't you?" He challenged.

"Hey, this fin thing is in my head too you know," she responded to his glare, pulled her hair back exposing the scar on her head and pointed at it.

"Fine. Pull up a chair. It's going to be a long night. No more talking out of you, unless I ask."

"Fine."

"Fine!"

Sondra was sitting at home watching everything occurring in her office from her security monitors. Cameras were strategically placed inside her office to provide several angles. Monitor number two presented a view to the computer monitor on her desk at Milton. She wished she had it wired for sound so she could hear what her little twins were discussing.

Nothing was as it seemed to be yet Sondra's plan was unfolding exactly as she laid it out nine months ago. Actually the plot was eighteen years in the making but the execution of the plan began nine months ago, and was moving along with perfection. She thought, *Wait until they find Ben's journal. Time to put your big boy pants on Adam.'*

"This is not very encouraging," Adam said as he read the text in the file, **"Severe risk is associated with the removal of the device. Side effects include headaches, hallucinations, nausea, vomiting, weight loss, memory loss, speech impairment stroke, coma and death."**

"Why would anyone do that to her own children?" Amy's eyes welled up in tears at the feeling of abandonment.

"This thing is hard-wired," he said aloud.

"Adam, she had a remote control and would press a button to control me into submission to her," Amy was crying.

Adam put his arm around her to console her. They had more in common than he ever imagined. Twin children of a sick and twisted controlling mother that let a mad scientist use them as lab rats for his own personal experiments. *'For what?'* Adam thought to himself.

"She told me it was for the betterment of mankind. A cure for Dementia, Alzheimer's and other mental illnesses," Amy responded, "What crap did she lay on you?"

"The same story...wait a second, were you answering a question?" Adam asked.

"You said, 'for what'," Amy replied.

"No, I **thought** 'for what'," Adam gulped, "Amy I think you heard my thought."

She grinned and said, "Well, we are twins, aren't we?"

"Yeah, but we also both have some kind of bio-electronic chip in our skulls, hard wired to our brains. People just don't go around reading minds you know," Adam was beginning to connect some dots.

"She made freaks out of us," Amy began sobbing again.

"Let's use it to our advantage and take control of the situation. And don't worry, we'll be fine," Adam's voice was soothing and reassuring. Amy observed a confidence in him she had not seen before.

"We need to keep looking for answers," Amy said as she used the sleeve of her scrubs to wipe the tears from her cheeks.

Adam was clicking and scanning files at a pace that Amy could not comprehend. He was reading whole pages at a single glance. Her eyes and mind barley saw the file open and he was on to the next one.

"How do you do that?" She asked.

"Do what?"

"Read so fast?"

Adam paused from scanning the files to answer, "Oh. My mind takes a picture of what it sees and then processes the image whether it's pictures or words and delivers a comprehensible message of understanding instantaneously." Adam immediately went back to scanning files.

"That clears it up for me, thanks Adam," Amy giggled and affectionately punched his shoulder. She was beginning to appreciate that she could finally have a brother in her life. She hated Sondra more and more for keeping him from her all those years. She wanted answers, and she wanted to find enough evidence of wrong doing to put Sondra in prison and lock her away for a long, long time.

"Amy?" Adam pushed away from the desk and the chair rolled to a stop when it bumped the wall behind him.

"Yes?"

"I found it!"

"Found what?"

"Skinner's journal. Someone scanned it into electronic files and stored it here."

"Did you read it already?"

"No. It scares me a little to proceed. I am not sure if I am ready for what I might find."

Amy assured him, "I am one hundred percent in this with you."

"What is the file called?" "Maybe there is a clue in that."

Adam liked the way she thought. Everything is done for a reason, thoughtfully.

"The file is called, *Monomania*."

"Does his journal have a title page?"

Adam clicked and scrolled forward, "Yes."

"And?" Amy waited in anticipation.

"The title of the journal is, *The last one to die*."

Amy leaned over his shoulder and stared at the screen for several seconds. A chill ran through her, from the back of her head to her tailbone. Her fingers tingled and she felt queasy.

Sondra leaned forward to get a better look at the monitor. *'Looks like they found it'*, she whispered under her breath. She snickered and thought, *'They are paralyzed with fear'*, then Sondra laughed out loud. She took a sip of coffee, set the cup on the table next to her and spoke to the monitors as if her children could actually hear what she was saying, "Nothing is as it seems to be kids. I am not what you think I am. None of us are for that matter.

Don't be too quick to judge. We are all simply doing what we need to be doing. We've been pre-wired for this adventure and we are on this ride together, like it or not. And oh, by the way, you'll never have all the answers, so don't spend your whole life trying to find them. Learn to accept things the way they are."

The step-daughter of the great Doctor Benjamin Skinner turned off the monitors, looked at the ceiling of her home office and laughed. And laughed uncontrollably. And laughed some more. Until it hurt. The irony of it all was overwhelming.

CHAPTER 21

Adam copied the files he wanted on to a zip drive and took it with him to review more at a later time. It was getting late and he needed some sleep. Amy dreaded going back to the house where Sondra would be waiting for her with a thousand questions about where she was all night and 'blah blah blah'.

"Can I stay at your foster parents house and get some rest?" Amy pleaded, "Please don't make me have to go deal with that witch right now. I can crash on your floor. I won't bother anyone. Please?"

"Yeah, I'll let Chuck and Doris know you are my long lost twin sister. That should be fun to explain," Adam shook his head but relented and decided he'd cross that bridge with his parents when he came to it.

The sun was rising when they reached Adam's place. Chuck and Doris were still asleep so he snuck Amy into his room and had her lay on a blanket at the side of the bed away from the door so Doris if poked her nose in she wouldn't see her.

Adam took off his shoes and laid back on his bed and he fell asleep within seconds of his head resting on his pillow.

It is dark and Adam's vision is crusty. He hears sounds but cannot distinguish their source. He has a dusty taste in his mouth. There is a rancid odor. He gags. His vision clears and it is too bright for him to see. The sun is bright and hot. He can smell his own body odor amongst the rancidness lingering in the air surrounding him.

Everything is coming into focus and Adam can clearly see what is causing the gagging odor. A lion lay dead at his feet. Adam's hands are covered in blood, not his own blood, the creature's. He hears a growl and a roar. Sitting atop a hill is another lion. A giant beast. It looks angry, or hungry, or both.

'I need to wake up,' Adam knows it's a memory dream.

The memory shifted scenes and Adam found himself presiding over a host of villagers. His interpretation of all the commotion led him to believe they were waiting for him to make some kind of ruling. There was bantering and arguing amongst the men.

Adam walked past his own reflection in a mirror. He stood and watched as he passed by himself. In a flickering moment they looked into each other's eyes as their path's crossed. Darkness faded into the light as Adam turned and walked the other way.

Adam awoke and said, "I never realized until now that Samson was judge over Israel for twenty years."

Chuck and Doris just stood frozen, eyes fixed on him. There was dried blood covering both his hands. His hair was long and curly and his body was dusty and sweaty.

"What are you guys staring at?" Adam asked as he looked next to the bed to see if Amy was there but she was gone. She must have left early so no one noticed.

He jumped up and looked in the mirror. He turned to ask them why they were staring and they were gone. Other than pillow lines on his face, Adam had no idea what was so shocking to his parents. He called out to them as he got himself dressed, "Hey mom and dad, where did you go? What's with the disconcerting looks?"

"He doesn't see it," Doris said to Chuck.

Adam walked into the kitchen where his parents were whispering to each other across from the dinette table. They exchanged knowing glances and turned to him and smiled.

Doris spoke first, "Adam," she said as she handed him a slip of paper, "You should go meet with this woman. She spent a lot of time at Milton when your father was there. Her information was given to us recently. That's about all we know about her. She might have some answers for you."

"She's at a group home?" Adam looked puzzled. He felt like it could be a waste of time if the woman had lost her marbles.

"It's worth a try," Chuck encouraged.

"You might want to quick shower before you head out," Doris said hoping he would wash up the mess from his dream.

His hair was looking ok, but the dirt and blood needed a rinse.

"Good idea," he responded and went off to take a quick shower.

After five minutes Adam reappeared all cleaned up, grabbed the note, shoved the paper into his jeans pocket and headed out the door, *'How the heck do they know about this?'* he wondered to himself.

He jogged over to the bus stop and rode the public transportation to the street closest to the address on the slip of paper Doris handed him. As he exited the bus, the driver looked him square in the eye and said, "Good luck." Adam shrugged it off and headed for the group home to meet the old woman.

The house stood out from the rest of the homes on the block as it was freshly painted. A screen door hung crooked from rusty hinges and the screen was torn and dangling from the rotted wood frame. A vacant swing was swaying back and forth creaking on metal hooks like someone had just stepped off of it and went into the old structure.

"You look just like him," the voice of an old woman echoed from inside, just past the screen door. Her image became visible as she got closer. She was holding a glass in each hand, "Can you get the door for me please."

Adam opened the door and she handed him a glass of lemonade and sat down on the swing.

"Well, come on now, join me", she beckoned him to sit next to her, so he did.

"I've been expecting you," she said.

"Oh did Doris call you?" Adam replied as he sat next to her.

"Doris? I don't know any Doris. I've been expecting this visit since the day you were born."

Adam was a bit confused but rolled with it, "So you knew my father," it was a statement not a question.

"Tom Dory. Handsome one just like you," she cackled a hoarse laugh. "Nice man. Very mysterious though. Always deep in thought. Conversations were always very philosophical. He was an idea man that's for sure."

"How long did you know him?"

"Long enough. His whole life actually…" her voice dissipated as Adam got lost in his thoughts. He suddenly recognized the old woman. It was her. The one that kept appearing in his dreams and memories over the years.

The longer he thought about her, the deeper he went into his cognitions of her… "You are my great-grandma!" Adam snapped out of his ruminations with a bursting epiphany.

"Yes, Adam, I am she."

"What did Tom Dory do for a living?"

"He was a carpenter when he was younger. He had taken shop classes in school and always preferred working with wood over metal. He would say that steel is man-made, rigid and unforgiving, but wood, wood is God-made, pliable and very forgiving if you make a mistake," she continued with a steely eyed look, "You know Adam, Jesus was a carpenter."

"Yeah, but Tom was no Jesus."

"Of course not, but follow your father's wisdom for a moment. Wood, being God-made and forgiving was what Jesus worked with. He was also hung on that same material by unforgiving men, nailed to the wood with man-made steel."

Adam interrupted, "What happened to my father?" then hung his head not certain if he wanted to know the truth. He expected if anyone would share the truth, it would be grandma. Grandma's don't lie.

"He was a Monomaniac…"

Adam interrupted, "A WHAT?"

"He got himself stuck on this idea, a far out idea, that he could move from person to person while sleeping. He believes you were conceived in his dreams. Claims he and your mother stopped physical intercourse two years before you were born."

"This is nuts. I think you might be nuts old lady, otherwise why else would you be in this home!" Adam was freaking out.

Grandma replied, " I understand your apprehension. A big reason we all kept our distance from you all these years was to protect you from the truth."

Adam snapped back, "Why now then. Why has everyone decided they don't need to protect me anymore, from the truth?"

"You are an adult. You need to move forward with your life. When we noticed you were starting to look for answers, we felt it best to see how much you could handle. This has been planned out for some time. We've just been waiting for you."

"Waiting for me for what?"

"To ask," grandma said. She sipped some lemonade and smacked her lips and sighed in affirmation of its refreshment.

Adam was feeling very thirsty, hot, even dizzy from the whole experience. He began gulping his drink until there was nothing but ice remaining. He took a cube in his mouth and crushed it between his molars, drinking in the chips and liquid. His composure returned.

"So what exactly happens to a Monomaniac. And who says that is what Tom Dory was?"

Grandma replied, "As I started to explain, Tom got it stuck in his head that he was a 'jumper' I think he called it. A 'soul jumper', that's it, that's what he called it," she was pleased with herself for remembering.

She closed her eyes and enveloped the thoughts and memories of her grandson. A frown swept over her face as she considered the last days. How quickly Tom had deteriorated. She sat by his side as he descended into a deep catatonic state.

"Even until his last breath, his eyes were closed and his eyeballs fluttered under his eyelids. They called it R.E.M. sleep. You know, dream state. He never stopped dreaming. I watched him for hours at a time, his eyes never stopped moving and at times it was like we would communicate. I would doze off and we would talk in our dreams..."

Adam was already off the porch and walking down the street as her voice faded and she called out her final remarks, "You enter the world helpless and leave this place helpless. Realizing that you are helpless the whole time is the key. Knowing that you cannot truly get by or through it all without God is the wisdom captured in the knowledge of the Holy One. God has knit you and woven you together. He has created who you are, your soul. Only through His word and a relationship with him can you nurture that being."

He stopped next to a large old oak tree and leaned his left hand against it, whispered, *'What am I and who are these people?'*. Adam hung his head, placed his hands on his knees, breathed in and out three times and vomited. He stared down into the fluid. It was clear with swirls of dark red, almost blue colors. He thinks, *'It must be the vitamins. They have a purple tint to them. It can't be blood.'*

He sees an outline of a face in the liquid. It was as if he was looking into a cracked mirror. He closed his eyes tight as a brain piercing ringing stabbed his ear drums. Everything started spinning and he broke out in a cold sweat. He dropped to the ground on one knee. Pain shot through his thigh and into his hip. His arms flailed in attempt to catch himself and as he collapsed on his side his head struck the tree and slid down the trunk leaving a streak of blood on the bark.

CHAPTER 22

Adam is surrounded by hundreds of men. Each one holds a weapon of some sort. Spears, shields, ropes, knives, all very ancient in appearance. Bodies are splayed all over the ground. Blood and guts emanating from each lifeless lump. Hundreds of them, everywhere.

Vultures are circling above and the heat of the sun reflects off the sandy dirt. The men still standing look hesitant, afraid. Several retreat and run the other way. One man drops to his knees, throws his weapon at Adam's feet in surrender.

Adam is holding a bone in his right hand. He studies it carefully. It is a jawbone. A piece of torn flesh hangs from the tip. The flesh of a man. The smell of death is strong and hangs in the thickness of the desert air.

A vulture lands at his feet in submission, respect. Adam nods, granting the creature permission to peck at the mangled remains. The bird cackles calling out to the kettle circling above. It's wake of scavengers join in a feeding frenzy, picking and pulling at muscle, ligament and intestine of a thousand fallen men.

Adam knows instinctively that he is not finished. His muscles feel sore and fatigued, yet a desire to eliminate the remaining men in his midst burns in his core. A voice, *'Them or you'*. His own thoughts guide him. Everything slows down and his vision is crisp and multi-dimensional in texture and color.

Men begin attacking him from all sides. Energy and power flow through Adam's veins, muscles and in every fiber of his flesh. He feels the strength of ten thousand men with the fury of a hundred hungry lions.

Every swing and swipe of the jawbone is perfectly timed and with precision accuracy it crushes through the skulls and tissues of each assailant and in rapid succession bodies writhe and fall..

Clarity turns to blur, power converts to exhaustion and sound fades to the drone of a woman's voice, "Samson. Samson. A thousand men with the jawbone of an ass! We must get him water. Quickly."

Cheri was standing over Adam's body in disbelief. She had rushed over to the group home as soon as Doris had informed her were Adam was. The house was down the street and an old lady sat on a porch swing sipping a cold drink. She looked back down at Adam.

He was breathing but it barely resembled him. His clothes were torn and tattered and he had blood and dirt on the side of his face. She wondered how long he had laid there unattended. The streets were vacant and void of other people. Just the old lady on the swing.

Cheri noticed Adam's arms were huge, muscles bulging and forged like an Olympian body builder. Adam had a nice physique, but nothing like this. His right hand was frozen in place as if it were gripping something, yet nothing was there. There was a siren in the distance and the sound of it amplified and faded in the eddying of the warm breeze.

Unsure of herself, Cheri stepped back and carefully studied Adam's body to be certain it was really him. It was only earlier today she was with him, yet his body was transformed and he looked like he was mugged by a brutal gang. The siren ceased, or faded, she wasn't sure, but she knew the moment was swept into the emptiness of sound.

Adam began coughing and spat up some saliva and blood. He sat up and opened his eyes. They were gray in hue and as the clouds covered the sun, his iris' turned emerald green and his pupils dilated to the size of dimes in the shape of diamonds. When the sun broke through the clouds, light sparkled from his eyes in blue and yellow, then clear and pure.

His voice was dry, parched and cracked, "Cheri?"

"Adam?"

"None other," he coughed a chuckle and groaned and winced from a stinging discomfort in his head. Adam noticed he was still holding the jawbone so he tossed it aside. To Cheri it looked like he was merely shaking his hand as if to awaken it.

He offered his hand and she grabbed hold, hoisting him from the ground. He was still weak and his legs wobbled but Cheri allowed him to fall into her embrace, "I got you."

Adam smirked. He felt what she felt. It was good. She was more than just his friend. It was a profound, deeper connection. A romantic one in that moment for sure. She was soft but strong enough to support him until his bearings were straight and he could stand on his own. He would have liked to stay in that embrace forever, but they had to move on.

Synchronously, they looked back at the house. Grandma was gone. Simultaneously they thought, *'She must have gone back inside.'* Only Adam knew different.

Cheri said, "Come on. Let's go," as she tugged him from the scene and toward her father's car. Adam kept his eyes affixed on the porch swing until the vehicle drove them from its sight.

Cheri wanted to ask him about his newly sculpted physique but didn't know how to broach the subject.

Sondra was at her computer scouring the internet for information on any recent government activity. It was a daily routine of hers and whenever she came up empty she would use her old NIH access to back door her way into the other databases of the multiple government intelligence agencies. She always looked for the same thing. Her son. Adam. Did he surface on their radar?

She was more concerned than ever since he went off and changed his name as soon as he became an adult. She couldn't let them near him. Lab rat was an understatement for what they would do to the kid. Hiding him in the foster system all those years as Skip Chalmers was the best thing for him. Right under their own noses. The most obvious was the least obvious.

'Click', Sondra entered the missing person database. The one used by the FBI, CIA, Homeland Security and NSA used to track down potential enemies of the state that rolled off their maps and disappeared.

She scrolled rapidly through the photos, sorted by most recent. Her mind began wandering, thinking about Tom again when she paused, scrolled back and there he was. It was an older photo from when Adam was about fourteen or fifteen, but it was definitely him but his name was not on the file. He was listed as a John Doe. It was recently posted under missing persons. They were getting close. Too close.

Sondra lowered her head and wept. Everyone including Adam always thought that Adam's mother died giving birth to him. In a sense she did. She no longer existed as his mother when she gave him up to protect him and placed him into hiding all those years. Yet, now here she was, running the same experiments, trying to put together the same puzzle that eventually drove his father, her husband, insane.

'Now what? Now What?' She thought, her mind racing to assemble the contingency plan. She would need to accelerate the trial. Juice up the memory chip in Adam's head to see if they could derive answers quickly and then deactivate the chip. Without an active device in Adam's cranium, the government would lose interest fast.

She was the only person that knew how to disarm it, but there was risk. Skinner documented the risks to Adam's mind and body. Possible insanity or death. Sondra had decided years ago that the risks were worth taking versus the alternative. Her experiments were nothing compared to what they had planned. *'Why is it always about a weapon?'* she thought, *'Have to have a leg up on the enemy.'* Tom's voice echoed in her mind.

Tom began by wanting to cure memory loss and then became convinced there were more capabilities to be unleashed and that those powers could make for a safer country and a better world. He was insane.

Sondra knew they had only scratched the surface. Tom would share his findings with her, most of which were below the surface of his mind. Neither of them had any clue of how deep below that surface they could travel. Tom believed it was infinite and that scared her. It tested her resolve because Adam was now displaying those same tendencies.

Adam wanted to go as deep as he could as fast as possible, just as his father did. Sondra found herself watching a rerun of a miniseries that has an unhappy ending yet she can't turn it off and she didn't know why.

Sondra believed that when Tom went insane, he dove into the depths of the infinite caverns of the human mind, never to return. She had to get back to the lab and get Amy back in there with her. Most importantly Adam had to get there right away. Neither of them trusted her, and for good reason. She knew she'd have to figure out a way to rectify that. *'The truth.'*

As Cheri turned the corner near Adam's house, he grabbed her arm and said, "Take me back to Milton."

"WHAT! Are you crazy," Cheri was shaking her head.

"Do it Cheri. I have to finish this journey. I'll call Amy and convince her to meet us there." He began dialing before Cheri could say another word.

Cheri veered to the curb and slammed on the brakes, "I cannot be party to this, Adam. It's too dangerous. Sondra is too dangerous."

"A mother is incapable of harming her own child."

"That's not true," Cheri blasted back, "Crazy women are plaster all over the news doing horrifying things to their children."

"I can handle her. If you don't take me there, I'll take the bus."

He felt he needed to give her an explanation, "When I was ten years old, I was with a man and woman who treated me like shit," Adam was explaining when Cheri interrupted, "What did they do to you?"

"That's not the point," Adam sneered. He hated when she focused on the irrelevant.

"Okay, sorry," Cheri replied. She never understood why he couldn't share the details of his childhood with her. It must have been really bad. She couldn't stand it anymore and if they were to stay together and be anything, even friends, he was going to have to open up more.

Adam knew what she was thinking so he said, "I tell you what is important. I don't want to freak you out every time we talk."

"I won't freak out!" Cheri exclaimed.

"Oh, like the scar?" Adam was frustrated. He just wanted to make a point and she was trying to take him down a different path.

"Since the scar, not very much freaks me out. Since you woke up with the body of an Olympian weight lifter, since all the scary nights at Milton, no, nothing really freaks me out anymore."

Adam shook his head and emphatically said, "Anyways, the woman would drop me off at Sunday school every week. Eight weeks in a row. I remember a song. A proclamation. It stuck with me. I never understood it, but it is making sense now that I have spent time reading God's word, digging in, meditating on it."

"What was the song?" she asked.

"The only words I remember were, 'All hail the Lion of Judah', like a chant. It was about Jesus."

"What about Jesus? He is the Lamb of God," Cheri was insistent, "He was spotless and pure, and shed his blood on the cross for each of us. He was the sacrificial lamb of God."

"He was from the lineage of the tribe of Judah."

"And?" Cheri was waiting for the punch line.

"And," Adam paused and swallowed, "Jesus is the Lion and the Lamb. When the Lamb and the Lion have fulfilled their roles, they will lie down together."

Adam pulled out a pocket bible and handed it to Cheri. She opened to the page that was dog eared and read it out loud, **"Then I saw in the right hand of him who sat on the throne a scroll with writing on both sides and sealed with seven seals. And I saw a mighty angel proclaiming in a loud voice, "Who is worthy to break the seals and open the scroll?" But no one in heaven or on earth or under the earth could open the scroll or even look inside it. I wept and wept because no one was found who was worthy to open the scroll or look inside. Then one of the elders said to me, "Do not weep! See, the Lion of the tribe of Judah, the Root of David, has triumphed. He is able to open the scroll and its seven seals." Then I saw a Lamb, looking as if it had been slain, standing at the center of the throne, encircled by the four living creatures and the elders. The Lamb had seven horns and seven eyes, which are the seven spirits of God sent out into all the earth. He went and took the scroll from the right hand of him who sat on the throne."**

"You are right Adam. I never realized this before, but why are you telling me this?"

Adam turned his head and smiled the words, "Tonight I will be Judah, the ancestor of Jesus." He was not afraid. The genetic memories were consistently linear. The path to the beginning had been cleared.

CHAPTER 23

Cheri pulled into the parking lot at Milton Medical Center and she stared straight ahead, not wanting to look him in the eye. She could not believe he wanted to go back to that place and those people. So many lies, so much at risk. The fake smiles and phony pretenses. Cheri didn't know what to believe anymore. She left the engine running.

"Aren't you coming in?" Adam asked with tilted head and squinted eyes.

Cheri didn't answer and she refused to look at him, she merely shook her head no. A lump formed in her throat and tears wanted to wet her eyes but she fought them back. It was his deal.

Adam opened the car door, stepped out, closed it behind himself, offered a back-handed wave and mumbled under his breath, "You can pretend to care, but you can't pretend to be there."

Cheri heard him say it and it made her weep. She gathered her composure and sped away from the clinic wondering, *'Why does he insist on re-entering that nightmare?'* and the sky darkened.

151

Sondra was working in her office trying to figure out how to get Adam and Amy back when her door burst open, "What the hell is a 'soul jumper'?" Adam said as his lower lip quivered.

"Sit down son."

"I prefer to stand, thank you."

"So polite," Sondra sneered.

"I'm all ears mother," Adam was losing his patience, "You know what, forget it," he turned to leave.

"Wait, I'm sorry, please sit, this could take a while."

Adam didn't chose the chair opposite his mother but rather the more comfortable chaise lounge in the corner of her office.

"Start spinning your yarn Sondra, or mother, or whoever you are. Tell me all about soul jumping."

Sondra didn't know where to begin. She only knew what Tom had shared with her about his experiences, so she decided to start there.

"Well Adam, I only know what your father told me..."

"And what might that be mom?" he interrupted. He was getting angry just thinking about the sick and twisted place called Milton.

"Tom believed that while he was asleep he could embody another human being while they were asleep and in effect wake up inside their body," Sondra's tone was just above a whisper.

Adam shifted in his chair. He felt ill, like his body wanted to expel something nasty. He was cold and sweaty and his skin crawled. He talked himself down from the encumbering anxiety attack. Sondra noticed Adam's physical response so far and wasn't sure he could handle anymore, "Drink some water Adam."

He stood up and helped himself to a cold bottled water from her office refrigerator. He downed the whole pint and began feeling better. She handed him a piece of hard candy to help with his blood sugar.

"When's the last time you ate?" Sondra asked?

"I have no idea what day it even is," he replied as he dropped the chunk of sugar in his mouth. He felt very tired. He had been waiting for her to ask about his change in physical stature and she sat there like nothing even happened. *'How can she not see that I am twice as muscular as I was last time I was here. It's not humanly possible and so obvious yet she's oblivious.'*

"I can see you are larger Adam."

'Did she just hear my thoughts?'

"Do you feel any better?"

"Yes mom, I'm fine."

Sondra picked up the story where she left off, "And he would roam around inside their bodies until he decided it was time to get back to his own." She paused to give Adam a moment to process it all.

He leaned forward and lifted his eyebrows as if to ask, 'and'.

"And," Sondra continued, "He believed it."

"Was there any way to prove it? Did you believe it. Did you ever soul jump? Was he the only soul jumper?"

"Whoa. Let me take those one at a time," they laughed synchronously.

"He came back from his dreams with markings, blood stained skin, dirty, he even brought physical objects back with him from his sleep, but he never showed up as someone else in my presence, so I don't know"

"I know what I saw when he woke up and I wanted to believe him, but he was going insane. So I guess that answers the next question, and no I never experienced soul jumping and no one else ever mentioned it."

Adam asked, "Who did he say he embodied?"

"He claimed he was able to jump into anyone he wanted as long as they were present in his dreams. He even alleged that he could enter other people's dreams. He talked about a traveler."

"A what"? Adam was struggling to make sense of the notion of embodiment and Sondra injected another concept.

Sondra stood up and reached over to her bookshelf. Third shelf from the bottom, in the center she retrieved a small booklet. She paged through it and then slide it across her desk toward Adam, "His journal. He explains it in there. Read it."

Adam looked at his father's handwriting. He could tell the man's hand trembled as he wrote. The words were descript and

blurry. He could picture his father trembling as he wrote.
Losing his mind, yet trying to capture his thoughts for others to
hopefully someday interpret their meaning. Tom must have felt
scared and lonely. Adam wondered if his mother stayed by his
side to the very end or left him and his mind to rot cold, empty
and alone.

He read the words aloud, **"The fact about the Traveler is
that unlike me, he is a wanderer. I have purpose.**

**There are many wanderers that never travel and many
with a purpose that never jump souls. There is only one
pure Traveler and one unique Soul Jumper and they are in
a constant struggle to understand each other and
themselves.**

**The Traveler desires a purpose and therefore seeks to
displace the Jumper. On the other hand, the Jumper seeks
to fulfill his purpose and therefore desires to define it."**

He slid the journal back toward Sondra and said facetiously,
"Well that explains it." Adam sat back down shaking his head in
an attempt to resolve himself of the mysteries of his parents.

"He's there now," Cheri explained to Amy through the car's
Bluetooth audio system, "And he's alone with your mother."

"I'm on my way over there now," Amy replied and
disconnected the call.

"Did you bail on him?" Adam asked with a steely eyed gaze.
He was sweating and realized his fists were clenched as well as
his teeth. His jaw was beginning to sting.

"What is that supposed to mean?" Sondra shifted into a
defensive posture and leaned back in her chair. She waited for
Adam to speak next. The silence was growing louder as both of
them had to restrain the volumes of negative thoughts about the
other.

"Let's take this up later. Right now I am tired and ready to go
back in time, so take me to my room and hook me up. And I

want you to jump start the memory chip. I understand the path so clearly now that I want to accelerate my travels to the final destination," Adam spoke quickly as he stood and headed for the door.

Sondra followed thinking, *'He sounds more and more like his father every time he comes here.'*

Adam stopped abruptly and Sondra crashed into his back unexpectedly. He turned, their faces less than an inch apart, and he breathed the words, "I heard that."

Sondra acted like nothing happened and calmly ushered him to his room where Amy was already waiting for them. The three of them exchanged glances and then methodically went on autopilot hooking up wires and flipping switches preparing Adam for his night's adventure.

Adam closed his eyes and began his decent. He could feel the bed pulling him in and away from the conscious world. A rushing sensation, euphoric, peaceful, tranquil, almost final. He noticed a blue light in the distance... and then there was a flash.

Amy looked at her mother with a pale expression, "You've never hooked up a third lead to the memory chip!"
Sondra responded with a calm confidence, "He wasn't ready until now."

Cheri was sitting in her car in front of the clinic sobbing, unable to muster up the courage to go inside and attempt to obstruct the madness. Raindrops the size of quarters began pounding the vehicle. The sound was calming so she closed her eyes and prayed.

CHAPTER 24

Adam began convulsing. Sondra administered straps to his arms and legs to keep him from harming himself during the seizure while Amy stood back in terror watching her brother shift and jerk so violently the bed moved across the room.

Sondra's eyes widened in terror and Amy screamed. Adam's eyes were melting and smoking inside his head. Burning flesh sizzled as his eye sockets blackened.

Adam is restrained. Strapped in chains. A soldier is pressing hot steel into his eyes. It is so painful it does not hurt. He smells his own burnt flesh and hears his eyeballs dissolve in the heat.

A man shouts, "Not so strong now Samson, ha ha ha." He hears more laughing.

Amy reached to disconnect the wires from Adam and Sondra grabbed her arm and shoved her away.

"He will remain that way, or you'll possibly kill him if you disconnect him now!" Sondra yelled, "His body will not understand the rapid variance and will immediately attack to defend and rapidly destroy his brain. His skull will be filled with brain puree. He needs to move into another dream, another memory and regenerate."

Amy backed away and complied. She turned and looked away, frightened for her brother's safety. *'How do I know she's not lying like she always does?'* Amy looked back at her brother and he was still. She stared at his chest to make sure it moved up and down to signify he was still breathing. He was.

Adam's eyes began repairing themselves. His skin and eyeballs were healing and transforming back to their original state.

Adam jerked upright, only as far as the straps allowed, his eyes burst wide open, his torso slammed back onto the bed and his eyes rolled around in R.E.M. but with the eyelids still open.

"Oh crap," Sondra rushed to close his eyelids, "He's dreaming with his eyes open again."

"Why is that bad?" Amy asked.

"He's deep inside himself, his past, his father's past, farther than he's ever gone so far. It's like he jumped right to the moment in time he wanted to be, bypassing all previous memories, to begin at the one he selected," Sondra explained.

"Why is that bad?" Amy kept probing.

"It's just a little dangerous to make single jumps like that. He must have figured out he needed to get out of the place he was, and fast."

"How do you know all this, Mom?"

"Your father jumped around, and look how that fared for him."

Amy felt paralyzed. She slowly walked toward Adam and stood over him as he slept. In the moment she felt like she had no life. All she knew was Milton. She spent all her time there. A few interactions outside of the clinic, but nothing more. She couldn't even recall her high school years anymore, even though they had recently ended.

Adam's hair was visibly growing longer right before her eyes. He donned an instant five o'clock shadow that morphed into a full blown beard within seconds. His hands were growing larger and his forehead extended. There was a noticeable shift in his bone structure, yet he lay still.

"Mom, look," Amy tugged at Sondra's lab coat.

"Amazing!" Sondra gasped.

"No, scary. WTF!" Amy screamed.

Adam's body was outgrowing the restraints and his feet were hanging over the edge of the bed. Sondra quickly released him from the straps to keep his blood circulating properly. He was no longer convulsing so there was no need to keep him pinned down.

Adam is pleading with a group of men that are about to kill a young man. He is asking them to let the boy live. He feels anguish in his being as the other men push the younger man into a deep hole. He steps away as the others point and laugh.

They are tossing around a colorful robe and playing tug-o-war with it. He begins walking away and the others soon join him. The sun is setting and the other men encourage him to pick up his pace. They are all jogging into the darkness.

"Was that there before?" Amy asked, pointing at Adam's arm.

His flesh was open and muscle was exposed. Sondra grabbed a universal tissue sampling device, extracted a piece of his exposed bicep and secured it in the container. No sooner than she pulled the device away did Adam's arm heal itself and seal the wound.

"What was that?" Amy pressed against her mother's chest.

"An integrated soft-tissue collection and preservation system used for collecting samples from any plant, animal or human. It was invented in Europe. It eliminates the need for traditional tools like scalpels," Sondra explained as she stepped back.

"What will you do with the sample?" Amy wanted to know.

"Examine his DNA."

"For what?"

"Did you see his arm repair itself?"

"Yes."

"That's what."

"Is that why the government is looking for him?"

"Yes Amy."

"Mom?"

"What?"

"Is Adam going to die like dad did?"

"Not if I can help it."

"Why don't I believe that?"

Sondra didn't respond. They exchanged a long hard stare into each other's eyes, piercing one another's souls. A standoff. Amy was no longer the weaker. Sondra was her equal. Yet neither of them noticed that Cheri was standing in the doorway watching quietly for the past few minutes. Amy was about to speak when Adam grabbed hold of her leg. Startled by it, she yelped.

Sondra and Amy both struggled to free her leg from Adam's grip, but to no avail. Amy began to cry out in pain. Cheri jumped into the struggles as the three of them wrestled with a sleepwalking hulk.

A young man entered the room. His name badge read *Tyler*.

"Who are you?" Sondra questioned him, "What are you doing here?"

"I heard the commotion so I came over right away. "I'm Tyler Gordon. This is my first night on the job, let me help."

Amy tumbled to the ground as the four of them pried Adam from Amy's leg.

"Man that dude is strong," said Tyler.

Sondra looked at his name badge and saw that he was actually with the security company that Milton had recently contracted with. '*Great*,' she thought, '*now what*'.

Amy stood up and patted Tyler on the back side of his shoulder and said, "Thanks Tyler, really appreciate it. We got it from here."

"Um, yeah, ok," he replied as he shuffled out of the room and back to his post watching the security monitors.

He wondered why they were the only ones in the clinic, but then again it was just his first night so he picked up the comic book he brought with him to pass the time. He read with fervor, letting his mind wander into a magical adventure while the event with Adam faded from his cares and concerns.

"That was weird," Cheri stated to the other two women.

"Not really," Sondra replied, "He's far more advanced than Tom ever was. We need to figure this out quickly and get him back to normal before our inevitable visit from the NSA."

"Back to normal! Are you serious mom?" Amy raised her voice.

Sondra administered an injection into the side of Adam's neck and responded, "I am going to run some tests on the sample I took, log the data and when I get back we need to make sure he's awake so you can get him out of here Cheri," Sondra barked her orders. The other two didn't notice her giving the shot to Adam.

"Yes mam!" Cheri sarcastically replied and added a salute. Amy chuckled at the fact that her mom was not able to get to Cheri anymore either. Little did they know.

Sondra bolted out of the room and headed quickly to the lab. Amy wanted to follow her, but felt it might not be safe to leave Cheri alone with Adam.

"Go, I'll be fine here. He no longer seems to be a threat. Besides, I know he would never hurt me," Cheri encouraged Amy to watch over Sondra.

"Ok, but if anything starts to happen, if he even appears as though he will act up again, press the red button on the wall and I'll be here in less than a minute," Amy said.

"Will do," Cheri smiled and nodded, "Now go see what she's really up to."

Amy took off down the hall after her mother.

Adam slept.

Cheri wondered what she had gotten herself into.

Snow blew across the window pane in Adam's room. It was dark and cold outside. Cheri wondered what it was like where Adam was. She would ask him when he woke up.

Sondra was looking into a microscope when Amy found her in the back of the lab.

"Since you're here, come take a look," Sondra waved Amy over to the scope.

Amy looked into the high powered scope, stepped back, blinked her eyes several times, looked again than said, "Put it on the monitor."

Sondra fired up the projection equipment and the sixty five inch display lit up with colors and crystal clear, high definition images.

Among the cells were alien looking creatures moving about. They looked confused, yet purposed. They moved about very rapidly and mechanically. Amy noticed one that was still, so she zoomed in. It had six spider like legs. A small round ball extending from the body of the structure looked like an eye. It had antennae and two small arms. It looked like a small spaceship, no, an insect, not really either, but both.

"What the hell is it!" Amy's eyes were wide with terror.

"A nanobot."

CHAPTER 25

"Skinner developed an advanced set of nanobots. He designed a Nanofactory that created a hybrid version of micro robots consisting of nubots and other microscopic nanoprobes. They were able to sense their environment and adapt accordingly. They were activated by small amounts of electrical energy. He built in complex algorithms so they could perform complex mathematical calculations. These creatures moved, communicated, and functioned to conduct complex tasks such as molecular assembly. Skinner tested and proved that his nanobots could repair and even reproduce themselves," Sondra explained.

"Then what did he do with them?" Amy quivered.

Sondra went on to explain, "The nanobots were originally programmed to rebuild the memory cells and when we injected them into Tom Dory, we had no idea they would so efficiently pass through to his children. They reproduced and embedded their um, for sake of explanation, eggs, in the genetic code."

"How do the nanobots survive?" Cheri asked from the doorway. Neither Sondra or Amy noticed she had been standing there listening.

Sondra appeared to be mildly irritated but took a deep breath and replied, "When asleep, the human brain cells shrink and the body has a self-cleansing mechanism that would dispose of any waste from those cells in a regeneration process. The nanbots feed on that waste."

"Why does Adam look the way he does physically? He's changed. Again," Cheri was pointing at Adam, her finger was trembling.

Sondra stepped in between Cheri and Adam and responded, "Adam has 'partial trisomy', so he experiences an advancement or acceleration in his muscle structure and physical shape when the nanobots are activated. Dr. Skinner triggered them when he first implanted the chip. That's why Adam was able to live and thrive without any stimuli over the years."

"Why did you re-activate them?" Amy chimed in.

"They've always been active. We gave them a little boost. Like an energy drink for microscopic robots," Sondra almost chuckled, "Listen, I need to run some other tests on this muscle tissue, but I need you to take notes on the activity and movement of the nanobots. Watch for multiplication or attrition. Both are important behaviors worth noting," Sondra's voice was fading as she quickly walked away.

Adam was resting peacefully in his room. Cheri had fallen asleep in the chair at his bedside. Inside Adam's body, the microscopic robots were feverously working to repair, rebuild and regenerate their world. Adam was becoming a new creation. The creatures disposed of the old and manufactured the new. It was going to be the way it was intended to be.

Sondra returned, gave Amy a quick glance and in unison they asked, "What did you find?"

"You first mom," Amy chuckled. A part of Amy's inner emotions couldn't help but love her mother, even though she hated her. The dichotomy was chilling at times, but this time it was refreshing for her.

"Adam's non-coding RNA is off the charts, well above the ninety percentile," Sondra's voice was scratchy. Neither of them had anything to drink for hours.

"I don't understand what that means," Amy's hoarse response was because her throat was equally dry. She was tired.

"Yes, of course. You see, the theory used to be that any DNA regions that were not part of the protein-coding genes were nothing more than junk. Doctor Skinner disproved the idea of junk DNA when his nanotechnology interacted with Tom Dory's non-coding DNA. The nanobots were able to somehow translate the non-coding DNA into RNA."

"Studies of the human genome have shown that around eighty five percent of it is made up of non-coding RNA molecules. When looking at those intergenic regions in Adam's code it is apparent that the functional and structural activities are such that it alters his physical state."

Amy nodded in understanding, "Which explains why he changes before our eyes."

"Correct."

"Ok. I get that it alters Adam, but since I am his twin sister and the code passes generationally, that means those little fucking bugs are inside me!" Amy screamed in a raspy, wispy growl. She stood inches away from her mother trembling with fear and anger, again. She thought, *'How did I ever become a character in this nightmare?'*

Sondra held her ground and decided to explain, "You only have one X chromosome. Unfortunately you are the weaker of the twins Unlike Adam, you needed the chip to stimulate the nanobots to keep you alive. However, Adam's reaction to the nanotechnology was consistent with their original intent supplemented by activation or stimulation through the chip."

Amy relaxed a bit and paraphrased what she just heard, "So the nanobots are keeping me alive."

"Yes."

"If that's the case then why did your little remote control always alter my behavior? Sounds like more bull crap to me."

Sondra explained, "We used the remote control device as a way to stimulate only when necessary. If you were to continue down certain paths of behavior, we could trigger the nanobots to redirect or activate them to repair the structural changes that were causing the behavior. Those behaviors are symptoms of cellular degeneration in certain areas of your brain that are rapidly decaying which would lead to an aneurism and instant death."

"I don't even know what is real anymore. Let's go check on Adam," Amy mumbled as she exited the lab.

Sondra followed closely behind in silence. The two of them, tired and thirsty, shuffled their feet as they headed back to Adam's room. The florescent lights in the hallway buzzed and flickered.

Amy wondered, *'Why are we the only ones ever in this place?'* She turned the corner and headed down the hall opposite of Adam's room, picking up her pace into a jog, a run, a dash and burst through the door marked emergency exit.

Cool refreshing air enveloped her. Her lungs drew it in and her body felt a rush of energy. Her head tingled and a surge of tranquility entered her soul. Then she collapsed. Her head struck the concrete sidewalk with a thud.

Sondra was seconds behind and arrived just in time to watch her daughter crash to the ground. She froze for a moment as Amy lie limp, face down, blood pooling up around her head. She reached in the pocket of her scrubs, removed a hand held remote control, pointed it at Amy's head and pressed a green button.

Amy's fingers twitched. Then her legs wiggled. Her back moved up and down as her breathing returned to normal. To the naked eye, the blood on the sidewalk appeared to be evaporating.

In the microscopic world, the nanobots were eating and digesting the dying blood cells until every last molecule was absorbed. Then, like an army of ants, in single file the infinitesimal mechanical wonders marched back into Amy's skull at the point of injury and her wound vanished.

Sondra turned and went back inside.

CHAPTER 26

"How's he doing?" Sondra was leaning against the door frame in Adam's room. She took a sip of water from a frosted plastic bottle and waited for Cheri's reply.

Cheri jerked at the sound of a voice. She had fallen asleep and Sondra's presence startled her. Cheri noticed that Adam started shifting around on the bed. She looked over at the mad scientist standing in the doorway and replied, "Just fine until you came in and woke us up."

As he awakened, Adam was struggling with ram shackled thoughts in the abyss of obscurity. Blue light in the darkness reaching out to him, calling for him, flickering, dimming, blurring to white, then shadows, outlines, people. Sound. Voices. Reality.

"Whew," Adam gasped and sat upright with a confused look on his face.

"Good morning bro," Amy said from behind Sondra. She stood there as if nothing ever happened. She knew, but didn't care anymore. It didn't matter. It was as it was. She had a part in this play but she didn't write it so she could only live her life imperiled by the script.

Amy smugly said to Sondra, "Is this a good time to let Adam in on the little nanobot secret?" Nothing really mattered to Amy anymore. The illusion of reality augmented by a distribution of abstract images clouded her perception of her own existence.

Sondra thought, *'I should have left her lying there,'* then answered, "If he wants to hear about it."

"Wait," Adam was shaking his head trying to clear from the fog of his sleep, "Who should you have left lying there, Sondra?"

Sondra replied, "Not sure what you are talking about Adam." She tried to keep her thoughts focused on what she would actually say next so he couldn't distinguish between thoughts and speech. It was a trick she learned with Tom Dory. Tom eventually stopped reading her mind, hopefully Adam would also.

She continued by responding to Amy, "Let's talk about microscopic technologies. Little robots that weave their way into and throughout the several billion chemical inscriptions of the human genome. While we're at it lets also discuss mutations and the reparation of them. Maybe we can toss into the discussion how we tried to calculate the date of origin of mankind through your father."

"Ok," Adam smiled, "Lets."

"Five thousand years," Sondra was looking at the ceiling. She couldn't look him in the eye. It panged her to finally reveal to him how she, along with Doctor Skinner, used her husband and son as lab rats.

"Is that what Tom was after?" Adam asked.

"Yes. He wanted to be in the moment. He sought after the origin of humanity. Then the wheels came off, so to speak"

"I am almost there. I sometimes skip a few generations, but I am on a linear path and the wheels are firmly on the tracks," Adam stood as he spoke and reached out to take his mother's face in his hand. He held her by the chin and gently turned her head so they could see into each other's eyes. He wanted to look into her soul.

Adam gasped, dropped his hand and stepped back so fast he almost fell over the chair next to his bed. His eyes remained locked on hers. Her eyes acted like a mirror. He was looking into his own soul. He was flummoxed by what he saw. It was like the scene from a movie and he played the lead role.

Adam was hearing distant shrills and screams and he began to sweat from the heat of his soul. In the distance he could see a fiery gate with flames of red, orange and blue on all four sides. Beyond the gate was a world colored in bright orange and yellow.

"Adam!" Cheri abruptly called his name because she noticed he was sweating, "Here, drink some water."

Sondra blinked first and broke the connection. Adam sat down on the bed and said, "Tell me about the mutations."

Sondra explained, "The nanobots constantly and consistently repair any mutations inside the DNA. They reassemble them into their original state, so when we try to locate a common shared ancestor it's like the clock never ticked. In the most recent sample of DNA I extracted from you today it became evident that the technology is enabling you to participate in your genetic past as if you are present in real time."

"So the tiny robots inside of me are reconstructing my genetic code into its original state," Adam replied matter of fact.

"Yes."

Amy and Cheri stood in the background listening and taking in the conversation between mother and son. They exchanged glances occasionally and appeared to be thinking the same thing when Amy spoke first, "Tell Adam about me."

"Your sister cannot ever reach an advanced or accelerated state of being. The technology simply keeps her alive. It has never been able to keep up with the degeneration of mutations and her autoimmune response constantly destroys the nanobots so their numbers have been declining since her birth."

Adam took it all in without responding. He cared about these people, but only trusted Cheri. The other two seemed self - serving. His sister less so than his mother. Amy seemed to care, but she still went forward with her life in a way becoming of a martyr which made him cautiously trusting.

Sondra spoke softly to Adam, "We need to get you away from here for a few days. They will be coming for you."

"Who?" Cheri and Adam said in unison.

Amy answered, "The government. Mom's experiments are child's play compared to what they will want to do with you."

Sondra sighed and shook her head in disappointment at Amy and the way she delivered information.

Adam asked with sincere concern, "What about Chuck and Doris? Will they look for me if I am gone for too long? Are they in danger?"

"Start packing Doris, it's time," Chuck yelled down the hall. They had been preparing for this event the moment they agreed to take Adam into their custody. Doris' emotions took her back to the first day they met Adam. He was a younger teenager, skinny, frail in appearance, innocent yet independent.

She took to him immediately and Chuck forewarned her this day would come. He would say, "Don't get too fond of the boy Doris. They will come for him one day and we'll have to follow the plans given to us".

She couldn't help it. She loved Adam, like a son. The son she never had. The child her and Chuck never conceived.

"Let's get rolling out of here Doris," Chuck's command snapped her from her thoughts. She began stuffing only the essentials into the two knapsacks they were allowed to carry with them. They had to travel light and leave no evidence of who they really were.

Chuck was packed and ready to go. He said, "The car is running, I'll meet you out there. My best guess is that we have less than fifteen minutes and they will be swarming all over this place. Which means we need every second of it to get as far away as possible."

Tears welled up in Doris' eyes. She started to sob when Chuck declared, "Don't," then he grabbed her bags and headed out the door. Doris quickly followed.

Tim Dunn

"They will be fine," Sondra answered, "The contingency plan has them getting out of town as we speak. You need to do the same Adam."

Adam asked with heartfelt concern, "What about Cheri? Won't they come after her and her family. They know me."

Cheri gasped, "What are we all supposed to do?"

Amy said, "My vehicle is out back, let's get in and go."

"Where?" Adam asked.

"We have a cabin a few hundred miles south of here. Chuck and Doris will be meeting us there. We will hold up there until the plan unfolds and the trail runs cold. No one knows who you are but the five of us."

"But my parents," Cheri chimed in.

"They have never spent more than a few moments with Adam and you always referred to him as Skip Chalmers," Sondra explained.

"You're right," Cheri said then asked, "Do I need to go with you?"

"No," Sondra replied, "You need to go on with life as normal. They won't even know to look for you.

"What about the public records?" Amy asked, "When Adam changed his name?"

"Chuck and Doris worked for the county. The documents have been structured to divert attention away from Skip and Adam and send them on a cold dead trail. They changed his birth certificate to show that Skip died after one day, so after his name change the records died also. They also destroyed the files with his new identity."

"So our models estimate about two weeks until this blows over, hopefully for good," Sondra said while scanning their faces. Then she nodded toward the door and looked back at Cheri, "You, wait here for an hour after we are gone, then go out the side exit. Walk to your car and take the long way home."

"When...?" Cheri started to ask but Sondra finished, "Don't call us, we'll call you."

Adam looked at Sondra with bewilderment and wondered to himself, *What is going on? Who am I?* It was a recurring thought.

CHAPTER 27

He is in a crouching position inside of a tent. He sees an old man lying before him. The man is speaking. The voice is clear and the translation is crisp in his mind. Adam understands the words as if they are being spoken in English. He looks into the eyes of the old man and it is as if he is looking into and at an extension of himself. The man's hand in resting on his arm. The man's hand is cold, weak and trembling.

His voice is soft as he whispers to Adam, "Ah, the smell of my son is like the smell of a field that the Lord has blessed. May God give you heaven's dew and earth's richness— an abundance of grain and new wine. May nations serve you and peoples bow down to you. Be lord over your brothers, and may the sons of your mother bow down to you. May those who curse you be cursed and those who bless you be blessed."

Adam leaves the tent and runs into the field outside. He sits looking at the sky wondering who he is and what era he has entered. An older woman approaches, sits next to him and says, "Your brother Esau is planning to avenge himself by killing you. Now then, my son, do what I say: Flee at once to my brother Laban in Harran. Stay with him for a while until your brother's fury subsides. When your brother is no longer angry with you

171

and forgets what you did to him, I'll send word for you to come back from there. Why should I lose both of you in one day?"

Adam knows he is getting closer to his destination. He is in the crisp clear memory during the time of Jacob and Esau. He is Jacob. He stole his brother's blessing. He knows he must travel into the desert and wrestle with God tonight. He understands it is part of every man's journey and his journey will be an example set forth for future generations.

Adam was lying on his back with his eyes and mouth wide open. He was motionless with amazement. He sees a stairway resting on the earth, with its top reaching to heaven, and angels of God are ascending and descending on it.

He hears a sound. It is audible, but like a thought: "I am the Lord, the God of your father Abraham and the God of Isaac. I will give you and your descendants the land on which you are lying. Your descendants will be like the dust of the earth, and you will spread out to the west and to the east, to the north and to the south. All peoples on earth will be blessed through you and your offspring. I am with you and will watch over you wherever you go, and I will bring you back to this land. I will not leave you until I have done what I have promised you."

"Adam," Amy screamed. She thought he had died by the way he laid there. She ran down the stairs and shook him until he responded.

Adam blinked as his vision faded and blurred and Amy came into focus. It took a few seconds for his mind to process that he was in bed at the cabin. He was recalling they arrived in the dark of night and he had immediately fallen asleep.

He noticed Sondra was wearing a white robe and standing halfway down the staircase. Amy was wearing white pajamas. The staircase had a brass railing and at the top, the sun was shining through a large picture window leaving a glow around his mother.

"I'm fine Amy," Adam declared.

"You were so still it freaked me out."

Sondra chimed in, "What were you dreaming about?"

"God. He has a plan for me. He promised he will never leave me."

Amy kissed him on the cheek and said, "I'll make some breakfast."

"What is all the commotion?" Chuck inquired from the top of the stairs.

Adam sat up, smiled and asked, "Is Doris with you?"

She poked her head around Chuck's broad shoulders and said, "Here I am Adam. We are all here. For you. How are you feeling?"

"The bottom of my feet burn, like I was walking on hot sand for a week," Adam grimaced.

"He's getting close," Doris whispered into Chuck's left ear. Chuck cleared his throat as she spoke to make certain Adam didn't hear her. Doris was always a bit louder than she realized.

"Drink some water and eat and it'll subside," Sondra handed him a cup of cool liquid.

The heat of the sun was rapidly warming the cabin so Sondra opened the door to let the fresh wholesome air energize them. Birds were chirping and singing to each other and to the one who created them.

Adam stepped away and into the bathroom to take a shower and clear his head. The water was warm and cleansing and he stood under the waterfall of refreshment for twenty minutes. His mind took him everywhere yet nowhere and time stood still.

"I don't see what the big deal is," Doris defended herself.

"You told him we were all here for him, when in fact he is here for all of us," Chuck quipped back.

"Shhush," Sondra whirred to stop the conversation because she heard the bathroom door opening.

Adam sat down at the table and ate the eggs, bacon and toast that Amy had prepared for him. He glanced around with a puzzled look and then noticed the dishes in the sink. The rest of them had already eaten while he was in the shower. He didn't realize he was gone that long, but none the less he devoured his food.

He sat back and took in the surroundings. It was dark when they first arrived and this was his first chance to appreciate where he would be staying until things blew over. If they blew over.

He looked around and the walls were bare and he was alone. He rubbed his eyes and shook his head. He drank the rest of his water and everything came back. Amy, Sondra, Chuck and Doris. The cabin was donned with rustic decor. Everything was made out of wood. The furniture, lamps, walls, it was truly a cabin.

He noticed a sword on the wall hanging above the bed he slept on. The weapon appeared to be antique like the rest of the wall swags. It seemed odd that there were no photographs anywhere, but then again, it was a hideout. There was a large mirror in the room. And his bed.

"Why is everyone else sleeping upstairs while I sleep alone down here?" the question was for all of them.

They exchanged glances and no one answered so Adam bustled, "Don't all speak at once. Forget it. I think I know why."

Doris sighed in relief. Too loud as always which sparked a stink eye from Chuck and Sondra. Adam was on to his next thought and didn't catch any of it.

"Well, now what!" Adam exclaimed to break the silence, "How about I go for a walk." And he put on his shoes and headed out the door.

Amy started after him and Sondra grabbed her arm, "Let him be."

Amy shook loose, leaving her mother with a look of disgust and caught up to Adam a few feet outside the cabin. She bumped into his back because he stopped abruptly. He stood staring at the majesty of the sunrise over the hills and the rays of sunlight bursting through the trees. Squirrels ran across his path and colorful red and blue birds rested on branches around him.

"This kind of stuff doesn't happen by accident."

"No it doesn't."

"Amy, Why do some people not believe in God?"

"I don't know. Did you always believe?"

"I guess I always knew there was something, but now I know it is someone and He wants a relationship with me. He wants me to know Him. He is revealing himself to me. When I stepped outside and saw this scene I knew He was saying, 'good morning.'

"And what did you say to him?"

"Thank you."

Adam shifted his thoughts and said, "Hey Amy. Did you or Sondra remember to bring the vitamins?"

"Vitamins?"

CHAPTER 28

It had been a few days since she was with the Dory clan and Cheri was concerned about Adam's safety. She was sitting in the front row of the congregation listening to her pastor teach from the word of God. He held the bible in his hand and spoke the words with authority and conviction. It was a beautiful sound.

The pastor's words hung in the air and danced like musical notes along the stained glass window panels. The building was full of people that all looked differently the same. She recognized each of their faces but could not name any of them.

"For our struggle is not against flesh and blood, but against the rulers, against the authorities, against the powers of this dark world and against the spiritual forces of evil in the heavenly realms," the pastor's voice clearly resounded in Cheri's ears and mind.

She was beginning to understand the nature of humanity and the struggle is not with each other but rather with unseen forces. Adam's words were also starting to make sense. Cheri realized that Adam could see those forces in his dreams and that he was actually participating in the struggle in the heavenly realms while everyone else slept softly and then went on with their day.

'I have to find out if Dr. Skinner is alive,' her thoughts drowned out the pastor and in the background of her mind was a droning

hum like an old furnace, *'Adam said that Sondra told him Skinner and Tom both died at the same time he was born. I do not understand why she would say something like that. Maybe it is true. She is a snake and I do not trust her.'*

Cheri was staring ahead at the platform where the pastor had been standing and there was a glow of shimmering white light with black flakes like onyx swirling and twisting around it. Sparks flashed as the black flakes bounced off the solid white glow and it zapped and buzzed like a bug light.

The black flakes turned to ash and fluttered inflight as they descended to the ground. An odor like burnt flesh hung in the air leaving an acrid taste in the back of Cheri's throat. Inside the white glow she could make out the shape of her pastor. He was smiling.

She looked around in disbelief as to why no one else was responding to what was happening. The rest of the congregation stood faceless, nameless, with only their skeletons showing through a white glow. The black onyx flakes were weaving their way in and out of the motionless crowd. Flashes and pops, sparkles and sparks. More burnt flesh.

Cheri cried out but there was no sound. The skeletons all had smiles. She looked at her hands and only saw bones inside a white glow. Her legs felt like they were attached to the floor and her body felt like it was being held in place by a powerful force of pressure becoming wrapped like a mummy.

'Adam, where are you?' She cried out, inside, *'God help me, please help me!'*

Then she woke up.

"Can I call Cheri and see how she is doing?" Adam asked Sondra.

"Not yet," Sondra replied.

"I have a bad feeling. Like she is in trouble or something."

"I said, not yet. It's not safe yet."

Cheri sat up and looked around. She was stunned and sweating. Her back was drenched, but her hands were ice cold. She began to recognize her surroundings and established that she was in her bedroom. The familiar wooden dresser in the corner, the window with the blue flowered curtains. Her clothes were in a pile on the floor next to her bed. She was at home. She was safe.

She sighed with relief and decided to get up and take a shower. She remembered the dream and her thoughts of trying to find Dr. Skinner.

'But why do I need Dr. Skinner?' she questioned her own thoughts.

Cheri attempted to climb out of bed, but she couldn't move. Something was holding her tight to the bed. It felt like a giant hand on her chest, pressing her into the mattress. Her arms were heavy as if someone or something was holding onto them. Her head hurt. Sharp pains stabbed like ice picks through her eyes and to the back of her skull.

Her furniture launched into a melting sequence that found its way around the room until she was left inside a blanket of blurred globs, a rainbow of colors meshed together, not knowing if she was outside down or inside and up. No gravity to hold her and no longer a force containing her, she floated motionless in the sea of colors, shrunken and insignificant.

"I can't stop thinking about Dr. Skinner," Adam said to no one in particular.

"What about him?" Sondra responded.

"You tell me. Why do I feel like he is behind all of this?"

"I never said he wasn't."

Adam looked at his mother with slight disgust and replied, "So you just leave out the facts and details that might tell the whole story. Is that it?"

Sondra huffed, "That's how you see it."

"Okay. I'll play your game your way. Hmm, let's see. What did Skinner do before he worked at Milton?"

"He was a contractor for the government's defense department. Worked with the weaponry division."

"Is that where he first developed the nanobot technology?"

"No, it's where he perfected it."

"What do they want with me?" Adam inquired.

"He happened to take that part of his research with him. He told his colleagues in the government that he hit a wall with his studies and he retired from service. From there he went into private practice at the clinic. They watched him for a while and gave up after about eighteen months."

"They never knew he injected the technology into your father. He did that immediately and then studied Tom as a psychiatric patient. They believed he was fading into the sunset with his psychiatry practice," Sondra cleared some phlegm from her throat and paused.

"Is he still alive?"

"What does it matter Adam?"

"I may need him."

"If you want him to be alive, then he's alive."

"Is that a yes?"

"Yes."

"How do I find him?"

"What will you say if you do find him?"

Chuck, Doris, Amy and Sondra were standing in a semi-circle around Adam. The sun's rays were emanating above and between their bodies. Sound became muffled and he could not distinguish who was speaking but he could hear the thoughts, the words, inside his head.

Adam looked into each of their eyes. He never realized before that all their eyes were blue. He could no longer make out their faces. They all looked like porcelain dolls, shiny, smooth and artificial. Replicas. Darkness.

"What are you doing here?" Cheri asked Adam.

"I was about to ask you the same thing. How did you find the cabin?" Adam asked.

"Cabin? I was wondering what you were doing at my house." Cheri replied.

Adam and Cheri exchanged a puzzled look and approached each other with bewilderment. Adam reached forward to touch Cheri's face and his hand stopped short. Cheri reached forward and put the palm of her hand on the glass.

They were both standing on the backside of a mirror. No reflection. The reflection was inside, and they could see through to the other side. Simultaneously they turned to look around and both experienced the same thing. Darkness with a blue hue in the distance.

They both stepped toward the glass, their faces were inches apart. In unison they opened their mouths and puffed a breath on the glass, but it did not fog. Adam chuckled at the irony and thought, *I cannot even fog a mirror.*

Terror filled Cheri's eyes and face and she let out a scream, without noise. She screamed again and again in an echoless dungeon of darkness, void of sound. She banged her fists on the glass and watched Adam do the same.

Adam tried to fog the mirror again and failed. He observed Cheri doing the same. He chuckled, she chuckled.

She screamed, he screamed.

He turned and walked away, looking over his shoulder. He noticed that she did the same. The mirror began to fog on its own. Words formed in the foggy glass.

Adam heard a voice reading the words, *The last one to die.*

CHAPTER 29

Cheri sat upright in her bed and glanced around her bedroom. It was daylight. She could see herself in the mirror above her dresser. She quivered, *'Forget about the dream.'* She threw on some clothes and dashed out of the house .

When she arrived at Chuck and Doris' home the sun had hidden itself behind some clouds and the street possessed a dinginess. The neighborhood was absent of activity. Everyone must have been at work already.

She walked around to the back door so she would not be seen. She gently tapped on the door hoping Doris would greet her, but there was no answer. She tapped a bit louder and wiggled the door handle and the door creaked open.

The place was a shambles. Furniture was overturned, cupboard doors were strewn open, dishes and glasses were scattered and broken, papers lay everywhere. It smelled like gas. She noticed a dial on the stove was on so she turned it off.

Cheri feared she would find Chuck and Doris murdered in one of the other rooms, *'Should I call the police?'* She knew she had to be careful and get away unnoticed as soon as possible. She could not be around when the police arrived or it could lead the wrong people to Adam. *'What if they found him?'*

Cautiously, she entered Adam's bedroom. It was in worse condition than the rest of the house. There was not a clear spot on the floor. It was like walking across a land fill of trash. The only thing that appeared in tact was Adam's bed.

Cheri lifted the mattress and found what she came for. Adam's diary. She grabbed the book and sprinted for the rear exit of the home. When she turned into the kitchen, her left foot landed on a puddle of orange juice and her legs went out from under her.

A flash of light and sparkles glistened as her head hit the corner of the counter, ripping a gash just above her right eyebrow. Her arms went limp and her left cheekbone planted squarely on the floor. The diary lay safely under her belly.

Cheri is standing in front of an old man. He is calling her by the name Sarai. He is telling her that they are going to have a child. She is going to have a child. She begins to laugh, uncontrollably. The old man tells her it is a message from God.

Adam is standing in front of an old woman. She is laughing hysterically.

She says to him, "I am ninety years old Abram, it is not possible."

He replies, "And I am One Hundred, but nothing is impossible with God."

There is a sound of crunching glass. Cheri blinked her eyes several times and realized she was face down on Doris' kitchen floor. She heard voices coming from another room. She quietly brought herself to her knees and shoved the diary under her blouse and tucked in into her jeans.

She was only a few feet from the door. It was gently swinging back and forth from a light breeze. She knew she could get out of their yard and into the neighboring yard without being seen if she could get out of the mess without being heard.

Keeping her body near the ground she scurried toward the narrowing outlet. The cool breeze felt nice on her face but the gash in her head stung from the sunlight.

She ran as fast as she could through several neighboring yards, dodged around a hedge of bushes stumbled through a garden and didn't stop until she reached the street on the backside of the sub division.

Cheri slowed her pace so she wouldn't attract unnecessary attention. Her breathing slowed and her heartbeat diminished its pounding in her chest and head. Everything around her appeared normal once again. She headed for home where she could feel safe.

"Good morning Adam," Amy spoke softly into his ear. She stood over him with a steaming cup of coffee, "That was the most uneventful night of sleep I think you've ever had."

"I didn't realize I had fallen asleep."

"Do you remember anything?"

He did, but answered, "No. I don't."

Amy gave him a second look that implied he might be withholding information, but Adam didn't flinch so she let it be and handed him the coffee.

He took a sip. It tasted odd. He set the cup down on the table next to him, stood up and did a long morning stretch. He inhaled deep breaths and felt a surge of energy. As his body awakened, so did the nanobots.

As the microscopic life forms awakened they roused his memory of the previous night's activities. His mind wandered into a daydream, reliving the experience as he recalled it. His eyes were open but he traveled inside his soul, riding on the technology train that was implanted in his body when he was a child.

Inside of his memory he is speaking to the woman, "Stop laughing Sarai."

"You laughed as well Abraham," She smiles and hugs him.

He is standing inside a makeshift tent. There are animal skins on the ground, like carpet. The sun is high in the sky outside and the tent is hot. He is sweating. The woman is sweating in his arms. He is the patriarch Abraham and the woman is his wife Sarah.

Her voice is familiar to him, "Like the sand in the desert, our ancestors will be too many to count? That's what God told you Abraham?"

"Yes," He replies. He has held her before. He recognizes his feelings, her feelings, her shape in his arms.

His whole being is living in the depths of his day dream. He can smell the odor of the wet skin emanating from their bodies, the dustiness in her hair, the damp animal furs below his feet. He can hear voices outside of his tent. The smell of animal manure floats in the breeze through the opening in the archaic shelter that would be identified as his home.

A little boy enters and calls him father. The woman in his arms shoos the child away. The boy hangs his head and walks out of the tent. It hurts Adam's heart and he feels conflicted.

"Why did you send him away?"

She stands up and pushes off of him in disgust. He reaches for her as she hurries from the tent. He knows why. He remembers the boy. Ishmael.

Forever are the scars of pride on humanity and the casualties that travel alongside, wounded and unforgiving. The desire of the creatures to take the position of the creator leaving a trail of lost souls that wander, searching for what has been and always will be right before them. The scars of sinful man.

"Earth to Adam," Amy was waving her hand in front of his eyes. She could see that he was deep into a trance, thinking about who knows what. His body was rigid and his breathing shallow.

A cloud moved away from the sun and when the light traveled across his eyes Amy witnessed a glitter and a reflection of fire emanating from his dilated pupils. The cloud covered the sun and Adam's eyes constricted. Adam was experiencing the reverse effect of light on the human eye, *'But why?'*

Amy gently tapped Adam on the shoulder. No response. Again, this time a little harder. No movement. She blew a puff of her morning breath into his nostrils. He shivered, tensed, relaxed, turned his head back and forth and acknowledged her presence, "I'm here, sorry about that."

He faded away into his thoughts again.

He is standing in a room full of people he recognizes yet doesn't know their names. He looks around until he sees John and Billy standing together with drinks in their hands. Billy notices him and waves. Johnny holds up his middle finger and Billy spews some of his drink as he bursts out laughing.

Adam counts the number of people in the room. Twenty four. A banner hangs above a table lined with food and drink. It is cold and musty in the room. An old wooden floor, like a gymnasium, rests solemnly under Adam's feet bragging black scuff marks on warped and chipped floor boards.

The blue letters on a white background of the banner displays, 'Welcome Milton Graduates'. He recalls the article about the program at Milton. He is number twenty-five. Tom Dory is number twenty-five. *'Why the reunion? Why now?'*

He moves his gaze from the banner back over to John and Billy. They are next to each other. They are sitting in wheelchairs, heads twisted, eyes bugging from their skulls and foamy drool dripping on their laps. A third wheelchair rests quietly next to them. Rust spots cover the exposed metal components of the chair. The backrest is worn and tattered.

The chair is empty. Adam knows the chair belongs to Tom. To him. Terror encapsulates his soul. He must not end up in the chair. Not again. Not this time.

A transparent image appears in the empty chair. It fades in and out of dimension. The face is distinguishable. The image is a reflection in a mirror. He watches his father's face slowly move to and fro in agony. Their eyes meet. He moves deeper inside the image. He is being pulled, transported into another world.

His eyes were changing color as his pupils enlarged and shrunk. She could not break free of her gaze into the mysteries that encapsulate the mind of a man transporting in and out of his own psyche. Amy believed she was on a ride along with him, as an observer visibly but a passenger spiritually.

When Cheri arrived at her house she locked herself in her room so no one could bother her. Just her, the diary, her laptop and a quest for answers. Who was Tom Dory. Who was Ben Skinner, Who was Sondra Farber, Amy Farber, but most of all who was Skip Chalmers? She knew him as Adam now, but the secret to him sleeps in his past. All of their pasts'. It was her desiring to awaken them.

She booted up her computer and opened a web browser. A flood of advertisements filled the screen on her home page. She clicked inside the field of her favorite search engine and typed, BENJAMIN SKINNER, 'click'.

The screen displayed an error message, *WEB PAGE NOT FOUND*. She tried again. Same response. She decided to try a different name, SONDRA FARBER. *WEB PAGE NOT FOUND*. *'Ok. What the heck is going on?'*

WEATHER, 'click'. Two hundred fifteen thousand results. BEN SKINNER, 'click'. *WEB PAGE NOT FOUND*. She looked over at the diary and back at the computer screen. *'I need a drink of water, and some food I am going to be at this for a while.'*

CHAPTER 30

Adam's diary lay open on Cheri's desk. Crumbs from her sandwich sprinkled the pages but were lost in the words, *'Amy and I were mining data from Sondra's computer today. We found the Skinner files. We also found the files for Tom Dory. I now understand who I am and the destiny that awaits me. It is with the utmost resolve and urgency that I take this journey and if necessary, travel it alone.'*

Cheri's bible lay next to the diary. She opened it to a random page. Mark, chapter eight, 'For whoever wants to save their life will lose it, but whoever loses their life for me and for the gospel will save it. What good is it for someone to gain the whole world, yet forfeit their soul? Or what can anyone give in exchange for their soul?'

She struggled to make sense of it all. God was speaking to her, but about who? Adam? Skinner? Tom? Who sold out? Is Adam about to forfeit everything or is he truly saved? She needed to get to him, talk to him, but first, she looked away from the bible and continued to page through the words in the diary;

'Everything in life has been coded. Nothing is capable of coding itself. There is a master programmer. A creator of everything. An omniscient being, planning a purpose for all of life. A living God.

The code exists within, I simply need to follow it. My father Tom tried, but he went insane. Doctor Skinner perfected the type of micro technology that would enhance the ability to decipher the code, but Tom Dory went in another direction. Tom was focused on the power instead of the glory.'

Cheri felt she should read the whole diary before she made any more decisions on how to proceed. Her parents wanted her to hang around the house more. They had been expressing concerns about her going with Skip all the time.

'What would they think if they knew he changed his name to Adam and I didn't tell them?' Cheri's thoughts whispered in her mind.

She continued reading, gaining deeper understanding and appreciation for Adam Dory, Tom Dory. The more she read, the less appreciation she had for Ben Skinner. The fine doctor could care less about anyone but himself. She read on,

'If I could get to the memory of Enoch, the decedent of Noah, I may get a glimpse of God. Enoch walked faithfully with God; then he was no more, because God took him away.'

"So far so good," Chuck shared with the group, "The area is still clear and nothing seems to be leading anyone in our direction.

We can hold up here for about another week and then we need to move on. Will that be enough time Adam?"

"Time for what?" Adam asked.

They all exchanged glances. No one spoke. Their chests moved as they took in and exhaled air, but there were no audible sounds.

'Why does this always happen? The absence of sound during relevant moments,' Adam could only hear himself think.

"Time for me to complete my memory path?"

Still silence.

"Yes. More than enough time, thanks," Adam looked into each of their eyes, minds, souls. Distant, almost empty. Fading. Dim. No one more dominating than the other. Diminishing into nothing more than shells of something that once was but may no longer be.

"Yes, we'll be finished soon. I need to rest and let the nanobots go to work. I am going to lay down now," Adam received no response. The four others stood zombie-like in the room of a cabin in the hills, away from civilization, while he lie down and slept.

After she stopped reading Adam's daily diaries for a while, Cheri decided she needed to get to him, but had no idea where to find him. Sondra told her not to contact them, but she knew if she called he would answer. She sensed something was not right and wanted to be there for him. Cheri felt a pull. Adam wanted her there.

He is working side by side with an older man. The older man calls him 'son'. They are building something. Adam steps back, away from the project to take a look and better understand who he is, what he is building, and who is his father.

He steps farther back because of the enormity of the structure he still cannot take it all in. The old man, his father, laughs, "What are you doing? Admiring our vessel. It will work. It is designed by the Lord."

Adam stops when he sees what it is. A ship. The ark. Noah.

"Shem, come back here, we have much work to do," Noah beckons him.

The air is humid, yet clean and crisp. Adam looks up and sees a glow of the sun. It is easy to look at. It is covered by an opaque film of vapor. No clouds, just a consistent covering. A water canopy. He feels protected by it.

The old man hugs him around the neck and asks, "Do you trust?"

"Yes," he replies, "I do."

"Seal this up and prepare the inside. The animals will be coming soon."

"Yes father," Adam replies.

Adam is waking up. He senses that he has entered another dream because he sees giant humans everywhere. He is standing atop the boat as it rests on dry land. With a bird's eye view of the surrounding lands he observes the events taking place around him.

The men look similar to the giant Goliath that he saw when he was the boy David. Their presence is stronger than Goliath, yet he does not fear them, he despises them. They are stunning, athletic, almost perfect in form. The women are elegant and beautiful. All the people appear subject to them, attending them, performing despicable acts of sex and masochism together. He feels a tightness in his belly. Nausea.

The old man, Noah, approaches and stands by his side. Noah shakes his head, not in judgment or disgust, but rather in pity and sorrow. Adam is horrified by the public display of orgies and pagan rituals. Human sacrifices. Blood. Dirt. Bodily fluids. Screams mixed with laughter. Pedophilia. Bestiality. Complete defiance of civility. No shame. Utter rebellion and chaos. Selfishness.

"What are they father?" Adam asks, pointing at the giants.

Noah looks straight ahead and solemnly replies, "Nephilim."

Buzz. Buzz. A cellphone was vibrating. Sondra reached over and looked at the screen. incoming call from Cheri.

"Not now," She griped.

Doris asked, Who is it?"

"It's her."

"He must want her here."

"It is his party."

"Do you think he knows?"

"Maybe. If not, soon enough."

Amy chimed in, "What are you guys talking about?"

Doris looked at Sondra and said, "I thought she knew."

"Knew what? What do I know, or not know?" She was glaring at Sondra. Dang it her mother was evil.

"She knows, she just doesn't understand."

Amy grabbed her mother's bicep and squeezed, growling, "Stop talking like I am not here. I am standing right here. Talk to ME!"

Adam groaned and the four of them quickly turned their attention to him to see what he would do next. Doris held on to Chuck in anticipation. Amy released her grip on Sondra. They all sensed something was occurring, they just didn't know if it included them, yet.

Long, stringy facial hair was appearing on Adam's sideburns, lips and chin. His skull grew larger and more defined features of bone protruded at his eyebrows and cheekbones. His eyes became sunken and sullen. Skin stretched and tightened like finely tanned leather across his forehead.

His arms made cracking noises as they extended in length and girth. Adam's whole frame developed larger and heavier before their eyes. Doris gasped. Chuck swallowed hard. Amy wept silently.

Sondra exclaimed, "They found him!"

CHAPTER 31

"What do you mean they found him? Who found him?" It was Amy speaking through her sobs.

Chuck answered, "The government."

"How? Where are they?"

Sondra started in, "Remote access. Through the nanobots."

"Now I'm confused," added Doris.

Chuck rolled his eyes. Amy shook her head in disbelief. Sondra held up a hand as a gesture to calm them down. The sun dropped below the horizon in the west and appeared again in the east as the group went on with their discussion, oblivious to the time and space alterations.

"Actually, they've been tracking him all along, waiting," Sondra sighed the words.

"Waiting for what?" Amy wanted answers.

"For him to reach a certain point in his memories so they could take over the experiment."

"What experiment?"

"The one where they create a new kind of soldier."

"What do they need a new kind of soldier for with all the technology they have today with drones, and unmanned weaponry?"

"An army will always need foot soldiers."

"Why not robots? Why does it have to be Adam?"

"Robots have limitations. They lack instinct. And Adam is simply the first of a kind. The physical transformations he has been experiencing are exactly what they are after," Sondra paused so they could take it all in.

Chuck decided he should add some color by saying, "And the only one who can stop them is Sondra."

"Do it mom, stop them!" Amy cried out.

"I can't."

'Why?"

"If I shut down the nanobots now, it would kill him."

"How would it kill him. How do you know that?" Amy asked. She wasn't going to accept the easy answers anymore.

"They have hacked into his code," Chuck chimed in.

Sondra added, "That's right. As we speak they are altering his genetic code to derive the end result that they have sought since before he was born."

Amy asked, "And how exactly are they hacking his genetic code, and for what?"

Sondra said, "Let me take this one Chuck."

"Remote access. Machine to machine communication. They are able to use the nanbots to go into the deep recesses of his DNA and find the exact location of separation from one ancestor to the next. They follow the branching and once they locate the branch of the family tree they want to follow, they lock down the code and that is the direction Adam's memories will follow."

Sondra continued, "I didn't realize they had set the protocols inside the nanobots. They must have been pre-coded when Skinner was still working with the defense department. All these years they've been tracking him, waiting for the opportune time."

"And then what?"

"Then they can actually isolate the section of code they want to keep. They'll freeze Adam's mind and body in that locale and use his genes to reproduce more creatures like him."

Amy gasped, "Creatures? What creatures?"

"Nephilim."

Doris asked, "What are Nephilim?"

"The heroes of old. Men of renown."

"Mom, you have to stop it," Amy pleaded, "Stop them from doing this to Adam."

"Like Chuck said, they have control of his code now. How could I be so stupid? I never suspected they had remote access to him, so anything I would try now would certainly kill him. I was afraid this day would come and a decision would have to be made."

"What are you saying? Are you actually considering killing your own son?" Amy turned pale at the sound of her own words.

"Noah"! The voice shook Adam's inner being, "I am going to put an end to all people, for the earth is filled with violence because of them. I am surely going to destroy both them and the earth."

Adam shakes violently in his bed and wakes himself up. In his hand is a tablet. On the tablet he has dimensions written in a scratch pad application. He begins to read them. 300 cubits (length) 50 cubits (width) and 30 cubits (height) – Cypress coated with pitch. He begins to feel dizzy, cotton mouthed and his hands are throbbing with pain. Looking down at his palms he sees calluses beginning to form.

He walks into the bathroom to grab a glass of water. Trembling with soreness he goes to turn on the faucet. Nothing. No water is coming out. He looks up into the mirror and notices the hair on his head is beginning to grey and he has much more than a 5 o clock shadow grown in.

'I just shaved this morning,' he thinks to himself. Now very confused, Adam walks out of his bathroom and through the living room heading towards the small kitchen area. As he walks through the living quarters he looks through the large window and sees three men and four women standing outside staring at him through his window. Adam pauses for a moment and looks past them. In the distance of the valley beyond the people he

sees two of every animals and creatures that move along the ground, all of them slowly approaching him and funneling at the tip of the heard, climbing the hill behind the house.

Adam is sweating now and wipes his forehead with his forearm. When he looks up again the people and the animals are gone. A stench is in the air, sour, the same smell Adam used to smell in his shop class in high school when they would use the saw blades to cut the wood.

He is no longer thirsty but can smell the stench on his own skin. He walks back to his bathroom and gets in the shower. As the water fills near the drain, he sees a dark tarry substance rinsing off into the pool of water as it gets darker and thicker. His tub is stained by the substance.

He climbs from the shower tub area and he dries off and puts on his robe. He shifts over to his sink, the mirror is fogged over from the heat and steam of his shower, he wipes it with his hand. Through the moisture he can see he has a full beard and his hair is significantly longer, all of it grey. His skin is like leather and looks very sun beaten and dry.

Outside he hears a large crash of thunder and all of the lights go out in his cabin. Adam rushes to the living room to look out his window. Outdoors there is a powerful storm of lightning and in the distance he can see rain approaching.

Again he sees the three men and the four women standing outside in the storm. Adam opens his door, "Everyone, get inside! It is getting violent out there."

The group of them calmly walk inside Adam's house and the wind slams the door shut violently.

"Father!" A voice calls out.

Unknowingly Adam yells back, "Yes Japheth?"

"Look father, the sky is darkening and there are beams of light shooting from the heavens!" Japheth answers.

"Are they all inside?" Adam inquires.

"Yes two of each as was specified, the Lions were last".

Adam realizes he has moved backward in his memory again. From Shem to Noah. He was Noah's son, now he is Noah.

They are standing at a colossal entrance looking out and down upon miserable world. People are shouting to them and at them, raising their fists and throwing things in their direction. Other are laughing and gesturing their apathy and dismay.

The previous evening, while all were asleep, young animals entered the boat two at a time. Each of its kind. The boat is like an ocean liner made of wood. An ancient cruise ship, perfectly architected for what was about to occur.

As Noah, Adam observes the sins of mankind unfolding as far as the eye can see. Murder. Men killing other men with their bare hands. Adultery. Woman performing sexual acts with multiple men. Visible open sores and wounds are abrading their genitals.

Idolatry. Men women and children worshiping wooden statues and kissing the feet of the giants. Stealing. Dishonor. Endless and senseless efforts of labor upon the land. Cursing God for their strife. Lies. And coveting. The people want what Noah has. They want his boat.

"Close the door to the Ark."

The enormous piece of wood planks perfectly sized and weaved together to fit into the opening descends from above. The light and noise diminishes, fades, dissolves and disappears as God closes the door of the massive structure sealing them in and covering them with protection from the outside world. A world that will be no more.

He hangs his head in sadness. Sadness for the world outside but an even greater aching of his heart for the world to come.

"What is it Noah?" the woman asks

Adam looks through the eyes of Noah and into hers. He simply shakes his head. For he knows that soon after everything is destroyed it is going to start all over again.

Without removing his eyes from hers he sighs and smiles. She returns the beam. They both know that there is also hope, and redemption is coming soon.

CHAPTER 32

The whole time, as the group was discussing Adam's fate, the young man was undergoing physical and mental alterations. The nanobots, guided by a new source, were redirecting their efforts.

None of them heard the rolling rumble of helicopter blades in the distance. They were wasting precious time bantering about what already was instead of what to do next. Doris couldn't take it anymore.

"We have to get him out of here," She shouted. They all turned and looked at Doris. In the moment of silence the rustling winds from the chopper blades grew louder and they all looked away from Doris and gazed out the windows to see what approached.

Behind them, Adam lay still with shallow breathing. Adam's appearance was remarkably different. He had the structure of an ancient human, but in no way resembled a giant. His transformation had halted. At least temporarily. Amy was the first to make mention of it.

"Look, he's not changing anymore."

"We have to move him. Now. They will be here in minutes," Sondra directed the group.

197

"I'll wake him..."

"No, Sondra stopped Amy. He's locked into a memory and that is good for now. His bed is transportable with him in it. We have a bunker for the three of us. Doris and Chuck will stay here. They are the residents of this cabin and we have their cover story complete and ready to execute."

Sondra pressed on some foot pedals attached to Adam's bed, side rails popped up around him and castors were exposed on the floor and ready to roll. Amy took hold of the head of the bed pulling and steering while Sondra pushed and barked directions guiding them through the back of the cabin and into the woods.

The helicopters were circling above but the trees were thick with overhead cover so they were not exposed. The bunker was about one hundred and fifty yards from the cabin. It was a slight decline in the terrain so they were able to make goodtime.

Amy slipped on some mud and lost her footing. Her body hurled into the base of a large pine tree. The dry pine needles scraped her skin as she face planted into the leaves and dirt. She could hear the roar of the chopper approaching.

Sondra let go of the bed to help Amy to her feet and Adam began rolling down the hill unattended. The women turned to notice the runaway bed and dashed in rapid pursuit. Adam's body bounced as his horizontal carriage rumbled down the uneven terrain and abruptly rested against a large rock.

They were only a few feet from the entrance to the bunker, so they unstrapped Adam from the bed, Sondra grabbed him under his arms, Amy lifted his legs and they carried him the rest of the way

The shelter was hidden by a large aluminum door covered in moss, dirt, leaves and pine needles. Artificial but realistic. The women transported Adam down fifteen feet into the bunker via a large manual elevator platform.

Sondra grabbed a camouflage tarp from a shelf in the bunker then climbed a metal ladder that was attached to the cement wall back up to the surface. On the way up she grabbed a rake that was attached to the wall next to the ladder. With the rake in her hands she hustled back to the cabin, turned around and ran back into the woods toward the bunker, allowing the rake to drag along behind her and cover the wheel tracks and evidence of footprints along their path.

Sondra quickly collapsed the bed so it lay flat on the ground. She unfolded the tarp over it and spread leaves and pine needles across it for good measure. Their location was concealed so she joined Adam and Amy in the underground shelter and sealed them in. The rest was up to Chuck and Doris. The bunker was designed to block any GPS or other remote signaling devices. The only way their pursuers could find them would be to torture Chuck and Doris for information about the location.

The bunker was designed for up to six people with food and water to last six months. There were separate areas for people to sleep and eat and even exercise. One thousand square feet of space constructed for maximum efficiency.

Books, music, medical supplies and an isolated bathroom area for hygiene and waste disposal. The whole place was built for function versus luxury. Ventilation was tantamount, so electricity and the possible consumption of it was limited and conserved to avoid popping out a breaker.

None of them could leave. The plan was to stay put for two weeks and then Sondra would surface in the evening to observe and explore what took place at the cabin. Ideally Chuck and Doris would still be there and Adam could be moved back. Sondra was presuming that after losing the connection to Adam for two weeks the government would think he was dead.

His condition stabilized once the remote connection from the defense department was broken by securing him in the bunker. She observed radical physical changes since then but he was not transforming into a Nephilim. Not yet. She could only hope they did not locate and crack the ancient code.

"I can't believe he slept through all that," Amy exclaimed.

"Check his vitals. There is a kit in the dresser," Sondra instructed pointing at a piece of furniture in the corner.

Amy placed the cuff on his arm and listened to his heartbeat through the stethoscope. Slow but steady. Low but normal. He was resting.

Suddenly there was a spike in his readings. His heartbeat was fibrillating. He turned pale. His skin was clammy and he was sweating profusely. Liquid was dropping from his pores as if he was lying in the middles of a rain storm. It appeared as if his bed was moving back and forth, to and fro, yet the room was still. Amy was dumbfounded. She was still, the bed was still, but Adam moved like he was in a ship on the ocean.

Adam is awoken by a queasy feeling in his stomach. It feels like his whole world is tilting from side to side as he lies on his back. Adam hears the voice of a woman, "Noah, are we going to die in this place?"

A woman is snuggling tight against his body. They are alone together in a small room. He feels an upward and downward movement. The sound and vibration of thunder shakes his core. The ark is being tossed about like a stick on the ocean. He is nauseous.

Opening his eyes Adam can see sunlight beaming through the clouds and a rainbow in the sky. He gathers himself and stands up. He turns to her. He takes hold of her hand, lifts her to her feet and together they step forward.

All that surrounds them is water as he stands inside the wooden craft. A dove approaches him from the east and as it flies overhead it drops an olive branch that lands inside his boat. '*There must be land towards the east,*' Adam thinks to himself.

"No," he replies.

"Is everyone dead?" she asks.

"Not everyone. Everything. Everything on land except what's on this ship."

"The Nephilim also?"

"Yes, especially the Nephilim," he shivers the words.

He lays back down in a bed of hay. The sea is calming and the boat is drifting peacefully. He closes his eyes and falls away from it all into a deep, serene sleep.

CHAPTER 33

Adam turns on his side. He vomited on the floor of the bunker next to his bed and started choking, gaging and gasping.

"Get some water," Amy called over to Sondra and she rushed over to position Adam's torso in an upright position.

His gagging ceased. Sondra removed the plastic cap and delivered the bottle of water to Adam. He rinsed the remaining bile from his mouth and spit it onto the floor, then proceeded to down the remaining water, emptying the contents of the plastic bottle.

"Is he awake, conscious?" Amy asked Sondra.

"I think he's about to transition again. That's good news. He will travel to a time before the giants. It, I mean he, is getting close," Sondra replied.

"Does that mean they failed? The government failed?"

"For now, yes."

Amy asked, "When can we get out of here?"

"Soon. Very soon."

"Is it over?"

"Far from it."

Amy had a puzzled look on her face. Inquisitively she asked, "What does that mean? If they failed and we can get out of here, then it must almost be over."

Sondra shook her head and soberly replied, "Quite the contrary. It's getting close to beginning."

Adam made a snoring noise and his breathing went deep and shallow. His chest rose and sank in a powerful rhythm. His color was back and his face looked full and alive again.

"Where do you think he is now?" Amy asked.

There is a peacefulness. Quietness. A form of serenity. There is a feeling of joy in Adam's soul. He feels energy. Alive. More alive than ever before. He has no fear. He feels safe, secure, strong. Alive!

A voice, **"Enoch"**.

He is alone, yet the voice is clear, mighty, and transcends physicality, **"Well done my good and faithful servant"**.

He feels his essence being pulled away from the world as he knows it. The world is rapidly getting smaller and he is ascending from it. He is not going into space while the world gets smaller, he is moving into another space, a different dimension. The unseen world is becoming his new home and because everything he sees is smaller, he sees everything.

Cheri read through most of Adam's diary. She had enough, too much. She learned that Adam knew quite a bit about the various players in his life. He knew much more than he lead on. Adam had documented the things he discovered about Doctor Skinner when he hacked into Sondra's computer.

Deoxyribonucleic acid exists in every cell of the human body. Adam went on to write in his diary that it is the hereditary material Skinner was the fondest of tinkering with. Most scientists were using their own research to diagnose various diseases; not Skinner.

Doctor Skinner liked using other people's research and extending it, or manipulating it for his own cause. Well, actually for the government, which paid him handsomely, which in effect was his own cause.

Skinner followed the work of BIOGENCODE very close. BIOGENCODE was the Biological Genetics Coding Project that was funded by the National Studies for Advanced Biology and Genome Research Foundation. Because Skinner worked for the defense department he had classified access to all the data and familiarities for what was known as 'Supplemental Research'. What that really meant is that he had developed new technologies for the military to test in soldiers.

One of the primary discoveries he extended was from a research project that uncovered another language, a second code, inside of human DNA It was previously believed that the genetic code made up of Codons, a 64 - letter alphabet, had only one meaning. The new discovery uncovered a separate language, written on top of one another. Scientists labeled those Codons, 'Duons'. Codons always were known to describe protein features but the new language, the second code is specific to instructing the cell on how genes are controlled.

Ben Skinner went after the new code. His research and experiments highlighted just what a powerful information storage unit he had at his disposal; human DNA. He figured out how to exploit the second language. He manipulated the gene control instructions, in effect, re-programming them to re-sequence proteins, have them re-build themselves so they could restructure a human body into a physical machine. A Soldier. A weapon of war, or a defense warrior depending on how it would be utilized.

Duons were his pet project. Tom Dory was his first human test subject. Adam's father was an experimental mutation. Skinner had disrupted the live, active DNA in Tom by inserting the new gene control program. He unlocked Tom's genetic memory. Adam now has those memories, passed along through Tom's genes.

Cheri was beginning to understand why Adam's body was undergoing such radical changes. He was adapting to the memories and the code was altering the proteins so rapidly that the modifications in his physique were observable in real time.

It was obvious from the notes in his diary that Adam knew that Skinner embedded code inside the nanobots as a way to turn on or off certain elements and functions once inside his DNA.

Skinner used Quantum computers to break the code. It gave him the where with all to maneuver his way around proteins and set up Adam's DNA structure, lock it down at any point along the spectrum of his genes using genetic memory as the map to the pathways of human ancestry. The beginning.

It was getting late and things quieted down inside the bunker. Amy and Adam were both resting peacefully as Sondra sat quietly and read. Outside the air was damp and cool. Nocturnal animals wandered above looking for food in the safety of darkness. Sondra had a tendency toward the darkness. It was a symptom of the human flesh that was more dominant in some than others. She was one of them.

While Amy was sleeping, Sondra pulled a vial marked 'C10' from a cabinet and began drawing liquid into a hypodermic needle. She flicked the syringe with her middle finger and cleared any air bubbles to prep the needle for injection.

She glanced over at Amy just to make sure she was still sleeping before injecting the milky brown preparation into Adam's neck.

Sondra didn't realize that Amy had one eye slightly open. Since Amy learned about the memory chip in her head, she always kept one eye open when it came to her mother. The woman simply could not be trusted. This was proof of that once again.

Adam didn't even flinch as the needle punctured his skin and Sondra plunged the contents of the syringe into his neck. Amy was frozen to her bunk. Her mind wanted to jump on top of Sondra and prevent her from the act but her body was in paralysis.

Amy looked on the table next to her and noticed an empty syringe. Her mother must have gotten to her in a moment of sleep. Anger raged through her but all the adrenaline inside her body was not enough to push her from her paralysis.

"Don't worry. It'll wear off soon," Sondra spoke in a compassionate, motherly tone.

Amy couldn't even speak, she could only think, *'I am going to kill you.'*

Sondra answered Amy's thoughts, "No. You won't want to once I explain. I had to subdue you to keep you from stopping me. This had to be done to protect Adam. To protect us."

As Sondra was speaking Adam sat upright. He slowly shook his head and let out a belch that got the attention of his sister and mother.

"How are you feeling," Sondra asked him?

"I was leaving this place. I was going to be where the righteous exist. I was Enoch and was being taken up. Then something happened and I woke up," Adam replied in a scratchy voice.

Amy could only observe.

"I need to take a quick blood sample in about fifteen minutes if you are up for it," Sondra said as if she was going to let him decide.

"Yeah. Whatever," he responded as he lay back down and fell asleep.

Sondra immediately opened a fresh needle and extracted four vials of blood from the vein in Adam's right arm. She labeled them and placed them inside a small cooler packed in dry ice that she pulled from a box inside the freezer.

She looked over at Amy and explained that she would be leaving for a few hours. She had to get the vials express delivered to the government. She had cut a deal with them that if she followed their protocol they would leave her and her family alone forever.

The injection was a mixture of mescaline, proteins, duons and nanobots that would enter Adams DNA, follow his genetic memory and locate the code for the Nephilim. The mescaline and protein would provide his mind the boost needed to direct the nanotechnology. The blood she extracted would contain the messaging the nanbots collected from his DNA so the government could recreate it and begin a human soldier cloning project.

Amy could only watch and listen. Sondra exited the bunker. Adam slept.

CHAPTER 34

Adam is overseeing the inner workings of his own genetic code. He is floating in a timeless place that is void of gravity. Strands of DNA swirl above, below and past him in every direction. Bands of colors and coding sequences intertwine and connect into infinite loops of messaging and instruction.

The nanobots are working furiously to organize and change the coding structure. Armies of microscopic robots shaped like insect spaceships move in and out of the DNA collecting and moving pieces of various strands and arranging them into new sequences.

Adam sees it all. His mind is the command center and he sits at the controls. It finally dawns on him that he can allow it to continue or shut it down. He thinks. He is contemplating his observation of the movements and operations of each robot. He notices there are sixty four nanobots that are different than all the others. Sixty four. One for each letter of the alphabet of the codons.

The master robots provide instructions to their respective sub unit of robots to work specifically on that letter in the code. Hyper speed movement of letters in the code is occurring right before his eyes. Adam feels fine. He is unsure of what he should do. He watches.

The master bots simultaneously turn and face Adam. They see him. They are looking at him. All activity halts. All the nanobots are immobile. Code and DNA strands float, suspended in a clear liquid substance with the robots attached. The bots anxiously wait for their command prompt to direct them to where they should place the pieces of code next. Foreseeing a structural rearrangement to capture a specific sequence that can be used and replicated for expanded purposes outside of Adam's body.

Adam has been controlling them all along. His uncertainty leaves them without instruction. They are waiting in anticipation. Adam's mind takes in the comprehensive view of the microscopic universe that makes up his being. Flashes of colored lights and popping sounds of muffled thunder seep through the gaps in the disconnected code. The lights flicker and fade like LED Christmas bulbs dancing independently, disconnected from each other yet united in rhythm.

Through his thoughts, he instructs the command bots to discontinue their effort. In unison their microscopic legs take them a single step backwards. Instantly the collective armies begin assembling behind their sixty four leaders. Millions of nanobots are marching in unison toward Adam. They are getting nearer but remain the same distance from him. They are separating their distance from his DNA but are the same size in appearance and relative distance from him. Microscopic cells and robots operate infinitely remote from the mind of Adam. He is looking into the cellular, physical world from a viewpoint in the spiritual dimension of time and space.

Adam remains focused on the approaching bots. It is like looking through the opposite end of binoculars. As they move toward him they begin shrinking as if they are moving away. He is puzzled by the counterintuitive phenomenon. The march ensues, the bots are fading. The colored lights are forming singular lines behind the bots. The brightness and glow of the lights are fading. All except one color.

Reaching toward the remaining color, Adam remains suspended and detached from it, yet it encircles him. The sound of screeching, clanging, metal scraping against metal interrupts the serenity and warmth of the blue light.

The millions of dots that once were large, visible microscopic robots are rapidly ascending in a swirling line like a river flowing upstream. Adam can feel them leaving. They never said goodbye. They didn't leave on their own, nor did he banish them. They were taken.

The feeling in Amy's limbs were becoming normal again. She could raise her arms. She rotated her ankles and bent her legs at the knees. She looked over at Adam. He was mildly restless, but nothing drastic. There was an unsettling feeling in her core. Maybe it was the drug wearing off. Maybe it was a transfer of uneasiness from Adam. Maybe it was because Sondra left ten minutes ago with Adam's blood. She had to stop her.

Sondra was in the back seat of the Jeep. Chuck was driving. Both of them bounced in their seats as the vehicle's suspension strained to absorb the rocky terrain of the unpaved path that lay beneath it.

Chuck looked at Sondra's image in the rear view mirror. She looked older. Facial wrinkles he never noticed before. Grey streaks in her hair. She seemed almost unfamiliar to him. She noticed him watching her and she smiled, exposing her yellowing teeth behind dry cracked lips.

Chuck returned the smile. He looked back to the road ahead, the tires skidded as he swerved around a tree, Sondra was thrown to her left, but she held on to the handle above the door and the vehicle bounded on.

"How much farther Chuck?"

"Few more miles and we should be at the rendezvous point."

"Hand me the 9mm," Sondra's request was stoic.

Chuck reached into the armrest compartment and retrieved the hand gun. He tossed it over his shoulder and it plopped on the seat next to Sondra. She picked it up and ejected the magazine to make sure it was full, snapped it back in and chambered a round.

"I don't trust them," Sondra said to herself but Chuck felt inclined to respond.

"You work for them."

"I still don't trust them. Is your piece chambered and ready?"

"Which one?" He looked back in the mirror and smiled.

They were as ready as they were going to be. The agreement they made was to deliver the blood samples and be retained until the samples were airlifted to a lab where they could be tested and confirmed as Adam's. Then they would be released. There was indifferent comfort knowing that the government would have to keep them alive until the samples were confirmed, but Sondra believed they were disposable after that. She didn't feel the same comfort knowing they were dispensable.

"We're almost there. Let's run over the plan one more time," Chuck was a stickler for flawless execution, especially when it concerned life and death. In this case, life or death.

Sondra rattled off the highlights of the plan; They would meet a group of agents at the designated point, a helicopter pad, to deliver the vials of Adam's blood and temporarily surrender into custody. Sondra would take over driving and stay with the Jeep. The vehicle would remain in motion during the switch and Chuck would exit with an AR15, a 45mm SR11 with 2 extra clips, two smoke grenades, a boot knife and a compact 32 caliber for backup.

The military agents would outnumber them and each soldier would be equally armed. The only difference was the surprise factor. Undoubtedly the Jeep had a tracking device, but Sondra's friends in the government did not know about Chuck. She reminded herself to thank Adam later for Chuck.

Sondra would approach the scene and stop the vehicle short and walk into the snare with her pistol at her side and the vials held visibly in front of her with her other hand. The hope was they would focus on the vials just long enough for her and Chuck to go on the offensive.

If everything unfolded according to plan, they would hand over the vials, but not have to surrender themselves. Once the samples were tested clean, then maybe her friends in the government's defense department would just leave them alone. Probably not, but that's where Adam came in. Only he could end this saga. He could and he would. She was certain of it.

"Adam, wake up," Amy was pushing his shoulder trying to shake him awake, "Adam, we need to get out of here."

He didn't respond. His breathing was shallow and his eyes were rolling around under his lids. R.E.M. Adam spent most of his recent life there. She couldn't wait. She would have to lock him inside the bunker, inside his dream.

'Lock him inside. On no, no, no, please not be true,' Amy's mind sent a surge of anxiety adrenaline through her veins that forced a rapid rise and drop in blood pressure and she was overcome with dizziness. When the room stopped spinning she headed for the ladder and climbed to the top to check the latch. Locked.

"Shit," she blurted the curse and looked down at Adam, *'Now what?'*

A tiny silver dot is growing larger, becoming a distinct object. It has a round center and eight arms extending from it. There are bristles extending from each arm and unlike a human the limbs have multiple joints that have 360 degree movement. They act as legs and arms. It is growing larger.

A visible mechanical entrance into the object is moving up and down. It is a nanobot. However, it is no longer nano. Its presence overwhelms. It envelops Adam's essence. The entrance is a mouth. It wants to eat him.

Amy's face is inches from Adam's. She was screaming, "Wake up damn you."

Adam's eyes opened and he was staring into the back of Amy's throat.

CHAPTER 35

Gunfire erupted and a layer of smoke hovered above the ground. Shadows rippled across the cloud of opaque brown air, light from the helicopter flickered around the human silhouettes.

Tatta, tat, tat.   Pop, pop, Tatta tat.   The crackle of various cartridges exploding with each squeeze of a trigger.   Shouts, the scraping of boots on dirt and gravel.   More gunfire.   Screams.

"Grab the broad, I'll get the vials."

"Forget the wench, just get what we came for and get out of here.   Two men down already."

More gunfire.   The blades of the helicopter slowly beginning to turn, sending the smoke swirling in hopes to clear the scene to regain an advantage against the attack.

Chuck was nicely tucked away in the woods picking off agents.   His intent was to only drop them, not kill them.   Clear the area and get Sondra out of there quickly.

Sondra was becoming exposed every second that the air cleared from the swoosh of the chopper blades.   She had dropped the case containing the vials.   She rapidly scanned the area for any sight of it.   *There it is. Nope.'*

What she thought was the case was a dead jack rabbit. Collateral damage.   She fired off two more rounds to buy time to locate the vials.   Twenty feet at ten o'clock they were splayed across the ground. One of them was cracked and the contents had drained. It was empty. Only three left. The minimum they required was two. She was still ok. Hopefully their adversaries would forgive the ambush if nobody died.

'Click'. Cold steel pressed against Sondra's temple.

"You're coming with me bitch!" The soldier gripped her bicep, paralyzing the muscle and cutting off circulation to her hand until the 9mm dropped to the ground.

The man leaned away to retrieve her weapon with his other hand, still pointing his at her. Then his head exploded. His blood sprayed onto Sondra's face and side. Droplets landed on her tongue when she gasped. It was salty and warm. She swallowed hard, turned and ran. *So much for that plan.*

Sondra retrieved her pistol and ran toward the woods. Chuck laid down a spray of cover fire to assist with Sondra's retreat. He turned and headed into the woods, occasionally dropping a few rounds behind to allow safe distance between himself and the opposition, but not completely giving away his location.

"Here. The vials. I have them. Three of them look intact. One is broken," the soldier called out as he knelt his bloody, wounded knee into the ground to retrieve the goods.

"Leave it. Let's get out of here."

He felt a tingle in his leg as he stood up and obeyed the commanding officer

"What about Johnson?" he asked as he tossed the empty vial into some tall grass.

"Leave him. Dumbass. His head's gone anyway. He should have not put any distance between himself and the girl. That's how you end up when you stray from protocol."

Sondra and Chuck were in a steady jog together a few yards apart. The elder man was getting a bit winded and Sondra could hear it, "Let's rest here," she said, panting the words.

"What's the matter, can't keep up?" Chuck said as he bent over and grabbed his knees, thankful she relented for him.

In the distance they could hear the rumble of the chopper echoing through the woods as it lifted from the ground and climbed into the evening sky. Three vials. One casualty. Five pissed off wounded men.

"Let's go see if the Jeep is still intact so we can get back to the cabin. Get back to Adam."

Chuck nodded in agreement and took off in a steady jog back to the battleground. Sondra followed closely behind.

Adam's heart fluttered as his mind prepared the transition from sleep to conscious awareness. Amy backed away when she saw that her brother had woken. Her face came into focus and Adam recognized his sister and the surroundings of the hole in the ground they referred to as a bunker.

"Mom left with four vials of your blood. She's giving them to the government to use for cloning an army of giants. Almost perfect humans to be used as soldiers. She claims she had to do it to save all of us. A barter for our freedom," Amy spoke so fast the words ran together in a blur of sound.

"Doesn't matter," Adam replied with indignant indifference.

Amy sat with her jaw hanging down, perplexed by the reality of Adam's disposition and her surroundings. The bunker had a musty odor she hadn't noticed before. Adam's shirt was soaked in sweat. He needed a shower. They were locked in. Trapped. Caged. *'We are animals in our mother's circus and Sondra is the ringmaster.'*

"She's not," Adam said aloud, "Mom's not the ringmaster."

He took his shirt off, stood up and walked into the bathroom area. His urine was deep orange. He was dehydrated. Or was it mixed with blood. He wasn't sure. It didn't matter. He needed to go back.

When he returned from the bathroom Amy handed him a bottle of water. He downed it and crushed the plastic in his hand, the crunching noise reverberating in the small hollow enclave. He tossed it aside, laid down and counted backwards from one hundred until he fell asleep.

The men on the Black Hawk were disappointed with the result of their mission. Three out of four vials and no woman scientist to hold as collateral and help them with the cloning process if they needed any assistance.

A medic attended to the wounds of every man on the chopper. Chuck hit them all at least once. The medic tore open the fatigues of the soldier that retrieved the vials. He made room around the knee to assess the damage, stop the bleeding and stabilize the wound.

Hundreds of thousands of nanobots, carrying very specific encoded instructions, were wandering aimlessly in their new alien environment. The code they carried was much different than the code they were now reading. *If then, else if then, else then* analysis were being calculated and assessed at hyper speed. **REPAIR FIRST. EXPLORE AND EVALUATE. ATTACH TO DNA. READ AND INTERPRET CODE. OVERWRITE NECESSARY CODE AND ALTER TO PREFERRED STATE. NEW STATUS ASSESSED, TESTED AND CONFIRMED.**

The soldier turned away choosing not to watch the medic dig into his wounded knee. The physician sat idle as he observed the flattened piece of lead work itself from a hole in the soldiers leg. The blood surrounding the laceration coagulated and dissipated.

Tink. The bullet popped out and dropped to the floor of the aircraft. The wound closed. Pain dropped away with the exiting of the bullet. The medic blinked several times. Shook his head. Breathed in deep and exhaled.

"How did you do that?" The soldier asked as he looked at his completely repaired, fully functional leg.

No response.

A surge of adrenaline rushed through the soldiers veins. Every cell exploded with a surge of newly constructed proteins. He felt stronger and more alive. He brushed it off as the rebound effect from the bullet being removed and his body responding to the alteration of a damaged state into one of relief.

"We'll be touching down at 0300," the captains voice burst into their headsets, "Minus fifteen minutes."

"Hey doc, how about a little help here," one of the other men shouted above the din of the engines and hollow ruckus that dominates sound inside a helicopter.

The medic went about his procedures, as trained, nothing should slow you down in the midst of pandemonium, let go and move on. Every life and limb is valuable and sacred. Follow protocol and everyone has a chance. *But I never touched that soldier's wound,*' he thought.

Cheri paused in her thoughts. Her mind raced through all the events since she first met Adam. She was trying to piece it all together. The scar. The sleep walking. The foster homes. His father Tom. Genetic memory. Sondra, Amy, Chuck and Doris. The old woman. Herself.

She reached over and paged backwards to the beginning of Adam's diary. The story began when he first met her. It was written as if it was the sequel to an earlier set of exploits. *There is another diary! Another book is out there somewhere that captures the earlier years of Adam's life.*'

There was no time to dwell on that. She could always go back and find it later. Cheri knew she had to get to Adam. She looked at the digital clock resting on her night stand. It was 2:45 am. She had been up all night reading and reflecting. '

'Time to go. Adam needs you. How do I find him?'

Cheri thought about calling him but in the past it had been going directly to voicemail. She dialed Adam's number. It rang. A voice she recognized was on the other end of the line. It wasn't Adam's voice.

It was Sondra, "Hello Cheri. Do you have something to write with? It's time you come join us. Adam will be happy to see you again. He's asked for you."

"Go ahead, I'm ready. Where are you guys?"

CHAPTER 36

Cheri hurried to get to the cabin to be with Adam. She never told her parents she was leaving, she just took the car keys and left in a dash. She ignored the phone calls from her father. There was no way she could even begin to explain why she took off. She would ask for forgiveness later. Send him a text she was ok and explain it all later. First, she needed to get to the cabin.

A truck ran a red light and raced passed her scraping the front bumper of her car ever so slightly. A semi-truck didn't see the truck and they viciously collided. Cheri felt the boom in her chest, like the fireworks that explode in the air every Independence Day. The eighteen wheeler kept rolling as the light blue truck wrapped around its front end.

Cheri pulled over to observe the scene and determine if she could help in any way. She ran over to the blue truck and peered inside of what was left of the crumpled box of steel, plastic and glass. Thick red fluid was sprayed everywhere. Pieces of flesh were hanging from various places in the metal tomb.

Three bodies were inside. Two adults and a little girl. No movement, no breathing. Lifeless and limp. She thought she saw the little girl blink, but it was drops of blood splashing onto her eyelids from above giving the perception of movement.

Suddenly Cheri felt like she was a distant observer. Hovering above the incident, watching as the chaos around the scene unfolded. It was surreal. Everything that was happening she had read earlier in Adam's diary. In the book he mentioned having memories of two adults and a little girl, a truck, an accident.

Was she just imagining all this? Was she simply lost in a day dream as she raced down the highway on her way to a cabin in the woods?

Instantly she was no longer an observer but a participant. A hand touched her shoulder and a man's voice shouted above the noise of sirens, "Excuse me mam, you'll need to step away so we can attend to the situation."

She was rigid. Terrified at the reality of the event and the foretelling, no, the repeat occurrence of the event, no, she wasn't sure what was happening.

"Mam, please step back."

Cheri turned and ran back to her car and headed for the cabin. Her GPS indicated she had a several hours before she arrived, so she stepped on the gas and stayed between the white lines with one goal in mind. Get to Adam before it's too late.

Adam is cold. He cannot speak. The sounds he makes are merely squeaks and coos. He feels at peace, but also vulnerable and exposed. He holds his had in front of his eyes. His fingers are tiny and soft. He is an infant. *'But who am I?'*

"God has granted me another child in place of Abel, since Cain killed him," the soft caressing voice of a woman is speaking into the air. She turns and looks deep into the eyes of the child, into his eyes, into his soul. He feels her essence above and around him. Her face is soft, almost perfect in shape, tone and form. He feels safe.

He hears the declaration of a man, "I will call him Seth." The man's voice is deep and thunderous, yet calming, strong and secure. Commanding but peaceful. A presence he never experienced until now.

He tries to speak but all that comes out from his vocal chords is a light grunt. He feels the gentle rumble in his throat. The woman smiles and kisses him on the forehead. He feels the moist warmth of her lips touching his skin. It is real. She is real. He is almost there. He is one step away from the man who named him Seth and two steps away from...

"Where's Chuck? Did anyone follow you?" Doris asked Sondra. She feared they would be captured and tortured in their quest to protect the boy. But she was ready. She knew her role and had no choice but to fulfill it, even if it meant persecution.

Chuck burst through the door, breathing heavy and answered, "Everything went according to plan."

He glanced at Sondra and she delivered a return gaze to acknowledge she understood that was all Doris needed to know. No need telling her Chuck tapped a few rounds into someone's head tonight. Keep the anxiety to a minimum. Doris was already visibly shaken.

"Let's get Adam out of that cave and back into this cabin," Doris politely suggested.

"Let us catch our breath. And besides, I am in no hurry to open that bunker door with Amy lurking beneath. She is going to be so pissed off I'll probably need to use a Taser," Sondra replied.

Light shines on his eyes and cold, damp air flood across Adam's body. His lungs tingle from the difference in air pressure and he expends rapid breaths forcing him to turn on his side. His gut rumbles and he expels a muffled grouse of gas.

He sees a silhouette hovering between him and the light. Adam sat up and shook his arms and hands to release the tingling sensation. He took a few deep breaths and picked the sand from the corner of his eyes.

Amy was half way up the ladder of the bunker screaming inaudible, unrecognizable words at the people above the surface.

"Stop!" Adam yelled.

Amy's motion ceased immediately. She turned and looked down at her brother, realizing she was more concerned about ripping her mother's eyes out than Adam's wellbeing, so she began her retreat back into the bunker and sat on the cot next to him.

"Can't a guy get a little sleep around here?" Adam's frustration with everyone was clear in his tone. His journey was interrupted once again. "Water please."

Amy shuffled over to the refrigerator and retrieved a plastic pint. Adam downed the cool clear liquid in a single constant swallow, crushed the plastic and threw it at the opening to the bunker in an expression of his irritation.

"Come on out. The coast is clear," it was Doris' voice.

"So Sondra sent you. Figures. The coward," Amy yelled up to the opening as she grabbed Adam's arm. He resisted.

"Come on, let's get out of here before they change their minds," she pleaded.

"It's not up to them. Nothing is up to them. It's up to me. These interruptions, these changes in venue, the drama, the whole story that is unfolding. It's mine and no one else's," Adam tousled his words and peered two steely eyes into Amy's soul.

"Ok. Can we go now?"

"Yes," he replied as he led the way back to the surface. Life was hanging on in the forest surrounding them as winter was just around the corner. Plants, trees and animals were anticipating the temporary death that was straightaway imminent.

"I am going to kill her you know," Amy said to Adam, in reference to what would occur the moment they reached the cabin.

"You'll do no such thing."

"Do you have any idea what she has done to you, to us..."

"I know exactly what she has done. Every thought. Every action precipitated by a command. She does as instructed. You all do," Adam's interruption was brisk and controlling.

"What about you?" Amy's question validated that she still did not understand. She would not comprehend it until it's over.

Adam ignored her last question as he quietly stepped through the door of the house with Amy and Doris in a strict compliant march behind him.

The sunlight felt warm on Cheri's body. The windshield of a car always seemed to magnify the heat as it permeated through it. It felt good. She needed the energy it conveyed. She had been driving through the night and was tired. She was almost there. She could sense Adam beckoning her, calling out to her to be with him.

"No one was supposed to die," Adam was speaking directly to Chuck.

"Everyone dies sometime," Chuck responded.

"It wasn't always that way," Adam looked down at his feet, hanging his head, representing disgrace he whispered in his heart, '*Forgive me.*'

"What next son?"

"You gave Cheri directions, correct?"

"Yes. She should be here soon."

"Ok, then your purpose is almost concluded."

No one responded to him. They all stood around him in a display of obedience to his silent request. The door to the cabin hung open. The air outside was still and damp. Coolness crawled inside and along the floor of the cabin. The thickness of it wrapped itself around their legs, holding them in place. They could feel its grip slithering up and encircling their bodies, their beings. Their skin burst with goose bumps and the hairs on their stood at attention like the pull of static electricity.

Sondra reached over and took Amy's hand in hers. Chuck looked at Doris and nodded in affirmation.

CHAPTER 37

A voice in the back of Adam's mind said, *'The last one to die.'* He still didn't understand what it meant. Maybe it was referring to Tom Dory. Tom was the last of Skinner's trial patients to stick around. At least that was the impression Sondra gave him. Adam wasn't sure what the relevance of the thought could be. He believed it to be more than the name of Skinner's journal. It felt like a lingering thought of Tom's, embedded in his genetic memory bank, but why?

'The last one to die.' He wasn't comprehending what it meant. It felt like a lingering thought of Tom's, embedded in his genetic memory bank, but why?

His thoughts were beginning to get trapped in a loop. Same cogitation over and over again. A circle, as opposed to a line with branches. A toy train traveling round and round and round again. Was he the engine or the caboose? Were the nanobots eating his good cells?

His DNA was a spectacular stream of code. ***If then, else if then, else then***. Rules and decision paths all coded uniquely for him. Every choice guaranteed a unique journey. Two destinations but only one ending. That was the promise. Choose your path, make your decisions. Path, decision, decision, path.   Find the fork in the road and take it. Free will your way to the singular finish line.

He closed his eyes, *'There is nothing left in this world without a personal relationship with the one who created me. He knows everything about me.'* Adam knew that. Adam embraced it. Adam feared nothing and looked forward to the day where he could meet Him face to face. He had experienced enough of mankind's past to understand the promise of its future. Hope flowed through Adam's spirit. He would not face the second death. *'Who is the last one to die?'*

Cheri wouldn't understand. Sondra will be upset. Amy will miss him. Chuck and Doris will get over it. They all served their purpose in his life. He knew them and loved them all for their role in shaping him. They all guided him in their own unique way. They protected him, pushed him, challenged him and loved him. Love expresses itself in many forms and Adam was able to experience the uniqueness of expression delivered by the individual for the individual.

Because you do not see something doesn't mean it lacks existence. Because you do not think something, doesn't mean it lacks existence. There is more than the human mind can comprehend or imagine, but the spirit knows of an eternal presence. Every breath is a miracle. Feeling is believing. Not a physical touch type of feeling, but rather the intuition type of feeling led by the spirit. It knows, because it is part of Him. He sent it so mankind could be one with Him. Adam understood that. Adam believed Jesus was who He said He was.

Not everyone believes. Adam didn't always believe. Not intentionally at least. Not passionately like now. It took an understanding of how deep and personal that relationship with his creator really was. Faith is everything. Not everyone wants it. It's the choice that has been given. Adam chose to believe it is real.

He was standing in front of a mirror. He saw his mother and father in his features. Other images formed in the mirror and one spoke in a crisp, clear voice, "Of all the voices of doubt, regret and so on, which one is the loudest? What do you cling to the most. What is the one thing you cannot, will not, or are afraid of letting go?"

Adam was watching a conversation between his great grandmother and his father. She was the one speaking and Tom Dory was on his knees, tears streaming down his cheeks. Grandma's image faded and Tom turned and looked at Adam and, then looked upward and said, "I am so sorry!"

"I want Cheri to get here now. I want her to be here," Adam shouted to Sondra as he snapped out of the daydream. He was growing impatient.

She had moved away from him while he was in his trance and was now standing in the kitchen area of the cabin watching his every move. She was patient in her response, knowing he was summoning the curtain call.

"If you want her here, then she will be here."

"But you always made the decisions," he replied.

"I only made the decisions you wanted me to make."

Adam was pale and exhausted. He noticed there were no mirrors in this place. It was different then the cabin he was in a moment ago.

"Where am I?" He asked Sondra, "Where are Chuck and Doris. Where's Amy?"

"I am here," Amy replied from behind the shadows in the corner of the small house in the woods where they had resided for the past several days.

No one knew what was happening on the outside world, but Chuck and Doris had held firm in their resolve to keep the place a secret or they all would have been exposed by now. They were all fit for purpose, so Amy, Adam and Sondra would be safe. Sit and wait was all they could do.

Sondra's phone vibrated in her pocket. A text message on the screen read, `'The blood samples check out clean. The DNA is his. You kept your end of the bargain. All except for the part where you killed one of my men. If`

you help us with the cloning, all can be
forgiven.'

Sondra turned away from the others and typed in her reply,
'How can I trust you? How do I know you
aren't on your way to get us and kill us
all this very moment?'

A few seconds later her phone buzzed and the screen lit up
with the response, 'We need you alive. The
blood from one of the vials entered into
the laceration of one of the men you shot
in the leg. He's transforming. I can't
really explain it. You have to see it to
believe it. Join us again.'

Sondra put the phone back in her pocket without responding.
What had she done? Was it according to plan? She couldn't tell
the difference anymore. She could only hear the sound of her
own heartbeat fading like a drum, banging from a distant village,
resounding a final directive.

Her phone buzzed again, 'P.S. I'm asking
nicely', but she ignored it and decided not to read the
message.

The others were indifferent to what Sondra was doing with
her cell phone. They were focused on Adam, waiting for what
would come next. Sunlight left a glowing starburst behind
Adam's head, washing out his face and leaving them with only a
picture of the shadow of a man surrounded by rays of light.

Adam blinked three times and the cabin rearranged itself.
The large mirror reappeared. He wondered if the room changed
or if the camera of his mind's eye was no longer able to keep up
with the pictures it took of his environment and his processing
speed was slower than the shutter speed. It was like watching a
computer screen paint the home page of a newly cached website.

Sondra, Amy, Chuck and Doris. Every time he blinked his
surroundings appeared one object at a time. It took several
seconds for everything to reappear. He held his eyes open and
stared. Nothing else materialized. *Where is Cheri? Why isn't she
here yet?*

Cheri was heading up the road to the cabin. She was almost there. The accident slowed her down. She should have arrived half an hour ago. Time stood still at the accident scene. It only felt like a few seconds, but she was there for over thirty minutes.

It was a gruesome scene. That poor family was annihilated. *'Who were they?'* she wondered. She listened to the radio news station and the accident was never reported on, as if it never happened. Yet she witnessed it transpire. She pictured the bodies splayed all over the inside of that truck. *'Why do things like that happen in this world?'*

Her thoughts went back to Adam. She hoped she wasn't too late. She didn't know why she felt like she did. What she was going to be late for? Her stomach gurgled as the car bounced and the gravel spewed under the tires rattling against the undercarriage of the car.

Adam lay down on the bed and closed his eyes.

```
public void NanoConnecion (ref dna DNA,
List<proteins> Proteins)
    {
      NanBot bot;
         for (int i = 0; i < Proteins.Length; i++)
            {
         bot= new NanBot();
         bot.Element = Proteins[i].Replace("C",
"bot.Gstrand");
         bot.Location = new Point(10, i * 15);
         bot.Anchor = (AnchorTo.Strand |
AnchorStrand.DNA);
            }
    }
```

CHAPTER 38

Adam is calm, relaxed. He is sleepy but not tired. His breathing is shallow, there is a peacefulness that envelopes him. If tranquility ever existed in the universe, Adam has found it. The stillness of time, the harmony of being. The rush begins. He starts ascending backwards from himself, a light euphoric pulling sensation ensues. Adam is rapidly falling into a very deep sleep.

Adam finds himself walking in a glorious garden. The scenery looks like images that have been reassembled from a kaleidoscope. Everything looks, feels, smells, and sounds perfect. He knows he has reached the beginning of time for mankind. Crystal clear streams and vibrant colored flowers dominate the landscape. He looks up and there is a warm refreshing glow above. It appears to be a water canopy.

Adam walks past all kinds of animals. He fears nothing and nothing fears him. He stops to pet a tiger. Adam picks some nuts from a tree and feeds them to a deer. He continues walking along on plush green grass that comforts his bare feet. Each step feels like he is walking on air. Everything is vibrantly alive and fresh. The fragrance from the plants smells of lilac, fruits and roses. The roses have no thorns. Beyond the garden and atop a hill is a giant lizard eating fruit from a tree.

Adam crosses another flower bed and enters into a small wheat field. He looks down and sees a small mammal eating some of the fallen wheat. A line of red ants is walking around the mammal, leaving it to its business. The ants are removing wheat seeds from their husks and burying them in the ground. They are acting like an army of miniature farmers.

As he walks through the row of wheat, careful not to disturb the ants, Adam notices a fruit tree in full blossom. On the ground at the base of the tree are a few pieces of ripened fruit. A white bunny hops over and begins eating the fallen fruit. A coyote joins the bunny in eating of the fruit and they enjoy their meal, side by side. Such purity.

Adam feels joy for the first time in a long time. Unspeakable joy. Of all the splendor, the most intriguing thing he sees is a lion that is curled up next to a lamb. The lion is visibly friendly with the other animal. He smiles and laughs with delight. Descending from the emerald sky, a red, white and blue bird lands on Adam's shoulder and sings a beautiful melody. Adam looks down and can see his own reflection in the water below. His facial features are clean and chiseled to perfection. A glow reflects from his persona in the water. His image is more than human. Magnificent creatures are swimming below his image. He feels a connection to them.

In the distance he sees the most beautiful woman in all of creation and she is waving to him and smiling. There is an aura, a glow, and energy force permeating from her perfectly formed shape. She is human but presents a manifestation he never saw before. He is drawn to her. It is not the human carnal attraction he is used to experiencing, but rather a oneness, a unity of spirit.

Adam pauses and leans his head back and takes a deep breath, filling his lungs with the purity of the air and he instantly feels more energy. He realizes his vision is crisp and nothing blurs as far as he can see nor as close as it appears. Sound is flawless and pure. Nothing is corrupted in him, around him or through him. Gravity does not hold him but rather he commands it.

A spider web is hewn across two plants and there aren't any insects trapped in it but rather it is holding water that a hummingbird drinks. Adam scrapes his leg against a rock and it swells slightly. A mosquito lands on the injury and injects something into the site and it immediately heals itself. He continues walking in the rightness of it all.

As he approaches the woman he notices she is eating. A soft inviting voice flows through the air as if it owns the space, or is a creature of it, "בואו. אלכול." Adam translates the words to mean, 'Come. Eat.' The woman reaches over to a tree that is lush and emerald green with flowers and button shaped fruits. It is a cactus without thorns. She plucks a piece of the fruit, hands it to him and smiles. He holds it in his hand. He hears two very different voices. The louder voice says *'yes'*, and a soft still voice pleads, **'no'**.

The fruit tastes deliciously bitter. He wipes some juice from his cheek with the back of his hand. The woman is plucking more pieces from the tree and collecting them in her arms. Something doesn't feel quite right. Like something foreign has entered him. Something that has the capacity to change him, alter him, corrupt him.

As Cheri rushes into the cabin, the words of Adam's last diary entry are screaming in her mind, *'the noises inside my head are louder than my own thoughts'*. He was writing about a voice. A competing set of thoughts that he constantly struggled with. He wrote about choices and consequences. He was struggling to discern which path to take. As she enters the room Cheri calls out, "Adam, what have you done?"

'The forbidden tree?' Adam looks over at the lion and the lamb. The lion commences drooling and stands up over the lamb. 'ROOOAR'. Adam's breathing is slowing and everything he sees looks like it is at the end of a tunnel. Images and light

surrounded by a cone of darkness. The bird lays waste on Adam's shoulder and flies off.

Adam leans against the tree and the skin of the tree gains ripples and grows thorns. A thorn pricks Adam's skin and he begins to bleed. The grass where Adam is standing begins to brown like hay and scratches his feet. The rose bushes grow thorns and ensnare the red, white and blue bird. A mosquito buzzes annoyingly in Adam's ear, then bites his cheek, draws blood and a welt forms. It itches and stings.

The waters surrounding him turn cloudy and fish are floating on the surface. The wind begins blowing, a dust cloud is forming and Adam looks back at the wheat field. Red ants are crawling all over the small mammal picking at its flesh. Adam turns toward the sound of a whimper.

At the base of the fruit tree, the coyote shows fangs, drools and bites off the head of the rabbit. It's fluffy white fur is covered in red blotches. To his right, he notices the woman is on her knees. She's aged and blood is running down her thighs. She appears very human and scared. He has seen the woman before. He recognizes her in her humanity. '*Mother of Seth.*'

Adam's vision is oscillating in and out of focus. He hears the sounds of chaos. He watches dumbfounded as the lion opens its mouth and bites into the belly of the lamb, viciously ripping the inside out of its core and swallowing the animal's flesh in rapid, ravaging gulps. The tiger pounces on a deer's back and the helpless creature screams a hideous shrill for mercy. The tiger reaches around the deer's head and tears into its throat. Blood is spraying everywhere and a stench fills the air. He looks across the garden, '*Did the lizard just breathe fire?*'

Sitting on the nightstand next to Adam's body is an unopened, sealed jar of generic multi-vitamins. Amy picks up the bottle, peruses the label and recalls Adam's earlier confusions about the clinic and the experiments. His diary entries made it clear he had become more and more confused over time. He was being pulled in different directions.

Cheri wonders where everyone is. *'Why did they leave him here alone?'* Mounted on the wall above his bed is an old spear. It has dried blood on it. Cheri doesn't recall seeing it before. Adam's body is unscathed and he appears very peaceful. His eyes are wide open and moving rapidly while staring into oblivion. Nothing seems right.

Cheri checks Adam's pulse and listens for his breathing. His eyes are flickering but there are no signs of a heartbeat. No air from his lungs. His body is beginning to cool. She slides the palm of her hand over his forehead and pulls his eyelids down. She looks at the diary she is holding in her hand, Adam's diary, and sobbing she asks him, "Adam, why did you hide it from me?"

Cheri sees a reflection in the mirror on the wall next to Adam's bed, but the illustration staring back at her looks like Amy. Someone is standing next to her reflection. Sondra. Cheri stands frozen, staring into the looking glass.

"You don't get it yet do you?" Sondra says to Cheri.

Cheri appears confused and replies, "What are you saying?"

"You don't exist. Amy and I don't exist."

Cheri looks behind her and sees Chuck and Doris standing in the doorway and asks, "What about them?"

Sondra replies, "Apparitions generated by Adam purely for self-preservation fueled by the flesh."

The lights in the cabin are dancing on and off in short bursts. In the midst of the illuminating strobe, Chuck's persona changes back and forth from Tom Dory, back to Chuck and then dematerializes. Doris' face changes in rapid succession from the old woman, back to Doris, gone.

"What about us?" Cheri trembles as she pursues answers, "Will I cease to exist if Adam dies? Am I going to perish," she cries.

"No, you will survive as a memory. Things about you may change or appear different depending on whose memory you reside in, but you will continue on in that form," Sondra explains, "You were powered by his psyche. The rest of us are a subjugation of memories. Adam's memories. None of this is really happening in the physical realm. Everything is a reassembly of information stored in Adam's mind. Only Adam is real..."

"I don't believe you. I believe that you are the sick and twisted person Adam says you are," Cheri snapped back.

Sondra's image was fading but her response was clear, "Think about everything that has happened leading up to this point. Have you had an original thought of your own? Where have your thoughts come from? They just occur, correct?"

Sondra's voice continued, "And of course you believe what Adam says about me. It's all true...in his mind, as he constructed me," she went on to say, sound fading, "And look at you. You are so cute, kind, sweet and perfect for Adam, just the way he wants you to be," Sondra's final words floated through the air as her image dissipated.

Amy's voice, "Mother, take me with you."

Cheri continued to stare into the mirror. Amy stood there shaking her head, her reflection fading, dissolving into infinite dots of color, pixilating like a digital image, gone.

At that point, Cheri knew she would no longer exist as Adam had formed her. She would cease in that manner at his passing, when his mind no longer functioned, when the last synapses sparked. She would possibly, someday reappear, or maybe even co-exist in multiple forms in multiple memories. But for now...

Cheri vanished. The mirror was merely a reflection of nothing. Empty and void.

Adam sits down under the tree as the cool of the garden dissipates and humidity rapidly increases. He remembers his first love. He was a child when he looked into the eyes of the King of Kings. He already knew him. He will see him again soon. He will have to explain his decisions.

A rooster crows. Adam understands now. He observes the fallen world of man, yet knows his salvation is secure through God's saving grace. Through the seeking of forgiveness and faith in redemption.

In the distance he sees a single tree. It remains pure and absolved from the corruption around it. *'The tree of life'*. His eyes are locked on the essence of its presence in the midst of chaos and destruction. Lightning flashes and in the momentary flicker he sees the image of a man hanging from the tree with his arms outstretched. An image of love. Perfect love. The tree of life.

The sky takes on a greyish hue. The air filling his lungs is hot and heavy. His skin is crawling and he's itching from head to toe. He begins to shiver violently. His whole body screams with a burning sensation. He gags. Adam is descending into a darkness, a heaviness, an emptiness. He hangs his head as the smell of death and decay surround him. Adam is naked and ashamed.

EPILOG

Adam's life flashed before his eyes. Over the past year he had read the Bible from cover to cover and he also lived inside the characters as he traveled the journey backwards in time through the memories in his dreams. Inside every man resides a complex code written for each individual, universal yet unique. He trekked along the genetic memory that existed in him.

Adam's faith was tested throughout his life and during his adventure through time. He observed his own life, his father's life, many of his ancestors, and the life of humankind inside those dreams. His assurance of hope for something better was built one episode at a time. Memory by memory the building blocks were assembled. His spirit was strengthened and made whole. He lived, he saw, he experienced, he believed.

He grew in confidence in the things he believed. He had journeyed from the present day back to the beginning, but now it all made sense as Adam's mind replayed the story of the human race from the beginning to the end. It was not only his life but his complete genetic memory was flashing before his eyes;

In the beginning everything was perfect, just as it was intended to be. There was no death or sickness. No crying, no hurt, only the joy of being in the presence of the one who created him. He was in the presence of God. As Adam stood in God's holy presence he only needed to trust, follow and serve. But there was another voice present. A separate and distinct voice. A reassuring voice that he would later find to really be a jagged and corrupt voice.

Because Adam was designed inclusive of free will, he was provided with choices. He could continue on the same path and go on living the same way, in the peaceful co-existence with God, following God's plan. Or, as the other voice offered, he could possess the knowledge of good and evil. If he chose to try to do it his way and follow the path that tempted him, he was informed of the consequence...death. Physical absence of life yes, but more importantly and more devastating, spiritual death. Eternal separation from Holiness.

That other voice assured him he could be like the creator and not suffer death, so Adam decided that he wanted to exercise a choice. He wanted more. He didn't believe that he had everything exactly the way it was meant to be. He wanted to be the one to decide on how his life should be lived. He desired knowledge. He wanted to know what God knew. The voice convinced him he would not die. That other voice played on his vanity. Adam chose not to trust in the one who gave him life, but rather in the words of the one who steals it.

That is when his journey down a different path began. A self-centered life filled with pride. He would be in control and exercise many more choices. He was the man. Unlimited options over thousands of years. Death, destruction and a promise. Promise that a savior would be sent. However, the cycle repeated itself and each time the promise required trust.

During the journey through time he had observed an almost complete purging of humans. All but eight people remained. It were those eight upon which the human race would be rebuilt.

Men and woman populated the earth once again. A great nation was built and a leader emerged among them. Rules were provided by God as a way for people to govern themselves.

The nation needed to possess a land for themselves. They found their dwelling place and over time began to ignore the rules for good and right living. Then they lost their land, ignored their laws and did what each one of them saw fit in their own eyes.

They lost their leader and decided they wanted to be like everyone else on earth. They traded away the leadership of God for the leadership of man. The people were out of control and wallowed in the mire of their individualism. Eventually they lost their population.

During the course of all of it God still wanted his people back. His heart was breaking. There were pockets of restoration and a few elements of renewal. Some people still hung on to God's promise so he renewed it through an earthly King. King David of Israel. There was still hope.

Throughout time, blood was used as a payment for doing wrong. Spotless lambs would be sacrificed as an offering for atonement, but people still continued to ignore the things that were good and participated in the matters that were harmful to themselves and each other. Humans needed a savior. The promised one. A spotless, blameless substitute that would take the punishment for their misgivings. An advocate on their behalf, to God.

People needed real redemption. They were incapable of doing it on their own. So the redeemer appeared and walked among them. The son of God. His name is Jesus. He is the real leader that people need. He brings with Him a plan. He delivers the real law by giving humans the Holy Spirit, the law that resides in their hearts.

Crucified and hung on a cross, He paid the penalty as the sacrificial lamb of God. As judgment for our rebellion He endured a spiritual separation from his Father. He suffered as a substitution for us by taking our judgment upon himself. He also conquered death by raising himself from the grave. Then He ascended to heaven to sit with God and to be our advocate.

Jesus rebuilt the population. He delivered a new kingdom of redeemed people in a real land. A land that exists in the everyday lives of those that believe in Him. He simply asks that you seek his forgiveness, follow his ways and believe in Him. He tells you that you should love God with all your might and that you should love your neighbor just as you love yourself.

A revelation of judgment and glory was provided as declaration that humankind will experience redemption on earth. There will be a point where there is redemption in heaven and on earth and Jesus will stand on the earth again. It will be very clear when He returns.

The evil one, the other voice, will come back in human form as a last ditch effort to rule but God will bring his final judgment. God will deliver a new heaven and new earth. It will be available to all those who seek His forgiveness and who claim their redemption through faith.

In his final moment of physical existence Adam witnessed the life of humankind from the beginning of time until the end. He hopes and he trusts in what he has seen as well as the things he has not seen. His heart has turned away from earthly things and he has set his mind on things above. Though his body has expired he is fully and completely alive now, and knows he has a savior, a redeemer that lives. He believes.

On the far reaches of town, in an old worn down building, a heart monitor displays a flat line and sounds a steady 'beeeeeep'. A nurse walks up to an incubator housing a baby boy who appears to have taken his last breath.

She picks him up and cradles him in her bosom and says, "Wake up my little dreamer. Don't leave us now. There is something special about you."

She presses a blue button on the wall speaker monitor, "Dr. Milton, come down here, we are about to lose him."

Through his tunnel vision Adam notices a dim blue glow of light. It is glowing brighter. He feels welcomed. He feels drawn toward the light. It is soft. It is warm. It is good...Very good.

"Prior to the fall, mankind was wholly and totally subject to God and needed nothing else. As a result of the fall, humans corrupted the image of God within them and in exchange discovered, obtained and unleashed abilities found within the knowledge of good and evil. Free will allows men and women to squander those abilities, or use them for God's glory."

Excerpt from Adam's journal

You cannot change the past but you can change the memory of it...

ABOUT THE AUTHOR

Tim Dunn is a Midwest native, married with three children. He spends his free time during the evenings and weekends serving his community, writing, watching sports or movies and preparing for the next day's events. The First Edition of his debut book, *Monomania – The Autobiography of Tom Dory*, received Honorable Mention awards at the 2012 London Book Festival, 2013 Paris Book Festival and the 2013 San Francisco book Festival. Monomania takes readers on an adventure of the character's inner mind, explores the possibilities of the power and capacity of reason all while highlighting the ongoing battle between human flesh and God's spirit.

NEXT :

One Third

Adam saw things in his dreams. He also saw things when he was awake. Things that other people did not see. That's when young Adam knew he was different.

29662717R00141

Made in the USA
Charleston, SC
17 May 2014